The
BOOKSHOP
OF DUST
AND DREAMS

The BOOKSHOP OF DUST AND DREAMS

Mindy Thompson

VIKING

VIKING
An imprint of Penguin Random House LLC, New York

First published in the United States of America by Viking,
an imprint of Penguin Random House LLC, 2021

Visit us online at penguinrandomhouse.com.

Library of Congress Cataloging-in-Publication Data is available.

Manufactured in Canada

ISBN 9780593110379

10 9 8 7 6 5 4 3 2 1

FRI

Design by Lucia Baez · Text set in Weiss BT

For Russell,
the little star,
who guided me through the dark

Chapter One

November 3, 1944
Sutton, New York

The bookshop is feeling blue today. I sense it the moment my brother James and I arrive home from school. The lights are low, the ever-shifting wallpaper is a cheerless dark gray, with somber books on display— *Wuthering Heights*, *Old Yeller*, *A Little Princess*. The gloom sinks into my bones.

"Papa?" I call. He should be at the emerald-green front counter, but he isn't.

"We're home!" James shouts.

The soft sound of customers chatting trickles toward us through the fiction section, but Papa's booming voice, often too loud for the small, cramped space, is absent.

"What's gotten the shop into a mood *this* time?" James asks, as the heavy atmosphere settles around us.

Rhyme and Reason does tend to be moody, but it's all part of the bookshop's charm.

I pull the strap of my schoolbag over my head and hang it on the coatrack.

"There, there. Everything is going to be all right," I tell the shop as I gently press my palm to the wall. The floral paper shifts from gray to a soft cream beneath my touch as it's soothed.

A quote written on the chalkboard behind the front counter disappears, and new words emerge as the shop attempts to communicate its feelings.

"The little bird, always energetic and bright, felt like no one saw her for her beauty or her strength. They only saw her flaws." —The Tale of Little Bluebird, *Ramona Woolridge*

"I remember that picture book, Mama used to read it to us at bedtime." James nods toward the board, as he hangs his schoolbag beside mine.

I remember it too, and understanding rushes over me. That picture book tells the story of a boastful little bird who gets knocked down a peg by her friends and must prove her self-worth in the end. Whenever a customer makes a suggestion to improve the shop, it deals a similar blow to Rhyme and Reason's self-confidence.

"Will you tell Mama and Papa I'm going to Arthur's house? We're all meeting there to listen to *The Adventures of Superman*." James tilts his head, and his fine brown hair falls over his eyes. Nine to my thirteen, he and I could not be more opposite. He loves going to school, where he's friends with everyone in his grade, and he spends most of his free time outside with them, as if he doesn't want to be tied down by Rhyme and Reason.

I glance at my watch. The radio program starts in five minutes. "You better hurry, or you'll miss the beginning."

"I'll be home for dinner!" he calls as he rushes out the back door.

I turn my attention to the shop, a shiver running through me. The usual warmth has disappeared. The hanging bulbs are off, and pale light pours in through the front windows, illuminating the tall bookcases in a soft glow. Even the wisteria and climbing hydrangea, which drip from every shelf and surface, seem to droop.

"Someone has hurt your feelings again," I say as I unbutton my wool coat. The shop had a similar episode just last week. A customer didn't like the orange wallpaper Rhyme and Reason had decided on that day, and suggested we pick something more tasteful. Rhyme and Reason went into a spiral for hours before Papa could calm it down.

I check on the potted lemon tree by the front door, to see how it's faring in these conditions. The focal point of the shop, its tall branches almost touch the ceiling. The leaves are a deep rich green that matches the color of the front door, and the growing fruit are a luminous, crisp yellow.

As I reach for the water pitcher that sits in the window, one of the branches brushes my shoulder in hello.

"Hello to you too," I say.

Mama often reminds us that lemon trees are a symbol of healing and travel, both of which Rhyme and Reason specializes in.

The flip calendar that hangs just to the right of the entryway begins to shuffle through months, dates, and years. A customer is approaching!

Our shop isn't a normal bookshop, it belongs to the world of magic ones. Just like the others, Rhyme and Reason finds people from outside of our time and brings them to our door. It searches a hundred years into the future and the past to find customers who need the light and hope it can offer through books and community. Papa says bookshops are good for broken souls and wounded hearts.

The calendar stops shifting. November 18, 1989. A customer visiting from the future. The bell above the door rings out as it pops open.

Mr. Makuto, one of our regulars with a bright smile and loud laughter, steps inside. "Hey there, Poppy, how ya been?"

"Just fine, Mr. Makuto," I greet him, feeling like I need to shield my eyes from the bright green jacket he's wearing. "How are you?"

"Great. I finished the first book in the murder mystery series you recommended. I'm back for book two! Do you happen to have it?"

"Let's find out." I lead him into the fiction section. He was here a few days ago, and I remember exactly where to find the book he wants. I pull it off the shelf and hand it to him.

"That's the one." He smiles.

I start to respond, when I hear a shuffling sound behind me. The books on the endcap display shift, and one entitled *Tales of Woe* is brought front and center.

"Oh goodness." I suppose finding Papa cannot wait. The bookshop is growing more forlorn by the second. "There are four books in that particular series, but the author wrote a spin-off that has eight. They're all here; I'll give you some time to browse."

Mr. Makuto nods, and I move around him. After a quick scan of the area, I see that Papa is not in the fiction stacks. I cut through the fantasy aisle and emerge in front of the lilac hedge. It runs along the right side of the shop, all the way from the front to the back, concealing the children's section from the main floor. The lush green vines and bursting purple blooms morph into a doorway as I approach. I slip through, and the gap seals behind me.

The children's area, made up of short white shelves,

is lacking its usual color and life today. The mural on the wall, a vast painting of an enchanted forest full of glittering colors and ever-changing characters, shows a bleak, stormy landscape. The kites and airplanes, which usually circle the ceiling, lie lifeless on the floor.

I move around the corner, and see Bibine Zabala and her twin grandchildren, Kosma and Prosper. Bibine stands on the raised Storytime platform, acting out a fairy tale, the way she always does.

"—let me tell you, dear reader, of the terror that struck their hearts at the sight of the seven-headed serpent." Bibine holds a well-worn copy of *Basque Mythology*. She wears a costume from the dress-up box we keep beneath the mural. A paper crown adorns her head, and a red velvet cape cascades from her shoulders. Her grandchildren wear crowns too, and Prosper clutches a wooden sword. "The great serpent came out to eat only once every three months, and it was a terror to behold."

Kosma and Prosper sit, captivated by their grandmother, their cheeks red with excitement. They're nearly identical, with glossy dark curls and big brown eyes. The Zabalas visit us from 1937. Kosma and Prosper are refugees from the Basque Country. They were sent to live with their grandmother and grandfather in the United States after their parents were killed. Bibine spends hours inside the shop with them, telling stories and acting out plays. Shy when they first began visiting, the twins are starting to come out of their shell.

Bibine notices me watching and calls out the Basque word for hello. "Kaixo!"

"Kaixo." Heat rushes into my cheeks. I hope I have the pronunciation right.

A smile tilts the corners of her lips. "Very good, you've been practicing. Care to join us? We are just about to get to the best part of the story."

"I would love to, but I'm actually looking for my father. The shop is in a mood." As if in response, a flock of paper birds flies from the shelf above the picture books and swoop inches in front of my nose as they head off over the lilac hedge. "You haven't seen him, by chance?"

Bibine shakes her head. "Your brother was at the counter when we came in."

Al was at the counter? That must mean Papa isn't here. "Thank you."

"What happens next, Amona?" Kosma leans in toward her grandmother.

"Well, the great creature opened its mouth and let out a roar. It—"

I move through the lilac hedge and into the small reading area at the back of the shop. Made up of a mismatched assortment of tables and chairs, the space is lit by the large brick fireplace that stretches across the far wall. It's full of customers today; some talk in whispers among each other, and some read independently. I recognize a few regulars, but many of them I don't know.

"Poppy! Hi! I was hoping I would see you today!" Anna Rose Alperstein, with bouncy brown curls, pale skin, and eyes that always seem to glitter, is nineteen and visits us from 1956. She looks up from the book she's reading. "I landed an audition for a musical that's actually going to be on Broadway. It's only a part in the chorus, and, well, all right, it's not directly on Broadway, but it's *near* Broadway."

The hanging lightbulbs turn on above us, then flick off again.

"What's going on with your electric?" a customer browsing the westerns calls out to me. "It's been like this for an hour."

"It has been awfully dark in here." Anna Rose frowns, her face lit by the glow of the fire.

"I'm so sorry about that, we'll get it fixed as soon as possible," I tell the customer. To Anna Rose I say, "I want to hear all about your audition, but I need to look into this first. I'll be right back."

She nods and settles into her seat.

I finally reach the wrought-iron staircase that leads to the nonfiction on the second floor, then start up the steps.

"You're being a bit dramatic," I tell Rhyme and Reason as I go. The vines that grow around the railing shrivel away from my touch, the shop stung by my words. "I know you're sensitive, but you can't just shut down every time someone says something you don't like. If I did that, I wouldn't go to school ever again."

I reach the top step and hear Al right away.

"I'm sorry, like I said, we don't have any books by Henrietta Davis in stock. At least, not today." My older brother emerges from the nonfiction shelves dressed in tweed pants and a sweater vest; he looks so much like Papa I almost rub my eyes. A woman I've never seen before follows tight on his heels.

"What kind of a bookshop is this without Henrietta Davis? She was the greatest writer of the twentieth century, my dear. You haven't read a mystery until you've read Henrietta Davis." The woman has a tight pinched face and gray hair swept into a bun.

It's worse than I suspected. Not just a customer offering a suggestion for the shop, but a customer who is insulting the shop. Al sees me standing on the stairs and his eyes widen behind the lenses of his glasses in a *help me* sort of look.

"Henrietta Davis happens to be a distant relative of my grandmother's. If this shop were a good shop, it would have some of her work," the woman insists.

Al adjusts the knot of his tie in discomfort. "Let me show you to our mystery section. I can give you some fantastic alternatives."

The customer peers up at him. "I've glanced at that sorry excuse for a mystery section. Nothing caught my interest. Not to mention, I can't find anything with your filing system, books shoved every which way. It's a complete mess."

The soft white wisteria cascading down the nearest bookshelf shrinks as Rhyme and Reason hears her comments and sinks further into despair. The air grows cold around us, the chill settling into my stomach as the lights go out completely. She's really done it now.

"And what is wrong with your lighting?" she snaps. "You should really get someone in here to fix it!"

Anger surges through me. She can't talk to the shop like that. I curl my hands into fists, seizing any bravery I have. "I think Rhyme and Reason is beautiful. The green paint on the front door might be chipped, and our books might seem disorganized to you, but we like it that way. If you don't like it, then you can leave."

Her bushy caterpillar eyebrows shoot up, and she stares at me in horror. "Excuse me? Who is this *child*?" She puts extra emphasis on the last word, and I wither, the sudden courage leaving me. My knees shake, and I lean back against the railing for support.

Al holds out a hand, as if to calm her down. "That's

my sister, I'm so sorry for her tone. She—"

"I don't know what kind of establishment this is, being run by children! It's a joke!" She huffs and then storms past us, muttering more about Henrietta Davis.

When she's gone, the fireflies emerge, rushing up to greet me. Tiny glowing bugs made out of yellowed book pages and magic, they've long followed me wherever I go inside the shop.

"Hello," I greet them, holding out my palms for them to land. They brush against my skin, and instantly I'm filled with a soft sense of comfort.

Al wipes a sheen of sweat off his forehead. "You all right, Rhyme?"

The bulb above us flickers twice in response. *Yes.*

"I couldn't get her to leave. I tried to show her other books. When she didn't want those, I pretended I was busy, hoping that would shake her, but she followed me all the way up here."

"Where's Papa?" He's the one who usually handles tough customers.

Al adjusts his glasses and starts for the stairs. "That scrap drive was today. The one at Hazel Park. He and Mama volunteered."

Posters advertising the drive have hung around town for weeks. YOU CAN HELP WITH THE WAR EFFORT! DONATE PAPER, METAL, RUBBER, AND RAGS!

"Save scrap." I begin the slogan.

"For victory," Al finishes unenthusiastically.

"For victory!" I shout. "C'mon, it's how we do our part to help beat the Nazis." Al shakes his head as he moves to the first floor. I follow after him. "It's how we help Carl."

I regret the words as soon as I say them. Al stops on the bottom step, his shoulders tense at the mention of Carl Miller.

"I'm sorry," I say quickly. "I didn't mean—"

"It's fine." Al waves me away, but behind his glasses I see the worry in his eyes. It was silly of me to say that. Of course, collecting bits of scrap paper for packaging army crates can't help Carl. Not now that he's gone missing in action.

Worry eats at me too. I try to push it down as I follow Al through the shop, but I can't. Carl and Al have been best friends since they were born. He's spent so much time here, he's as much a brother to me as my actual brothers. I can't help but miss the way he used to burst into the shop, always pretending to forget my name, calling me Peony or Posey or some other flower as if he didn't know it was Poppy.

There's a table in Rhyme and Reason where Mama likes to keep family photos. Al and I move past it, and I stare at one of my favorites. A shot of me, James, Al, and Carl at the beach. Mama and Carl's mother, Victoria, are in the background, lounging on chairs in dark high-necked bathing dresses, with big sun hats shading their faces. They met in grade school and became life-long friends who did everything together. It was a co-incidence they had children at the same time, but they planned to raise them side by side. They just didn't know this war was coming and that it would change everything.

Missing in action, that's what Mr. and Mrs. Miller told Mama and Papa two weeks ago. Papa thinks he's probably been taken prisoner, which means always-laughing, always-teasing Carl is still alive out there. And that's something, I suppose.

"They're saying the war is going to end by Christmas." I repeat what my history teacher, Mr. Adams, told us at school today.

"They've been saying that for months." Al's eyes sweep over the shop, red rimmed in the fear he's trying to hide. I know he feels guilty too. He was disqualified from service, and now his best friend is missing and there is nothing he can do.

"I don't want to talk about it anymore." Al takes a breath and moves behind the counter. He pulls out a book from a box full of new finds. "We bought a few new titles today. Had a customer come in with a nice collection they wanted to sell. I got a few saved for you if you're interested."

"Really?" I beam at him and dive for the small stack

set to one side. A Nancy Drew mystery: *The Secret in the Old Attic*, which came out earlier this year. A book of fairy tales, and a book about Amelia Earhart and her disappearance, which Mama and I have been studying at night after dinner.

Once I've looked through the selection, I peer over at the box Al is inventorying. I'm not allowed to read things from the future until I get older, per Mama and Papa's rules. They say that it will confuse us, but I've secretly been reading the Chronicles of Narnia and have been on the hunt for book two a good long while. It's taking ages to collect them all.

"It's not there," Al says as if he can read my mind.

"What's not?" I play innocent.

"*Prince Caspian*. I've been trying to find a copy too."

My mouth drops open. "How long have you been looking?"

"For a few weeks. Don't tell Papa."

"Loose lips sink ships." I recite another slogan from the propaganda posters that have hung all over town since the war started.

Al laughs, a real genuine laugh, and I'm so proud to have made him happy.

He pulls another book out of the box, looks at the title, then copies it in Papa's ledger.

"How was school?" He glances at me.

I raise one shoulder in a shrug. "School."

It's hard to explain to him what it's like. Not feeling like I fit in with the other girls my age. They're different from me. They talk about how to get the perfect curls, take trips to the soda shop after school, and Meryl Clarke is always going on about the boys in our class. But my sandy curls are frizzy no matter how Mama tries to smooth them, and I overheard one of the boys in our class describe me as "heavy for a girl" last week.

"You look like someone just ripped the cover off your favorite book," Al says.

The lights of Rhyme and Reason flicker in fear, offended by his choice of words.

He ignores the shop and rests his arms on the counter as he leans in. There are five years between us, but he never treats me as if I'm some little kid. "Trouble at school again?"

I look down at my hands, trying to fight the embarrassment that crawls up my neck. "Meryl Clarke is having a birthday party this weekend, and I'm the only girl in our class who didn't get invited."

Al frowns. "Why?"

I sniff, trying to pretend it doesn't matter. "I don't know. I guess we're not exactly friends anymore." We haven't been for a while now. "It's on Saturday, anyway, and I always help Papa here on Saturdays. It's not like I even wanted to go," I add for good measure.

Al's hand is gentle as it covers mine. I start to pull

out of his grasp, but he stops me. "You know, the fire-flies in the shop didn't exist before you were born."

I've heard this story a thousand times before, but I stay silent and listen because it's my favorite.

"The shop didn't like you when they brought you home, on account of you crying so much. But then, after your first birthday, you decided you wanted to walk. On your first try you had a bad spill, and you were scared to try again. And then suddenly these fireflies appeared out of nowhere, a whole group of them that hovered in the air in front of you. So, you stood up, and took a step to try to reach them. But before you could, the fireflies backed away from you, and you had to follow them." He shakes his head. "We all just stood there watching it, this—this miracle as you made your way through the fiction section."

"So?" I say, not sure what this has to do with school and Meryl Clarke.

"So, the shop created a new life-form, just for you. Three generations of Fulbrights have lived here, but it did that because you are one of a kind." He pushes his glasses up his nose. "Those kids at school, they don't know what they're looking at when they see you. You can out-argue and out-quiz all of them." He takes a breath. "And as much as I hate to admit it, you know more about books than any of the rest of us."

My eyes widen in surprise.

"You tell anyone I said that, and I'll deny it," he teases. "The thing of it is, they don't know what to do with all of that. Not yet, anyway. Someday they will."

The ache of being left out starts to fade. "You really think I'm one of a kind?"

I've never thought of myself that way. I've always felt less than all the other girls.

"Don't let it go to your head, firefly." He gives me a wink and then drops my hand.

The muscles in my shoulders relax, as warmth spreads through me, the tension melting away.

"That's one of my favorite stories." Papa and Mama move in through the back door. I hadn't heard it open. "The shop taught you how to walk."

I smile. "How was the scrap drive?"

"Well, we collected lots of scrap." Papa laughs, and a cough rises in his chest. He turns and sets his hat on a hook by the door.

"It was fine." Mama rolls her eyes at Papa's joke.

"Did we miss anything interesting while we were gone?" Papa asks.

Al and I exchange a glance, both of us thinking about the customer who hurt Rhyme and Reason's feelings.

"I had everything under control," Al says.

"With my help," I jump in, not wanting him to one-up me.

"Now, now, everything doesn't have to be a competition between you two. There's plenty of room for both of you to help out around here." Papa moves toward the front counter, just as the calendar above the door begins to shift. It lands on today's date, and we all glance up as Carl's mother, Mrs. Miller, steps into the shop. Her eyes are red and splotchy, and my heart sinks.

"Victoria?" Mama asks.

Mrs. Miller moves her lips to speak, but nothing comes out at first. Finally, she hands Mama a small piece of paper. A telegram. My legs go weak.

"No," Al whispers behind me.

"'The secretary of war desires me to express his deepest regret that your son, Sergeant Carl Patrick Miller, was killed in action—'" Mama can't finish the rest, and Papa takes the telegram from her.

The pain is sharp and instant, like a knife in my chest. This can't be happening. Carl promised us he was going to come back from the war. He can't be gone.

"They're wrong," Al says. "They're wrong. It's a mess over there, everyone knows that. This has to be a mistake."

Mrs. Miller crumbles, and Mama goes to her, wrapping her up in her arms.

Papa finishes reading the telegram, tears in his eyes. "This says he was taken prisoner and was killed attempting to escape."

The words slam into me. That sounds like Carl. Never one to accept defeat.

"I just—I can't—" Al takes fast, shallow breaths, and then his knees buckle. He falls to the floor, his head in his hands. And then his shoulders start to shake with silent sobs.

The war seems distant from inside the safety of the shop. It's happening miles and miles away. It can't touch us here, not really. Papa hasn't wanted to talk about what's happening, and we've all agreed.

But we've been wrong. The war can't be ignored or pushed away; Rhyme and Reason can't protect us from everything. The shop may be magic, but even magic has its limits.

Carl had so much life left. He had this big booming laugh Mama said would fill up the world one day. I won't ever hear his laugh again. And neither will Al.

Papa stands frozen in shock, his face a sheet of gray. Mama comforts Mrs. Miller. And I drop to the floor at my brother's side. He looks up.

"He can't be gone, Poppy," Al says.

And then I pull him into me.

As Al sobs, I put my hand on his back and pat over and over again, as if I can take this burden from him.

Above us, I see the hanging lightbulbs dim and then go out.

Chapter Two

Saturday mornings, before the shop opens, have always been sacred in the Fulbright house. We sit around the table in our apartment on the third floor and talk about our plans for the day, how our week was, and the tasks in the shop that need doing. Al and I compete for the best jobs, like redoing the displays and picking books for weekend Storytime, which always takes place at eleven o'clock on the dot.

This morning we sit staring at cold toast. An ice-cold chill has wrapped itself around me, and I can't stop shivering, despite the fact that I've put on two sweaters.

Carl is *gone*. And I don't know how anything is ever going to be the same again.

The radio, which is on low, switches from music to a news report. "Our boys continue to battle through the Siegfried Line to reach the Rhine River. They fight for every yard—"

Papa reaches over and switches it off.

Mama takes a breath and looks up, her eyes red rimmed. "When they were little, people thought they were twins. They would cry whenever Victoria and I separated them. Have I ever told you that?" The ghost of a smile crosses her face. "Carl's first word was *Mama*, but he—he said it to me, not Victoria."

I picture Carl and Al, little boys who were brothers from the start.

James smiles at Mama. "That's why he called you Mama Number Two."

Mama laughs. "Yes, that's right." She blinks and looks at James as if she's waking from a stupor. "Is Al still asleep?" She asks him because the boys share the big room at the end of the hall.

"Let him rest." Papa sighs, his face tight with worry. He looks pale this morning, like he didn't get a wink of sleep. "I'll handle the shop today. Why don't you all just stay here and—"

"Morning! Sorry I overslept." Al breezes into the room. I'm not sure how I expected him to look after hearing the news about Carl, but not like this. Dressed in a clean gray sweater and neatly pressed slacks, he wears his hair slicked back, and his eyes are bright, as if nothing has happened. He glances at his wristwatch. "What's on the agenda today, Pop? Did you want me to start on that inventory in the fiction section?"

My eyes grow wide. Nobody expected Al to work today.

Papa and Mama exchange a glance.

"I—well," Papa stutters. "If that's what you want."

"Great." Al grabs a piece of slightly burnt toast from the table. "Beat you to the shop, Poppy." He takes off before I can say anything.

We all sit in shock for a moment.

"Why is he acting like that?" James breaks the silence.

Papa frowns. "I suppose everyone has to grieve in their own way."

I hear Al's footsteps in the distance as he rushes down the narrow stairs which lead to the second floor. "What do we do?"

Mama's chin quivers as she sets her shoulders back. "We go on living, for Carl."

Papa nods. "And we help Al through this the best we can. However he needs. If he wants today to be normal, then we'll make it as normal as possible." Papa looks at me. "You better go."

"What?" I ask.

"He's going to think you let him win, and we can't have that." Papa gives me a wink.

I nod and push back from the table. Normal. Al wants things to be normal. I should be able to manage that. But as I start down the front hall, all I feel is numb.

Rhyme and Reason is busy all morning. Customers move in and out of the aisles dressed in an array of different clothes from different time periods. Papa rings them up behind the front counter and asks me to work at the currency exchanger. It's a machine with a crank gear that allows customers to insert money from their time and exchange it for currency that works in ours. As I help people trade their money, it's easy to forget about Carl. But every time there's a lull, the ache comes back.

After lunch, when the rush dies down, I move toward the reading section to see if any books need reshelving, when I spy two of our regulars, Whitney Rivera and Katherine Moore, having a debate. Both of them have a hand on the back of the walnut chair with the needle-point seat.

"I got here first, and you know this is my favorite place to sit." Katherine, a shop regular for over a year, is in her thirties, with fair skin and green eyes. A suffragist from 1913, she is never without a great big Edwardian hat, and a SECURE THE VOTE FOR WOMEN button on her lapel.

"We got here at the same time." Whitney, also from 1913, is tall, with golden-brown skin. He lost his left arm below the elbow in a factory accident when he was a kid. He stumbled into the shop a few months ago and has hardly left since. "And it has recently come to my attention that this is the best spot in the house."

I stare at them, eyebrows raised. The shop doesn't tolerate unkindness; if this escalates any more, Rhyme and Reason may take the chair away completely.

The rules of the shop rise in my memory. I've seen them a thousand times, posted behind the front counter.

1. Bookshops exist to spread light, love, and hope to the world through stories.

2. As such, Shopkeepers must never use the magic of the bookshops for their own gain.

3. Bookshop and Shopkeeper work together side by side for the good of humanity.

4. Customers and Shopkeepers may not divulge the secret of the bookshops to the ordinary world.

5. Kindness is mandatory.

Whitney pulls the chair out from the table, but before he can sit, Katherine plops down with a satisfied grin on her face.

"How kind of you, Mr. Rivera."

Whitney frowns at her. "Well—I—there was a book I was going to get upstairs, anyway." He turns on his heel and walks away.

"What was that all about?" Al says from behind me.

"I have no idea . . ." I trail off. It's odd to see the two of them fighting.

Al shrugs and then hands me a clipboard. "I came to challenge you to an inventory-off. We'll do the historical fiction section. You take half and I take half. First to finish gets to arrange the front display for a month."

The front display is a constant point of tension between us. It's the window that customers see when they first enter our shop. And we are always trying to do it bigger and better than each other. I've been imagining an enchanted-forest theme and have been dying to put it together. Winning dibs for a month would really give me a chance to shine.

But I nervously glance toward the front counter. "Papa wouldn't like it if we race."

"He's upstairs on a break and left me in charge. He doesn't have to know." There's a gleam in Al's eyes that's contagious.

I snatch the clipboard from his hands. "All right, you're on."

He takes off through the shelves, and I follow close behind. As we round the corner to the historical fiction section, Al stops so quickly, I bump into the back of him.

"What is it?" I peer around his shoulder to see what's captured his attention. On the oak table beneath the window in the corner, Rhyme and Reason has set up a memorial for Carl. Two candles burn, their flames flickering in the dim light. Between them is the photo of Carl and all of us at the beach, the frame entwined in lush green vines and white blossoms.

"The shop loved Carl too," I whisper.

Al's blue eyes are distant as he gazes at it, his mind a million miles away.

"Al?" I say his name, and it's like he doesn't even hear me.

His lips move, and he mutters something I can't make out.

"Al?" I say it louder this time, but still, nothing. Just a blank, empty look on his face. I reach for his hand, and when our skin touches, he jumps.

"What?" He blinks, as if he's trying to clear his vision.

"Are you all right?" I ask.

Al doesn't answer, and we stand in silence staring at the photograph. Carl has a smile on his face, his unruly curly hair falling across his eyes, and the loss of him hurts so much I want to scream.

I take a deep breath. "It's not fair, that we live here in this place with all this magic, but it can't save him."

Al's eyes grow wide in horror, and he pulls away from me. I sense the panic rising in him as he stumbles forward, taking rapid, unsteady breaths. It's like the truth he's been trying to forget all morning is slamming into him all at once, and I worry about his asthma, that his weak lungs can't handle the weight of what's happened to his best friend.

"I hardly thought about him over there." Al's voice

is little more than a whisper. "Things have been busy here. We've been doing promotions for the shop. I—I went weeks without thinking about him, but then I'd see his little brother in town, or Mrs. Miller up in the kitchen having tea with Mama, and it would hit me that he was over there fighting. And I'd feel like the worst friend a guy could have."

There are so many things I want to say, but none of them can take away Al's pain.

"And now"—Al's voice hardens —"now he's dead."

Suddenly Al lunges forward, raking the memorial off the table. The candles and the frame hit the bookcase to the left, glass shattering across the floor as Rhyme and Reason extinguishes the flames before anything can catch fire. Al collapses into the wall and slams a fist against it. He pulls back his arm for another swing, and the cream paper shifts beneath his touch to a murky purple before he can punch again. I stand frozen in fear, the lights flickering frantically above us.

"Al?" Papa calls out.

"Poppy?" Mama emerges from the fiction stacks, Papa just behind her. They take in the scene and Papa reaches for Al, pulling him off the wall before he can hurt the shop again. Mama raises a shaking hand over her mouth.

"Let me go!" Al stumbles away from Papa.

The shadows beneath Papa's eyes are deep. "The

shop is delicate, son. We treat it with respect. I know you're angry, but—"

"I'm fine," Al snaps, stepping farther out of Papa's reach. "I—I need some air." He moves away from us.

"Al!" Papa calls, but Al doesn't stop. If anything, he moves faster, disappearing through the stacks. I stare at the empty space he's left, the weight of his grief heavy on my shoulders. And then before I have time to think it through, I run after him, trailing him all the way to the back door. I burst out into the frosty November air.

"Al!" His name rips from my throat. He stops at the bottom of the porch steps. "We all loved him." He has to know that this is a burden he doesn't have to carry alone. "We've all lost."

Al turns, his blue eyes meeting mine, empty and vacant. "Half the guys my age are dead." Flurries begin to fall around us. Fresh flakes land on the lenses of Al's glasses, but he doesn't seem to notice. "I should have been there with him. He shouldn't have been alone."

"Getting disqualified for asthma wasn't your fault," I say.

There's bitterness on Al's face. "I'm so tired of it ruining my life. Never allowed on sports teams, always getting picked last for neighborhood baseball, except for when Carl was captain. All the kids thought he was a meatball for picking me first, but he did it anyway."

I wish there was something I could say. Al had Carl his whole life, but I had Al. And I don't know how to help him.

"Come inside," I whisper.

He wavers, one foot on the step, the other on the snow-covered pavement.

A shiver courses through me. "Let me make you some cocoa and—"

"Cocoa?" He pulls back, his whole body trembling, teeth chattering. "Cocoa can't fix this, Poppy." He steps off the porch and moves away from me. "You've never had a best friend, you don't understand."

It's like a punch in the stomach, and all I can do is watch as he walks away from me.

Last winter, James and I hid here in the back alley with a pile of tightly packed snowballs. When Carl and Al emerged from the shop, we ambushed them, but Al quickly turned traitor, and together we tackled Carl to the ground, laughing so hard we could barely breathe as we stuffed snow down the back of his coat.

I don't remember the last thing I said to Carl. Good-bye and good luck, probably. I never had the chance to tell him how much he mattered to me, that I loved how he always got my name wrong and the way he treated me like a little sister.

I wonder if laughter will ever fill this alley again.

Chapter Three

I watch the clock on the wall above Mrs. Walker's desk. Twenty more minutes until the Monday school day is over. Papa wanted to let us stay home after everything that happened with Al and Carl this weekend, but Mama insisted we go to school. It's just my luck that Mrs. Walker is having us share poems in front of the class today. I've been keeping my head low, hoping she won't call on me.

"Poppy Fulbright," Mrs. Walker says. "Please present your autobiographical poem."

Applesauce! She saw me. Anxiety crawls up the back of my neck as I slide out of my seat. The poetry form we're following is supposed to tell people about ourselves. My classmates wrote about their love of baseball and their favorite colors and foods. It all seemed so dull to me. But as I stand in front of the class, I regret my decision to be different.

I start to speak, but nothing comes out. I clear my throat and try again.

"P-Poppy Fulbright." I read line one and move on to line two. "Hardworking, loyal, one of a kind." Someone snickers at that, and I swallow my fear. "Lover of happy endings and red nail polish. Who feels books make the best friends, and that magic is not just for fairy tales." My palms are slick with sweat, and I press on. "Who fears dragons, evil queens, and unbreakable curses. Who hopes to save a kingdom from the clutches of an evil sorcerer someday. Resident of Sutton, New York. Poppy Fulbright."

"Funny Fulbright strikes again," someone mutters, and the whole class giggles.

"Well," Mrs. Walker says. "Thank you, that was— unique. You may take your seat."

I clutch the paper in my hands as I move back to my desk.

"Ezra Meyers." Mrs. Walker calls on the next student.

When the bell to end the day rings, a piece of paper hits me in the cheek. I pick up the crumpled ball and open it. Someone has made a sketch of one of the Uncle Sam posters plastered everywhere for the war effort. But instead of saying *I want you for the US Army,* the sketch reads *I want you to fight the dragons.* The kids sitting nearest me burst out laughing as they collect their things to leave.

Meryl Clarke bumps my shoulder as she brushes past, a laugh trailing behind her.

Feeling ashamed of my poem, I tear it in half and drop it in the trash bin on my way out.

I work on my homework behind the front counter, trying to forget what happened at school today. A vine grows up around my hand, and I shake it off.

"I'm trying to work," I tell the shop.

Something falls from above me, landing next to my math textbook. I glance over at a lemon square. The shop can sense I had a bad day.

"I'm not hungry." I push the dessert away and return to the arithmetic problem.

The fireflies appear in the air, bobbing and glowing as they spin around me.

"Rhyme." I sigh. "I don't want to talk about it."

The fireflies land on my shoulder as the calendar by the door begins to shuffle, someone coming through. It stops on November 6, 1944. Someone visiting from today.

Most of the people who come to the shop are from the past or the future, but the shop also brings people from our time. Rhyme and Reason finds them the same way it finds anyone else. It senses their personality, their wants and needs, and only brings people it thinks it can help.

Ollie bursts through the front door.

"Jeepers, I'm running late again." She's the courier assigned to Rhyme and Reason, responsible for passing correspondence to and from the other shops like ours. A year older than me, Ollie has been working after school as an apprentice courier for six months, ever since our last courier quit. With bright eyes and light-brown skin, she's always a burst of light.

"I stayed too long talking to the Shopkeeper at my last stop, but I can't help it! People have so many interesting things to say . . . My supervisor is a real eggbeater about it. I guess someone complained about my punctuality." A collector of colorful and eccentric scarves, today she wears a checkered purple one.

She flips open the top of her satchel and skims through the letters inside. I catch a glimpse of seven or eight pins, all hooked to a leather keychain on her bag. Each one represents a shop on her route and allows her to move back and forth between them. The couriers have been in place for decades, traveling to each shop to deliver personal letters, requests for books, inquiries about running the business, that sort of thing. Unlike us, they're allowed to use the front door to travel among the shops.

"Take Mr. Goldstein at Books by the Sea. He's eighty years old! He has some dynamite stories, I tell ya. Things about the Great War and the turn of the century." Ollie has such big energy, it fills up the shop whenever she's here. Rhyme and Reason loves her too. As she leans against the counter, the vines and flowers swell up around her in a hug. She glances down and pauses.

"Hi, Rhyme, it's good to see you too." She pats the rosewood surface affectionately. "Enough about me. How are you, Poppy?"

"Fine." Ollie has always been nothing but nice to me. I would love to be friends with her, but I just freeze up around kids my age.

"What my mother wouldn't give to have a kid like you instead of me. She says I could talk a door right off its hinges." Ollie laughs and pulls two brown envelopes out of her bag. "These are for Rhyme and Reason. You got anything for me?"

I glance at the mail basket on the counter and find Papa has left one letter for her to take, which I hand her.

"Poppy?" Mama calls from the back of the shop. "Will you grab a lemon from the tree for the water pitcher?"

I look up at Ollie. "You want to stay for Monday Favorites?"

She tucks the letter into her satchel. "Rain check? This is my last stop, and I promised Mother I'd be home in time for dinner today. See you tomorrow?"

I nod, and then as quick as she came, she's gone.

"Poppy?" Mama calls again.

"Coming!" I push back from the counter.

Tonight is Monday Favorites. The best night of the week and a long-standing shop tradition. It's open to any of our regulars. Everyone brings something they've read recently that they'd love to share and discuss. There are always treats and laughter, and tonight, after the news about Carl, it's a welcome escape.

I pluck the juiciest-looking lemon from the tree and hurry through the fiction section to the reading area at the back of the shop. Mama and Papa have the radio going. A song ends and a news report comes on.

"The United States First Army shattered the Siegfried Line lull today with a new drive southeast of Aachen. Our troops faced strengthened German defenses and—"

Papa turns the radio off. He hates talking about the war. I think it reminds him of his time as a soldier during the last one.

"I was listening to that." Mama sighs and turns to see me standing there.

I hold out the lemon for her.

"Thank you, have you seen Al? He was supposed to help set up the chairs."

I frown. Al never shirks his jobs around the shop.

He always does what Mama and Papa ask.

"I haven't seen him since yesterday."

Mama sighs and moves to the refreshment table.

"While we have a minute . . . I got a call from your teacher, Mrs. Walker." Mama reaches for a small knife and cutting board. "She said there was an incident in class. That some of the other kids may have picked on you, is that true?"

I shrug.

Papa stops what he's doing. "Poppy, you can talk to us."

"We had to read a poem in front of the class. Mine was different than everyone else's . . . The other kids didn't get it." I glance up in time to see them exchange a look. "It's fine. Really."

"We're worried you're spending too much time in the shop and not enough time out there experiencing life," Papa says. "You should be doing after-school clubs, learning what you like and dislike, getting to know your classmates."

I blink. Where is this coming from? He's never said any of this before.

"But the shop is important. I—I don't want to be anywhere else."

Mama reaches for my hands. "There's more to life than the shop, Poppy."

The words burn as they hit me, and I pull out of her

reach. They don't get it. I want late nights doing inventory, long days filled with customers looking for the perfect book, and the magic—always the magic.

Shops pass down in families, I've known that my whole life. It's always been a given that Al will inherit someday. But Al doesn't have a connection with Rhyme and Reason the same way I do. To him the shop is an annoying younger sibling, but Rhyme is my best friend; we speak the same language. We're meant for each other. Why can't Mama and Papa see that?

The front door opens, the bell above it ringing loud and cheerful.

"Let's talk more about this later." Mama runs a hand over her hair, making sure it's set in place.

"Henry!" Papa greets the first regular to arrive. "I haven't seen you all week."

Mama hurries to help Papa get the chairs in order. I watch her go, anxiety bubbling in my stomach.

I press one hand to the wall. "They can't take you from me," I whisper to the shop. In response, the leaves of the climbing hydrangea coil around my wrist, Rhyme and Reason trying to comfort me.

"Hello? Anyone home?" Bright and happy, Katherine emerges through the fiction section, a plate in her hands.

"Katherine!" James bounds down the stairs. He has long been her favorite Fulbright.

"Hello there, James!" she greets him, as he plows into her with a hug.

"You brought apple tarts." He beams up at the plate she balances in one hand.

"I did indeed." She sets them ceremoniously on the table and looks around the room. "No need to ask for the recipe; it's an old family secret, and I cannot divulge it to anyone."

James dives for a tart.

"What if I bribe you for the recipe, Miss Moore?" Whitney asks.

"If it isn't Whitney Rivera himself," Katherine teases. "I'm flattered you would offer, but I'm sworn to secrecy."

An easy smile stretches across his face. "That's *Mr.* Whitney Rivera, to you. Haven't you seen the papers? They're saying I'm one of the most inspiring young entrepreneurs of the year."

"Ha, inspiring? More like fictionalizing. I saw some outlandish headline in that newspaper of yours last week. 'Puppy Born in Queens with Two Heads.' What kind of a headline is that?"

Whitney laughs. "What can I say? We write stories that appeal to the people."

"When are you going to print real news?" Katherine presses him. "Like the fight for women's right to vote?"

Whitney tucks his hand into the pocket of his waistcoat. "When you agree to an interview."

"I'll agree to an interview when you agree to print all the facts."

"People don't always like facts," he says. "We like stories, don't we? Isn't that why we're all here?" He looks around the room, and some of the others who have filtered in nod their heads in agreement.

"Poppy, will you get our customers some water?" Mama asks.

I do as Mama says, filling a few cups and passing them out to the other regulars who have arrived. Some of them I know well, like Bibine and her twin grandchildren; others I know by name, but little else.

There's Cameron from 2019, and Anna Rose from 1956, and Albert from 1880. All in all, a group of twenty or so, which is a fairly good number for Monday Favorites.

They each wear our pin: round and gold, it features a lemon tree and the words *Rhyme and Reason* written in script across the top. *Made of stardust and daydreams* is in the same font along the bottom. We give them to all of our customers so that no matter where—or when— they are, they can always find their way back.

I watch them interact with one another. Anna Rose talks to Whitney about her latest audition. Kosma and Prosper and James play a game of marbles on the floor. Everything has felt less bright since the news of Carl's death, but somehow, with the customers here, the ice around my heart begins to melt. Sometimes, I think the shop is only for them, but the truth is we all need each other.

"Welcome to Monday Favorites!" Papa calls out, and people begin to take their seats in the circle of chairs set around the fireplace. "As always, I'd like to remind everyone that this is an opportunity to share something you've read recently and loved. Please be mindful of the setting. Nothing that reveals big historical details or inventions, please. We would love to avoid cross-time contamination if we can."

Everyone understands the shop is magic, and they know the things they learn here must be kept secret. Rhyme and Reason controls access to books and information in a way that protects the sanctity of time. The regulars are respectful of that effort and try to do the same.

There's a competition for who wants to share first, and Bibine wins out, reading a passage about the Basque Country. Then Whitney takes a turn, followed by Katherine.

" 'Hope' is the thing with feathers." She begins to read an Emily Dickinson poem.

Light footsteps tread behind me, and I glance back to see Al moving down the aisle between the stacks. He wears his heavy wool coat with round wood buttons and a red winter scarf Mama helped me knit for him last Christmas. He stops when he reaches the group and blinks a few times as if he's forgotten what day it is. How very unlike Al.

"What is he doing?" James hisses in my ear, leaning around me to get a better look.

"I don't know," I whisper back, as Katherine finishes her poem and takes a seat.

Al reaches into his pocket and pulls out a piece of paper. His eyes skim over it for a second, and then he moves forward, making a split-second decision.

"I have something to share with you all. Just—give me—" He pushes his glasses up his nose and looks down at what appears to be a newspaper clipping. "This isn't usually how we do things . . . This is an article from our local paper, but the writing really speaks to me." He takes a breath. " 'We regret to announce the death of Carl Patrick Miller, age eighteen. Miller went missing a few short weeks ago. He—' "

"Al." Papa is on his feet, Mama right behind him.

Al stops and looks up. "This is sheer poetry. I want to share it. Isn't that what Monday Favorites is all about? Stirring renditions of emotional—"

"That's enough." Papa's voice is loud and sharp.

There's a long, loaded pause as the regulars stare at Al, who, with shaking hands and bloodshot eyes, is clearly not himself.

Mama stands in front of Al, as if she can shield him

from their gaze. "We're going to take a brief intermission. Please enjoy the refreshments." She motions to the table up against the front windows.

Bibine moves first; small, with a permanent hunch, she somehow commands the room. "Come on, everyone, if you haven't tried the lemon squares, you must."

The others do as she says, shifting to give our family privacy.

"What are you thinking?" Papa turns on Al the moment they're gone.

"Did you see this article?" Al glances back down at it. " 'Carl is remembered as a kind boy, quick to lend a helping hand to others. Cut down in the prime of his life, he was much beloved by his high school teachers and classmates. May we remember the sacrifice he has made.' "

"This is not the place for that." Mama clutches the collar of her dress.

Al ignores them. "He wasn't beloved by his teachers. They thought he was a pain in the neck. Half the fellas were jealous of him, and the other half just disliked him. He broke all the girls' hearts. You remember, don't you, Poppy?"

He's right, Carl was a troublemaker, often goading Al into breaking curfew and the rules. They never did their homework on time. But Carl had a big laugh and an easy smile, and he brought Mama a bag of apples from his grandfather's orchard once a week when they were in season.

Mama reaches for Al. "You can't do this here. Not in front of the regulars."

"This is exactly where we should do this." Al looks at Papa, his eyes wild and unseeing. "The shop—look what it can do. It brings customers from out of their time into ours. Why can't we use that to change what's happened?" Al looks at me, and I remember Saturday and the picture of Carl and how I said the same thing. "Poppy, you thought so too."

Papa turns toward me, eyebrows raised. I shrink back, not wanting to be pulled into this. Disappointment fills Al's face.

"I—I could go back and save Carl before it's too late. We can bring him here, let him hide until the fighting is over. He might be a deserter, but they would never be able to find him."

I suck in a breath, waiting for Papa's reaction. What Al is suggesting is against everything we are. Shopkeepers don't use the shops to change the past or the future. Papa has always said that the shops exist to share and preserve stories, to spread their light to the world.

"Al," Papa whispers.

"We'd be doing it for Carl," Al presses.

"We can't break the rules like that." Papa winces, as if the words cause him physical pain. "We are keepers of the magic, never users." Papa utters the mantra I've heard my whole life.

Al looks away in defeat, his eyes focusing on the front door for the briefest of moments. Whatever he sees there seems to give him courage to keep going. "We have time at our fingertips. The past, the future. We can go anywhere! What use is any of it if we can't change a thing?"

"We can talk about this later." Papa coughs, and he fumbles for a handkerchief.

Al's jaw is tight in stubborn defiance. I get to my feet, an icy rush of air brushing up my back as if the window is open.

"You know this is wrong," Al says.

"I said enough!" Papa's voice rings through the shop louder than I've ever heard it as his patience bursts. He coughs again, this time longer, and deeper. Al doesn't seem to notice.

"What would you have done if it were me? If I had been found in a grave in Germany?"

The strength Papa has been holding on to crumbles. He leans into clasped hands, shutting his eyes at the impossible question.

Tears blur my vision. I can hardly fathom that this has happened to Carl; the idea of Al gone too is enough to make my knees weak.

The lights flicker overhead, the way they always do when Rhyme and Reason is afraid. The warmth of Monday Favorites begins to fade around us, replaced by something else I can't identify.

"Al, let me take you upstairs." Mama reaches for him.

Al's lips tremble as he says one word, one sad, heavy word. "Please."

Papa's face shifts from anger to sorrow. "If I could, I would change it, but I cannot do what you are asking me."

Al gapes at Papa in horror. "You're just going to let him die out there? Cold and alone?"

Tears run in streams down Mama's cheeks, and James wraps his arms around her in a hug.

"He's already gone, Al," Papa whispers. "It can't be changed or undone. We have to accept it."

Al caves in on himself then, burying his head in his hands.

"I'm sorry, everyone," Papa says to the regulars. "Please, excuse—" He stops as another cough rips from his chest. He fumbles for the white handkerchief in his pocket and presses it to his lips.

I turn to get him some water, but all at once Papa staggers forward. He grabs hold of the black chair with the cream-cushioned seat and just manages to steady himself, the handkerchief falling from his hand. It floats to the ground and lands open, the white fabric stained with blood.

The breath catches in my chest, and I stand frozen, unsure of what to do.

Papa tries to take another step forward, but his legs give out. He falls to the left, into a row of empty chairs. A scream leaves my lips, and I'm on my knees at his side, rolling him over. He coughs again, but this time is unable to stop, and I watch in horror as he struggles to breathe.

The regulars shout and cry out behind me, and then Mama is here.

"Go get Dr. Kauffman," Mama shouts. "Hurry, Poppy!"

I am on my feet, stumbling through the fiction stacks, and bursting out the back door into the icy night. The cold air is like knives in my lungs as I rush around the shop to the corner of Marigold and Beaumont. Marigold is the main thoroughfare in Sutton. Dr. Kauffman's practice is one block over, and I have never been so grateful that he lives close.

When I reach Dr. Kauffman's, I pound on the door for all I'm worth.

After what seems like years, Mrs. Kauffman answers. "Poppy?"

She takes in the sight of me, shivering and sobbing.

"It's Papa." I can't grasp the right words at first. "He's—he's coughing blood."

"Jacob! Come quickly!" She shouts for her husband. "It's Vincent Fulbright."

Chapter Four

James and Al and I sit side by side in uncomfortable chairs at the hospital as we wait for Mama to tell us how Papa is. I pick up the newspaper lying on the coffee table in front of us. YANKS LOSE TOWN ON SIEGFRIED LINE, the headline reads.

The Siegfried Line has been in the papers for months. The Germans' last stand for the Fatherland, they're calling it. A bulwark defense, it stretches some 390 miles and is made up of bunkers, tunnels, and traps to keep us out. Our boys have been cracking it for months now. Battles have been happening up and down the length of it as they fight for every yard. Everyone knows the Germans are going to lose the war; the only question is *when*.

I set the paper down and notice there's a few flecks of blood on my dress from Papa's coughing fit. They're so dark they look black. I feel numb as I wonder if Mama will be able to get them out in the wash.

"This is my fault." Al speaks for the first time since we got here. "I shouldn't have pushed so hard."

I look over at him, sitting with his head in his hands, his glasses on the arm of his chair.

"It's not your fault, Al. Papa has been coughing for the last couple of weeks. We all thought it was just a cold."

Silence presses in around us. I stare across the waiting room at the front desk.

"Do you remember last summer, when you and Carl were teaching me and James how to toss a baseball? He threw it to you and hit you right in the face. We brought you straight here."

Al squints at me. His nose still bears a slight bend at the bridge, from the break.

"Mama was so mad at you for playing ball. She marched in ready to tell you off, but when she saw all the blood, she went after Carl instead."

A hint of a smile flickers across his lips. "She nearly twisted his ear off."

I can see Carl now, his ear flaming red as they helped Al into the shop after leaving the hospital.

"You folded her flowers out of book pages every day for a month." I remember the way the ink stained the tips of his fingers black.

"I had to do something. She really flipped her wig over that." He laughs and shakes his head. "It was just a broken nose. Not like I die—" he stops, the smile sliding off his face. Pain fills his eyes as he remembers Carl is gone.

"Al." I reach for his hand. He lets me take it, and I hold on tight, because it's the only thing I can do.

He looks up at me, his eyes searching my face. "It's all wrong, Poppy. It's like this shadow is hanging over me. I close my eyes and it's all I see."

I move my hand to his forearm and squeeze three times. It's our code, the way we've always said *I love you* without words.

The sound of footsteps makes me look up. Mama walks toward us, her heels clicking against the white hospital floor.

"How is he?" James jumps to his feet.

"He's stable." She takes a deep breath to steady herself. Usually well put together, her hair has come out of the rolls on the top of her head. "The doctor says he can have visitors now. He's asking for you." She motions for us to follow her.

Sutton's hospital is so small there's only three private rooms, and Papa is one of two patients tonight. There's one window, a narrow bed, and two chairs stuffed into the tiny space. He sits propped up against a few pillows, eyes shut. He looks so frail.

"Papa." James rushes forward.

Papa's eyes fly open, and the corners of his lips turn up in a smile. "There you are."

James leans in for a hug, then all at once his face is in Papa's shoulder and he's crying, his body shaking as if he's been holding it in for the last few hours.

"It's all right, son," Papa comforts James.

I can't get the image of him falling out of my mind.

"Poppy." He calls for me, but I hesitate. Mama gives me a push, and I move to the other side of his bed, leaning in for a hug.

"How are you feeling?" I try to swallow my fear.

"I'm feeling—" He stops to cough, and I anxiously wait for him to recover. "I'm getting there." Papa takes a breath. "They don't know what's wrong yet. They think I have a lung infection. They've got me on some medicine and want to keep me for a few days."

I can tell Mama and Papa are trying to be calm for us. If it were serious, they would say, wouldn't they?

The tension between Papa and Al hangs thick in the air. Al looks down at the ground. "I'm sorry about Monday Favorites. I don't know what came over me."

Papa sighs. "I understand, son, that you want to change the past. But the rules exist for a reason."

I look at Al, and the pain on his face fills me.

"But why can't we do it for Carl?" My mouth goes dry as I pull together the courage to ask.

Papa motions for us all to come in close. "Do you remember how I've always told you that the shops exist to spread hope and light through books to anyone who needs it? We are protectors of that light. Using the shop for our own gain corrupts that purpose." He takes a breath. "And the magic is complicated; it—it has more than one side."

"More than one side?" I ask, not sure what Papa means.

He continues like he didn't hear me at all. "The Council made the rules two generations ago. We protect the magic by following those rules. Do you all understand?"

James and I nod, even though I'm not sure I do.

Papa's eyes move to Al. "Do you?"

Al hangs his head. "I didn't mean to make a scene."

"Every now and then, life calls for a scene. But if you're going to become Shopkeeper someday, you must learn to obey the rules."

If you're going to become Shopkeeper. The words sting to hear. It's not that Al can't run the shop, it's that I want it more than he does. He was restricted by his asthma, and Rhyme and Reason was his prison during childhood. But it's always been my haven.

"Promise me you'll put the idea of saving Carl to rest?" Papa's gaze doesn't waver from Al.

Al rubs the back of his neck. "Okay."

Papa sags back into his pillows, all of his energy spent. I have so many questions to ask him. About the magic, about Al taking over for him, but now isn't the time.

"All of you should go home and get some rest," Papa says weakly.

"Who's going to watch the shop while you're here?"

I ask, eager to be the one in charge. I want Papa to see I can handle it.

"I'll do it," Al says.

"I'm the mother here," Mama speaks up. "I have things under control."

"But you have so much on your plate," Al tells her. It's true, she's been spending evenings with Mrs. Miller, trying to help her through the loss of Carl. Plus, Mama is the president of the women's organization in town that is fundraising for the war effort. And now this.

Papa studies us. "What if Poppy and Al take care of Rhyme and Reason together?"

"Together?" I glance over at Al.

"But—" Al starts.

"What if instead of competing with each other, you work together for once. That would really be something."

I start to argue, but Papa's eyes are heavy with exhaustion.

"All right," Al finally says. "We'll try."

"Good, it's settled." Mama gets to her feet. "Now I think it's time we let your father get some rest."

"Wait!" James lunges for his bag and frantically digs through it. "I thought we could read, like we do at home." James's ears turn pink as he shifts his hands, and we see what he's brought. *Charlie and the Chocolate*

Factory. A book from the future he's been begging to read for months.

"James!" Mama scolds, because we aren't allowed to read things from the future, much less bring them outside of the shop.

"Just this once?" He blinks at her with those innocent blue eyes of his.

"Of course not, you—"

Papa clears his throat, and Mama pauses. "This rule is our rule, not the shop's. I think tonight we can make an exception." Papa gives us a wink.

Mama sighs, too tired to argue. "Oh, all right then."

Papa shifts in bed and motions for me to sit down. Then he glances at the door. "Al, close that, will you?"

I can't help but smile as I climb up onto the narrow space beside him, while Al settles at the end. Mama moves her chair closer, and just for this moment, we're all together.

Papa has long been the one who reads books out loud in our family. The tone of his voice always makes the perfect narrator. But tonight, he looks at James.

"Me?" James asks, eyes wide.

Papa gives him a nod.

Staring down at the book as if it's sacred, James turns to the first page and begins.

Chapter Five

No matter how hard I try, sleep doesn't find me.
Papa's words circle around and around in my
head. *The magic is complicated. It has more than one side.* What
did he mean? Why does it have multiple sides? And
why can't we at least try to save Carl?

Every time I shut my eyes, I see Carl's face. But he
isn't laughing the way he always did. He's screaming
in pain on a battlefield somewhere. I can't shake the
image from my mind.

Just before seven, as the sun starts to rise, I give up
sleep. Sliding out of bed, I tug on my heavy plaid skirt
and favorite victory-red sweater. My legs and arms feel
heavy with exhaustion as I move out into the hall. James
and Al's door is open a crack when I pass, and I peer
in. James sleeps curled up on one side, but Al's bed is
empty. He must be in the shop.

Rhyme and Reason is dark, but the radio by the
fireplace is on, a news report spilling into the empty
reading area. "The Allies recaptured lost ground
today and fought back into the center of the Siegfried
stronghold, less than fifteen miles southeast of Aachen.

Bent on smoking the Nazis, our boys continue to push forward . . ."

I weave my way through the shelves, and see a soft light coming from the front counter. When I emerge from the fiction section, I find Al, sitting on the floor in the entry, his head in his hands, his back pressed against the door.

He told Papa he would stop thinking about saving Carl, but why else would he be so close to the front door? He's thinking about using the magic again.

I move closer, and it's so cold in the shop I wrap my arms around myself.

"Al?"

He startles and looks up. The ends of his bangs hang over his eyes, and they're coated in something that almost looks like ice crystals. He swipes a hand through his hair, and they disappear.

"What are you doing up?" he asks.

"It's morning," I say.

"Oh." He looks down at his watch. "I must've lost track of time."

"Couldn't sleep?" I ask.

"No." I wonder if he's slept since we saw the telegram.

"Me neither." I kneel on the icy wood floor in front of him, and Carl's face flashes in my head again, his eyes full of fear beneath the rim of his army helmet. Heaviness fills my chest. "I can't stop seeing his face."

Al laughs, sarcastic and low. "Really? I thought I was the only one who cared that he's dead."

I stare at Al in horror. "How could you say that?"

"I'm the only one who wants to save him." He leans against the door for support as he clambers to his feet.

I stand too. "Papa said he would do it if he could. But the magic—"

"Is corruptible, whatever that means." He scoffs.

I look between the door and Al, who still has his hand on it like he can't let go. *What's buzzin', Sunflower?* Carl's laugh echoes in my memory, and it hurts so much I press a hand to my stomach.

"Do you really think we can save him?"

"Yes." Al doesn't hesitate.

"But the rules—"

"Just because there's a way things have always been done doesn't mean those things can't change." Al's eyes flutter, and he rubs a hand over them.

"Carl's death, it's—it's wrong, Poppy. I can feel it. Ever since we got the news, it's churned in my head. I can't sleep, I can't eat." He pushes a hand to his temple. "I have to find a way to save him, even if that means using the shop's magic."

Papa has been Shopkeeper for twenty years. He

knows more than us about the magic, about the Council and the rules. My gut says we should listen to him, but it doesn't mean that I don't want to follow my brother too.

I hear the scritch-scratch of the quote on the chalkboard changing, and I turn my head to read what Rhyme and Reason has to say.

"There are some forbidden things that should stay that way, no matter how much we want to break them."—Artifice and Relic, *Anushka Kapoor*

"How would you use the shop to save Carl?" The words are so simple, but they send a shiver through me.

"Rhyme and Reason brings customers out of time to us because it senses that they need light and hope." He takes a breath. "What if it can work in reverse and send me to Carl?"

"You're going to step through the front door and hope it takes you to Carl? Once you're out there, how would you get back?"

Al reaches into his pocket and pulls out one of our pins. The tarnished gold gleams in the low light. "As long as I have this, I'll be fine."

"And if you find Carl?"

"I'll convince him to come here and hide out until the war ends. The shop would keep him safe."

It seems like such a small thing. Find a moment in

time where Carl is alive and then bring him to Rhyme and Reason for safekeeping until the fighting is over. It could work. There is power to the shop. I feel it all the time, the magic in the air around us. Is it so wrong to think that magic could save Carl's life?

"But we told Papa we'd take care of Rhyme and Reason while he gets better. He's trusting us." The rules are posted behind the front counter; they've been drilled into our heads, and the idea of breaking them makes my blood go cold.

"And we will, but it doesn't mean we can't try to save Carl." Al's eyes find mine, and I swear I see ice on his eyelashes again. "We can figure it out, together. If you'll trust me. Are you in?"

I stare at my brother, at the choice he's asking me to make. Following Papa and the rules and the Council or trying to use the magic to save our friend.

Before I can answer, the clock behind the counter chimes the hour and Rhyme and Reason turns the lock on the front door, opening itself up for the day. Within seconds, Bibine rushes inside without the twins.

"I came as soon as Rhyme and Reason would let me. Is your father all right?"

The door shuts behind her, and the knob turns again, the calendar flipping as Katherine and Whitney step through, bickering about who got here first.

"I've been so worried about all of you." Katherine tilts her head to one side, and the wide brim of her hat bounces from the movement.

"I brought some broth that my mother used to make whenever I was ill as a child." Whitney shoves a jar at me as more of the regulars who were in the shop last night arrive. We all shift, squeezing together to make room as another person steps in, and I end up shoulder to shoulder with my brother.

Al tries to talk over them. "He's going to be in the hospital for a few days, they—"

"How can Rhyme and Reason stay open without him?" someone calls out.

"He knows just the books I like!"

A chorus of concern surges from the regulars, and I want to shrink from it, but I can't because Al and I are in charge here. I have to be brave now. I try to speak up. "Al and I are going to take care of—"

"It can't run without him. Vincent is the heart of the shop!" Whitney interrupts me, kneading his forehead in worry.

"Holy mackerel, would you all cool it!" Al shouts, making Bibine jump. "Things are going to be fine!"

The light flickers above us in fear, and I look at Al in shock. We don't yell at customers, not like that, not ever. A heavy silence settles over the group. Papa would be horrified to see Al snap at them like that.

I seize my courage and start again. "H-he—I—we—" I stop myself, take a breath, and rush forward. "What my brother is trying to say is that we're going to do the best we can to keep things running while our father gets better."

The light stops flickering and the fireflies appear in the air around us, small orbs of light that zip in and out of the crowd, Rhyme and Reason comforting everyone. "Papa always says, when trouble happens, head for the nearest bookshop. They exist for times like these. To—to bring us together in order to get through the hard things."

They wait to see if Al will say anything, but he has a distant look on his face.

"Happy reading," I finish. "If we can help you with anything, please let us know."

The regulars slowly break up around us, uncertainty heavy in the air. Bibine gives my arm a sympathetic pat as she walks past.

Al rubs his forehead again. "I—I don't know what came over me. Their voices were buzzing in my head, and I couldn't make sense of any of it."

James emerges from the fiction section. "You ready for school, Poppy?"

I've forgotten about school, that I promised Mama

I would go today even though so much has happened.

"Yes," I tell James. "Let me get my things."

After we've both put on our coats and schoolbags, we head to the back door. Before we can leave, Al stops me. "Poppy?"

I pause halfway out of the shop.

"Think about what I said?" His gaze is steady, determined. He's talking about his plan to save Carl. He wants me to jump with him. I'm not sure I can.

"I will," I say, but the words turn to dust in my mouth as James and I step out the door.

Chapter Six

F or the rest of the week, all I think about is Al's plan
to save Carl—and go against the Council and Papa.
He wants a yes or a no answer from me, but I need
more information about the rules of magic, about all
of it. More than anything, I need to find out what Papa
meant when he said there is more than one side to the
magic. If we break the rules, what will be the cost?

I'm set on asking Al as much when I get home from
school on Friday. But when James and I arrive, Mama is
the one behind the front counter, not Al.

"—I understand that you're saying the treatments
aren't working, but there has to be something you can
do." She pauses to listen for a moment. "Yes, I'll be
there as soon as I can."

As the call ends, she slams the phone down onto the
cradle and shuts her eyes.

"Mama?" James drops his book bag, worry creasing
his forehead.

She startles. "Hello." She looks exhausted, after
dividing her week between home and the hospital. "H-
how was school?"

"Good," James says.

"Where's Al?" I ask.

"He's upstairs looking for a requested book." She runs a hand over her forehead. "Can you two hold down the front counter until he comes back? I need to freshen up quickly, before I head back to the hospital."

James looks up at her. "Can I go with you?"

Mama gives James a weak smile. "Your father's not up for visitors today."

"Why?" James and I ask at the same time, fear washing through me.

"Has he gotten worse?" I continue.

"He—it's—the medicine doesn't seem to be helping." She sighs. "Everything will be fine. This all just takes time."

But I see the worry in her eyes.

"I can handle things here," I tell her.

Mama pats my cheek, and then heads for the stairs. "I'll send Al down if I see him."

James and I stand in silence for a minute. "I'll check to see if anything needs reshelving," he says, wanting to be helpful.

"Great." I give him a nod. As he disappears through the fiction section, a customer approaches the counter with a book. I'm in the middle of ringing up their purchase when Ollie rushes into the shop, the ends of a bright yellow scarf trailing behind her.

She sighs loudly. "Golly, I've had a day."

"That makes two of us," I mumble.

"I've somehow misplaced my shop pins. I don't know if I dropped them somewhere on my route or what. I had to report it to my supervisor, and she gave me a strike. Two strikes and I lose my apprenticeship. She must think I'm a complete crumb." Ollie sags against the front counter. "What's new with you?"

Usually, I keep things to myself, but something about today, about the weight sitting on my shoulders, makes me want to spill my worries to someone else. Before I can stop myself, I tell her everything, about Carl's death, Papa getting sick, all of it. "And now my brother wants to break the rules and—" I stop abruptly, realizing I've said too much.

"Break the rules?" Her eyes grow wide.

I look around, making sure we're alone.

"He wants to use the shop to fix things."

"He shouldn't go there." Ollie lowers her voice to a whisper. "He shouldn't cross the Council. They're serious about the rules, and if your brother tries to challenge that, it'll mean disaster for you and your shop."

The Council is made up of six members, the job passing down in families the same way shops do. Our Council members are the direct descendants of the original Council.

"My parents run our bookshop, Copper and Ink, and they have friends in high places. They've heard things, like this story about a Shopkeeper who wanted to use the magic to make money by traveling through time. He made a plan, but before he could even go through with it, someone tipped off the Council, and they banished him from our world."

I look around Rhyme and Reason, trying to imagine it being taken away from us.

"Your brother might think he can get away with it, but they'd only find out in the end." She pulls back, her face more serious than I've ever seen it. "I'd stop him, if I were you."

She glances down at her watch. "Jeepers, is that the time? I've stayed too long." She flips open her satchel and pulls out a stack of letters. "Sorry to rush out of here, but I'm trying to turn over a new leaf and deliver everyone's mail promptly."

Though I've only known Ollie for a few months, I like the way she bursts into the shop every day.

"Our old courier was boring," I say. "I like your speed; it means you're an important person with important places to go."

She freezes. "I've never looked at it like that, but golly, you're right."

I laugh, and a grin rises on her face. Ollie's smile fills me with warmth.

She pushes her hair back from her face. "Do you have anything for me to take?"

"Not today."

"Dynamite, see you tomorrow!" She starts toward the door, then stops. "And, Poppy? If your brother doesn't listen to you, about the Council and breaking the rules, tell him to look it up in the Shopkeeper's Handbook. Your family could lose Rhyme and Reason if he doesn't listen."

Then she bursts out the front door, her yellow scarf trailing behind her.

"The Shopkeeper's Handbook," I say out loud. Why didn't I think of that before? I've seen Papa read it from time to time; it's a guide with all of the rules and regulations about the bookshops. Maybe I could use it to find out more about the magic and what Papa meant when he said there's multiple sides to it. More than that, we might be able to use it to find a loophole. Instead of breaking the rules, maybe we could work with them to get what we want.

I pull a sign out from behind the counter that reads BACK IN FIVE MINUTES and set it next to the register.

The quote on the chalkboard shifts.

"She had a way of finding trouble, and then being surprised when it got her." —Silence the Dragon, *Sarah Clearwater*

I ignore Rhyme and Reason's words of caution and

hurry through the shop, waving at Whitney Rivera, who nods at me as I pass through the reading section and up the stairs.

The Records Room is a tiny closet on the second floor, the door nearly hidden by a particularly dense thicket of climbing hydrangea that I have to push my way through.

I turn the brass knob, and the musty smell of old books engulfs me as I step inside. A single bulb hangs on a rusty chain at the center of the room, and I switch it on. Bookshelves cover all three walls, stacked with rows of notebooks in every shape and size. They're Shopkeeper's logs, kept since Rhyme and Reason opened in the 1870s. When I was younger, I used to sneak up here to try to read them, but I've always had a hard time making out the old handwriting.

Next to the logs are stacks of boxes filled with correspondence between Shopkeepers dating all the way back to my great-grandparents' time. On the highest shelf at the far corner of the closet, in a tarnished metal box, is where Papa keeps the Handbook. I've seen him take it out every once in a while. But I've never held it myself.

My hands shake as I contemplate what I'm about to do. Papa trusts us to run the shop, to keep things in order, not to go snooping around, breaking rules. But I can't stop thinking about Carl and Al, and if I find a loophole, then everybody gets what they want.

I stand on tiptoes and reach for the box. It takes me a few tries, but finally I knock it off the shelf. Once I have it, I slowly pull the lid open, the hinges creaking from the effort. Inside sits a small book with a rich crimson cover. Stamped across the center are the words *The Shopkeeper's Handbook: A Guide to Magical Bookshops.*

I flip open to the first page and begin to read.

> *The following is a collection of rules and regulations laid forth by the Council of Shopkeepers. The rules were put into place to protect the bookshops, their keepers, and their customers alike.*
>
> *The bookshops were established to spread light, love, and hope, across time and space, that we might bond the souls of men against the Dark. Let it be known that those who choose to break these rules and regulations face retribution. We are keepers of the magic. Never users.*

Retribution. I shiver at the word, remembering Ollie's story. I read the paragraph again and notice something else.

"The Dark," I say it out loud. "'Bond the souls of men against the Dark.' What is that?"

The minute I say the word, something in the closet shifts. A sudden cold gusts around me, slamming the door shut. I lunge toward it, grabbing the knob, but it acts as if it's been locked from the outside. I'm trapped.

The temperature drops around me as I turn back to the room. A light crackling sound fills the air, and I look down to see something dark and slick forming over the concrete floor. I back away as it spreads up through the walls. I reach a shaking hand out to touch it, and freezing cold spreads up into my arm.

"Frost," I say, letting out a shaky breath that's visible in the air. "What's happening?" I call out to Rhyme, but the shop doesn't answer.

The frost spreads over the door and the cold sinks into me, making it hard to breathe. I spin and knock with both hands for all I am worth.

"Someone help me!" I cry, hoping a customer in the nonfiction section will come to my aid. "Please! Is anyone there?"

"Poppy?" I hear Al's voice.

"Al! I'm in here!" I cry.

There's a pause, and then the knob turns from the outside, the door finally opening. I fall forward, into the heat of the shop.

"What's going on?" Al grabs my shoulders to steady me. "I heard you screaming."

"I was—locked in—so cold." I stumble over my words and point toward the closet, but when I turn back to the Records Room, the frost is gone. It stands still, as if nothing happened at all. "There was something in there with me."

"What do you mean, there was something in there?" Al frowns. "What are you even doing up here?"

Before I can answer, he sees the Handbook in my arms.

"I thought we could look into the rules," I say weakly. "Maybe find a loophole or something."

Al takes the Handbook from me, hope lighting up his face. "Of course, why didn't I think of that? There's got to be some way we can work around the Council. Did you find anything useful in here?"

I'm too afraid to say *the Dark* out loud again after what happened in the closet, so I point to the passage where it's mentioned. "Do you know what it's talking about here?"

"No." Al flips past the introduction. "You mind if I borrow this for a while?"

I stare up at him. I've never *not* trusted my brother. He's always been there for me. But his sudden obsession over Carl, wanting to break the rules, he—he's different these days. And I don't know what the Dark is, but I have a feeling we shouldn't test it.

"We should put it back. Papa wouldn't like us to move it."

Al pushes his glasses up his nose and blinks. "No, he wouldn't . . . but he's not here."

"Al." I reach for the book and try to take it from him. He tugs it away and somehow in the scuffle, the page he's on rips clean out of the book.

"Look what you did!" Al growls.

"Don't snap your cap at me!" I growl in embarrassment. "I'm just trying to put it back where it belongs."

He snatches the page from me. "Now I have to figure out how to fix this."

Heat rushes into my face. It wasn't all my fault; he's just as much to blame. Al starts to put the Handbook into his pocket. I grab his arm to stop him, and he looks up at me.

"I'm better at book repair than you." It's the truth and Al knows it. I started learning how to fix books when I was eight. It's an art Al has never had a knack for. "If I do it, then Papa won't be able to tell that it happened."

There isn't a way to fix the page quite that well, but Al doesn't have to know that. I hold his gaze, my head buzzing with adrenaline and fear.

"Fine. But I want it back when you've finished with it." The tension eases as he pushes the book toward me.

"I'm going downstairs. Turn the light out, will ya?"

I clutch the Handbook to my chest long after he's gone. I don't know what just happened between us, but something has shifted, something I can't name.

"What's happening, Rhyme?"

I back away from the Records Room, the Handbook in my pocket, and the fireflies rise around me, as Rhyme and Reason helps chase off the chill in my bones.

Chapter Seven

Worry settles into me, as I move back down to the first floor. The frost that swept through the room was so strange. I've never seen anything like it in the shop before. Maybe with all this talk of us breaking the rules, Rhyme and Reason is giving us a warning.

"Are you upset with me?" I ask Rhyme, wishing I had never tried to find a loophole.

The shop doesn't answer.

Feeling badly for what I've done, I sort the mail Ollie brought earlier, trying to distract myself. One of the letters is for Mama from a shop friend. Another is from the Council to Papa, with a sentence stamped on the outside: OVERDUE, RETURN IMMEDIATELY. I set it aside.

The last letter isn't addressed to anyone, just Rhyme and Reason. This would normally be Papa's business, but I'm desperate to do something right. I feel like I'm balancing between taking care of the shop for Papa and taking care of Al. It seems like I'm losing on both accounts.

"Should I read it?" I ask Rhyme and Reason.

The fireflies buzz around me. One lands on my

shoulder and some of the chill from the Records Room starts to ease.

The light above me flickers twice. *Yes.*

Encouraged by the shop, I slide my finger beneath the seal and tug the paper from the envelope.

To: Mr. Vincent Fulbright, Rhyme and Reason
From: Theo Devlin, The Woodland Winds

November 9, 1944

Dear Mr. Fulbright,
I'm writing to you on behalf of my mother. I know you're one of her good friends, and well, we're in need of some help at The Woodland Winds. She's too stubborn to ask, so here I am.

Our shop has been acting up recently, and I'm wondering if you have any advice. I'm not sure if you've heard, but Granddad died four weeks ago. It was sudden. He left the shop to my mother, and we're trying to fill the space he left behind, but we don't know nearly enough about how to run this place. Mother would never admit it, but Granddad did her a disservice, not training her proper, and all.

The thing is, we've been malfunctioning. The shop,

that is. Yesterday, the front door wouldn't open. A customer was trapped here for a few hours until it fixed itself. Maybe the Woodland Winds is angry that Granddad has died, but I don't know what to do about it.

I've searched all of Granddad's Shopkeeper's logs for help, but he never wrote about anything like this. I suggested to my mother we could ask some of the other Shopkeepers for advice on how to soothe the Woodland Winds, but she refused. I think she doesn't want anyone to know she's having a tough time with the shop. But I want to help however I can, so I've reached out to a few of her regular correspondents.

How can we run the shop if the door keeps malfunctioning and we can't guarantee our customers' safe return home?

Have you ever encountered a similar issue? Is there something we've overlooked?

I'd be grateful for any advice.

Sincerely,
Theo Devlin

I've met Theo Devlin. Once every four years, families like ours get together for Shopkeeper's Weekend. It's a time for us to gather all in the same place. It happened when I was four and again when I was eight, but there hasn't been one since the war broke out.

Theo was a scrappy boy with unruly curls and long skinny legs. I remember playing Peter Pan and the Lost Boys and long games of hide-and-seek.

I liked old Mr. Devlin. I'm sorry to hear that Theo's granddad has passed and that their shop is not doing well.

I look out at Rhyme and Reason, thinking about the frost, the way Al seems haunted by Carl, me getting locked upstairs in the Records Room. We've had problems too. Perhaps ours are linked to Papa being unwell.

"I c-could write him back," I say to Rhyme and Reason. "Since Papa isn't here to do it, and all."

The hanging bulb above me flickers twice. *Yes.*

But as I stare down at his letter, my heart rises in my throat.

"What if he thinks I'm just some silly girl who doesn't know anything?" I whisper.

I hear the quote changing on the chalkboard behind me.

> *"Life is either a daring adventure or nothing."*
> —The Open Door, *Helen Keller*

I blow a loose strand of hair out of my face. The only daring adventures I ever take are in books. I'm not sure I'm up for it in real life.

But I want to be brave.

"Okay, I'll write to him." My fingers shake as I reach for a sheet of paper.

"Dear Mr. Theo Devlin." I say the words as I write them. "I—"

"That's not how it's supposed to go!" A voice rings through the shop, startling me into dropping my pencil. I think it's Prosper's voice.

A few customers browsing the fiction section peek around the shelves to see what the commotion is.

"We better figure out what's going on." The light above me flickers twice, and the fireflies rise behind me as I rush toward the sound of raised voices.

The lilac hedge opens as I near, and I slip through it. Kosma and Prosper and Anna Rose play on the small Storytime stage. Behind it, the enchanted forest mural showcases glittering fairy hovels and glowing mushrooms. Storm clouds gather in the painted sky, threatening rain.

"I just thought it could use sprucing up," Anna Rose says. "Something like, 'Rapunzel, Rapunzel, throw your gorgeous locks out of the tower, that I might painstakingly climb up and—'"

"You're ruining our play!" Prosper tears off the

velvet cloak he's wearing and stomps off.

Anna Rose adjusts her polka-dot neck scarf self-consciously. "I was just adding a little embellishment. 'Let down your hair' has been done, don't you think? I could never audition with that line."

Kosma sighs.

"Where's Bibine?" I search for their grandmother.

"She's looking for a book upstairs. I offered to act in and direct the twins' play, but they don't seem to like my advice." Anna Rose sits down on the stage, and a loose chestnut curl flops into her eyes. She blows at it with a defeated sigh. "Really they can join the club. No one seems to like my acting these days."

Kosma leans forward and touches Anna Rose's hand. "You were great as Juliet, when you performed her monologue for Monday Favorites two weeks ago."

Anna Rose perks up. "Really?"

I watch Kosma comforting Anna Rose. Papa would know how to make everyone feel better, but I stand to the side, awkwardly.

"I-I'm going to check on Prosper," I say, because I'm not sure how else to handle the situation.

At first, I don't see him anywhere, but just as I'm about to leave the children's section, I spot his leg sticking out from behind the puppet show.

"Prosper?"

He glances up at me with tears in his eyes.

"What's the matter?" I sit beside him, tucking my skirt around my knees. "Is it Anna Rose? She didn't mean to ruin your play."

"It's not that." He swipes a hand under his runny nose. "Today is my mother's birthday." He seems to cave in on himself. "It's her birthday and I miss her."

Understanding crosses my mind. I forget how much Kosma and Prosper have been through. They came from Gernika, a town in the Basque Country that was bombed. They were sent first to England with other child refugees and then were able to move to New York to live with their grandparents in a country they'd never seen. According to Bibine, their parents were killed in the bombing.

"I miss her so much, Poppy."

Prosper's little body shakes with a sob, and it breaks my heart in half. I put my arm around him, and he buries his face in my shoulder.

I can't help but think about Carl, and war and the way it destroys us. He was always a big brother to me, always teasing me about being a bookworm. Sometimes, he and Al would let me and James tag along with them to the movies on Friday nights when they didn't have other plans. I wish I could talk to him, if only to say thank you.

And I see that's what Prosper needs now, a way to talk to his mother.

"Do you know that love is really just a type of magic?" I whisper in Prosper's ear.

Prosper looks up at me. "Like Rhyme and Reason?"

I give him a nod. "Quick, tell me what your mother's favorite color was?"

"Blue," he says. "Like the sea."

I reach out for the vine that grows down the bookshelf next to us. "Can I have a blue flower, please?" I ask the shop.

A delicate blue wildflower blooms above my fingers, the petals silky and shimmering. I pick it and hand it to Prosper.

"What's this for?" He twists the stem between his fingers.

"Hold it to your lips and whisper whatever it is you want your mother to know, and this flower will deliver it to her."

He blinks up at me, wonder on his face. "Really?"

"Really." I nod and nudge his shoulder. "Give it a try."

He sits up, wiping the tears from his cheeks. Gently he lifts the bud to his mouth. "Kaixo, Ama," he whispers. "Happy birthday. Kosma and Amona and I made cake for you and served it in clay dishes just like you taught us. I hope you had some, where you are. I miss you, Ama. We've found a magic bookshop here. I think you would love it."

He presses a kiss against the petals.

"Do you think she felt that too?"

Tears fill my eyes, and I try to blink them away. "I think so."

"Poppy, look!" Prosper points over my shoulder, and I glance back to see glittering wildflowers bloom up the side of the bookcase beside us.

Prosper grabs my hand and pulls me to my feet. We follow the wildflowers as they spread over the top of the shelves. They begin to climb across the wall, moving faster and faster, sweeping through the children's section, a sea of blue bursting from every surface, dripping from the ceiling and the shelves. They even appear in the enchanted forest mural, blossoming over the fairy hovels, pushing the storm clouds away.

Kosma squeals and spins in a circle. "They're beautiful, Rhyme!"

Prosper's eyes are wide with excitement.

"See?" I lean in toward him. "They're carrying your message."

He laughs, joy spilling into the air around us as he twirls with Kosma, his dark curls bouncing around his face. Peace rolls through me. I think Papa would be proud of us, me and Rhyme and Prosper.

I turn to leave them to their joy when something crunches beneath my shoe. Stepping back, I find a patch of wildflowers trampled beneath my foot, their stems wilted and black. I pick them up and the petals are cold, covered in a thin layer of ice. I drop them and spin, my heart leaping in fear. I expect to see frost exploding around us, but Kosma and Prosper still dance among shimmering petals, the magic intact.

Worry swells through me. I've never seen a flower die inside the shop, not in the heat or the cold, or with the change of seasons.

Leaving Kosma and Prosper spinning behind the lilac hedge, I search the other plants and flowers in Rhyme and Reason for frost, but they all seem healthy.

I sink onto the stool behind the counter and take a deep breath.

"Something is off, Rhyme." When the shop doesn't reply, I look down at the letter from Theo Devlin. With courage in my heart, I write back.

To: Theo Devlin, The Woodland Winds

From: Poppy Fulbright, Rhyme and Reason

November 10, 1944

Dear Theo,
I don't know if you remember me, but we used to play together at Shopkeeper's Weekends. We won a hide-and-seek tournament by burying ourselves in a coat closet. My brother Al looked for us twice but couldn't find us behind all the sweaters and jackets.

He and I still laugh about it. It was the only time I ever bested him.

I'm sorry to hear your granddad has passed away. He always made everyone feel special. I loved that about him.

I've received your recent letter about the troubles you're having at the Woodland Winds. Our front door isn't sticking shut, but we have had some trouble of our own, though I think our shop is in a state because my father has taken ill. He's currently in the hospital in town. My brother and I are trying to take care of Rhyme and Reason in his absence, but everything feels off.

I don't have much advice about your door. I wonder if it would help to remind the Woodland Winds that it's loved? I recommend a day with the windows open, a few hours of upbeat music, and a good cleaning. Perhaps saying the words out loud, "I love the Woodland Winds," all while spinning in a circle three times.

If that doesn't work, try some grease.

Kindest regards,
Poppy Fulbright

Chapter Eight

The next day, I sit at the repair station by the closet beneath the stairs, trying to fix the torn page of the Shopkeeper's Handbook. Sometimes we buy books to resell that need some fixing first. Papa always says to never turn away a book that needs a little bit of love.

I carefully tape the ripped edge, but there's no way Papa won't notice it. I suppose when he gets released from the hospital, I'll have to tell him what happened. I hope he's not too disappointed in me.

Once I've repaired it as best I can, I skim the introduction where it talks about bonding the souls of men against the Dark. There's a table of contents next, and I read through it hoping for a chapter that might tell me more about what the Dark is. But most of the book seems to be about the rules and various bookshop procedures.

On the last page there's one single paragraph: *As Shopkeepers, we must protect and defend the magic. The Dark lies in wait, somewhere out there, searching for an open door. Be watchful, be vigilant.*

"Hi, do you work here?" a girl asks. "I want to buy this book."

I jump to my feet, feeling like I've been caught reading something I shouldn't.

"Of course, I'll ring you up at the front counter."

A Saturday rush hits hard after that, and James and I struggle to get everything done, no thanks to Al, who is nowhere to be seen.

It isn't until later, when things have calmed down, that Al appears. Still in the same clothes he wore yesterday, with a stack of papers tucked beneath one arm, he descends from the second floor as James and I are cleaning up for the day.

"Where have you been? We got so busy James and I could hardly—"

Al's eyelids flutter strangely, and he swipes a hand over them. "I had things to do."

I frown. "Like what?"

"I've been looking through some of the old Shopkeeper's logs."

He's been in the Records Room this whole time? Anger crawls up my neck.

"You'll never believe this, Poppy. I found a petition from Great-Grandmother Aggie. It's dated 1890." He rifles through the stack of papers until he finds what he's looking for. " 'To the Council of Shopkeepers, I write to you on behalf of my missing daughter, Ada Elaine Fulbright. She disappeared from our home two days ago and has not been seen since. We fear she is in danger and beg permission to return to the last time we saw her in order to prevent her disappearance from occurring.'"

"Grandpa had a sister who went missing?" I whisper. I've never heard about anyone in our family named Ada Elaine Fulbright.

"That's not the point, the point is they thought they could use the shop to change the past. They wrote to the Council for permission, Poppy. *The Council.* It means I'm not wrong for wanting to use the magic to fix things. Our great-grandparents wanted to do it too." He tilts his head to one side, and his eyes flutter in a way that leaves me feeling unsettled. "Maybe Papa is wrong about using the shop."

"The Shopkeeper's Handbook says using the magic will—"

"*Forget* the rules, Poppy." There is desperate hunger in his eyes.

Al sees this letter as proof that Shopkeepers can change the past by using the magic. I skim it again and search for a sign this was ever sent to the Council, or approved by them, but can't find any.

"This isn't a solution, Al. This is a letter someone wrote out of grief. It doesn't prove that we can suddenly break the rules."

A shadow passes over Al's face.

"What if—what if we petition the Council the way Great-Grandmother Aggie did? We can try to get their permission." The thought makes my mouth go dry, but it would be better than facing *retribution.* "Maybe they'll say yes."

"They won't say yes, Poppy." His voice is hard and loud.

"I—"

"Poppy, Al, James?" Mama's voice makes me pause.

Al and I exchange a glance as she emerges from the back. "Where's your brother?"

"I'm here." James moves out of the lilac hedge, where he's been playing with Kosma and Prosper and Bibine.

"What's wrong?" Al asks as we take in her splotchy face.

Her chin quivers. "It's your father."

My heart sinks as fear sweeps over me.

"He—he's worse." Tears slip down her cheeks. "They've done all they can do here, and they've decided to transport him to the city. The hospital is much bigger there; they can do more for him. A specialist wants to run some tests. I'm going to go with him."

"When are you going?" James curls his hands into fists at his sides.

"Tomorrow." Mama swipes a hand beneath her eyes.

"What if they can't figure out what's wrong with him?" Al asks, his face white.

Mama takes a breath, as if to steady herself. "Then— then there won't be anything they can do for him."

It starts to sink in then, that Papa has some strange disease they have never treated before. He might die.

I press a hand to my mouth, feeling sick. None of this makes any sense. They told us they weren't worried, that he would get better, not worse.

The lights begin to flicker overhead in fear, as Rhyme and Reason takes in the news, and suddenly it's like I can't breathe. A pressure throbs in my head, and I stumble around Mama.

"Poppy." She tries to grab my arm, but I shrug her off. I need air.

I rush toward the back of the shop and burst out onto the porch. I stumble down the steps and make it to the sidewalk before I fall to my knees.

Haven't we been through enough? The war and Carl and now this? I try to gulp down freezing November air.

Footsteps echo in the alley behind me. I glance back to tell Mama I want to be left alone, but it's not Mama, it's Al.

He tucks his hands into the pockets of his slacks. "You still against using the magic?" he says smugly.

"Go away," I growl between gritted teeth.

"We could fix it." He speaks slowly. "Fix everything that's gone wrong. After I save Carl, we'll—we'll take Papa to the future and get him some better doctors."

And I picture what he's saying. It would be like nothing had ever gone wrong.

But the cost of such a choice. Ollie told me that breaking the rules could lose us the shop. The Council would take away everything. Would it be worth it?

"We could lose Rhyme and Reason," I whisper.

"Only if the Council finds out." Al's eyes flutter again, and I get to my feet.

"Papa is sick, he's—he's dying, and all you can think about is getting what you want." I rarely yell at my brother, but anger like I've never felt before blooms inside of me. "What is *wrong* with you?"

His mouth pulls into a frown. "That's what I've been trying to tell you. Everything is wrong."

Shivering from the cold, I push past him back inside the shop, where I see Mama and James holding on to one another behind the counter.

Rhyme and Reason has always seemed endless to me, something eternal. And Papa along with it. No matter where I look, he is here. His care, his kindness, his laugh echoes in my memory. He is the heartbeat of us. Without him, nothing will be the same.

My legs feel weak, and I reach for the nearest bookshelf to steady myself. It's freezing beneath my fingers. I lean into it and find it coated in a thin layer of black frost.

It doesn't have to be this way.

A voice that is not mine rises up inside of me, distant and thin; it presses into my head. My blood runs cold at the sound of it.

I close my eyes and Carl's face flashes in my memory, followed by an image of Papa, sickly and weak in his hospital bed.

I push away from the shelf and rush through the lilac hedge, desperate to escape the feeling of dread that floods through me. I get to the back of the shop, intent on finishing up the repair on the Handbook. The light above the workbench is still on, and I reach the table expecting to find things right where I left them.

But the desk is empty. The Shopkeeper's Handbook is gone.

Chapter Nine

❧

To: Poppy Fulbright, Rhyme and Reason

From: Theo Devlin, The Woodland Winds

November 11, 1944

Dear Poppy,

I'm sorry to hear about your father. Watching someone you love suffer is one of the worst things I've ever gone through. When Granddad was in the hospital, I hated knowing there was nothing I could do to help him get better.

I remember you from Shopkeeper's Weekends. If I close my eyes, I can still smell those musty sweaters from that coat closet where we won hide-and-seek. If I recall, your brother spent the rest of the day swearing up and down that he let us win.

I also remember your laugh, funny enough. It always made me laugh too. I miss those weekends.

I hope we can meet there again when the war ends.

I'm fourteen now—you're a year younger than me, right? It feels like the whole world has changed since I saw you last. The war's made everything different. It's funny how they've been saying it will end any day since it started. It seems like it won't ever be over, but I hope it ends soon. I miss the way life used to be.

The door of the Woodland Winds is still malfunctioning. I did what you told me in your last letter. I said the words "I love the Woodland Winds" out loud and spun three times. It was on the third spin when I realized you were joking, and boy, did I feel foolish. I also tried your suggestion of grease (on the hinges, of course), but it didn't seem to help. It's strange business that both our shops seem to have odd things happening. Maybe they're just in a bad mood.

Or maybe it's grief. The shops must grieve, too, right?

Sincerely,
Theo

I settle at one of the reading tables in front of the fireplace. It's early in the morning, the shop is empty, and my heart is heavy because we're going to the hospital to tell Papa goodbye before he's moved to the city. I read Theo's letter that Ollie delivered yesterday, and a soft warmth fills me. For this moment, this tiny moment, I don't feel so alone.

The fireflies float in the air around me, their light soft and gold, as I pick up my pencil to write back.

To: Theo Devlin, The Woodland Winds

From: Poppy Fulbright, Rhyme and Reason

November 12, 1944

Dear Theo,

I don't think the things going on around here are on account of the shop being in a bad mood. Don't get me wrong, Rhyme and Reason can have a temper, but this is different. Today one of our regulars was looking for a poetry anthology, and when we found it, there weren't any words on the inside; the whole thing was blank! It turned out all of the books on that shelf were exactly the same. Like the words had been wiped right out of them. And the pages were cold, as if the books had been left out in the snow. Can you believe it? I keep asking Rhyme and Reason to tell me what's wrong, but the shop isn't saying.

I think you're right about the shops feeling grief. The sicker Papa becomes, the worse things seem to be getting around here. Rhyme and Reason must be worried and sad just like the rest of us.

They're moving Papa to a hospital in New York City today. They don't know what's wrong with him and—I'm scared. What if he doesn't get better? What if he—I can't write the rest of that sentence.

My mother is frantic at the moment, packing everything they'll need in the city. My brother and I are supposed to be taking care of the shop, but he keeps disappearing for these long gaps of time. I look for him everywhere with no luck, and then all of a sudden, he turns up like he never left. I wish I knew where he was going . . .

I'm worried he's digging into things he shouldn't be. A few days ago, I stumbled across the Shop-keeper's Handbook and, well, he was very interested in it. Have you ever heard of the Dark? The

Handbook references it a few times like it's a bogey monster under the bed, but I don't know what it means. It almost sounds like it's waiting to get us at any moment. I've been reading through Papa's Shopkeeper's logs to see if he ever mentions it, but I haven't come across anything yet.

Sincerely,
Poppy Fulbright

Papa's hand seems so small in mine. I resist the urge to hold on tighter, to keep him here with me always. It's my turn alone with him, but I don't want to say good-bye.

His room is cold and drafty, the white iron bed pushed up against one large window that doesn't seem to hold out the chill. A glass bottle sits on a stand, connected to a thick tube that drips something into his veins. He looks worse than I imagined. His face gaunt and gray, like there's a shadow lingering beneath his skin. It's been a week since I've seen him, but it feels like so much longer.

"Poppy." He manages a weak smile. "How are things at the shop?"

I look down at my lap. I'm not sure I should tell him

my worries. About the sudden bursts of cold, the empty poetry books, the black frost. I want him to focus on getting better.

"Fine," I say. "We all miss you. Katherine gave us a recipe for a healing balm her family swears by. Whitney sends his regards, and Prosper and Kosma drew these pictures of Rhyme and Reason for you, to keep in your hospital room."

I hand him the papers, and Papa looks them over, tears welling in his eyes. After a moment he sets them aside. "How are *you*?"

The truth is that I don't know how I am. Sad, lonely, confused. I want to ask him so many questions about the rules, the Council, the Dark, but I don't know where to begin.

"I'm keeping things running for you." I try to sound confident, even though it really seems as if everything is slipping through my fingers.

Papa fills the silence. "It's not all on your shoulders, Poppy. It's okay to leave the shop sometimes."

"But I want to take care of things while you're gone." I can't tell him that Al isn't doing his part.

Papa nods. "I understand, Poppy. But there's more to life than the shop and the magic. There's normal life out there. You're allowed to find other interests and to want other things."

The shop *is* normal life. More real to me than anything in our time. I'm able to meet customers, talk about books, be myself. Mama and Papa don't understand.

"What are you thinking?" He pushes me.

"I—I feel like I don't fit in at school. It's so hard to pretend to be like everyone else." I attempt to express the thoughts that flood through me.

Papa starts to speak, but I stop him.

"I work in the shop and see things no one would believe even if I told them. I have captivating conversations, with marvelous people, and then I have to go to school and act like my life is the same as the other kids'."

"I'm not saying you have to be like everyone else." He takes a breath. "But I want you to see more of the outside world. The shop is our home, and it's full of so much good, but there are other things, Poppy. You mustn't be afraid to—"

"I'm not afraid." I cut him off, but it sounds like a lie, even to me.

"There's nothing wrong with fear. We're all afraid sometimes." He waves a hand at the window. "Look at this war. The whole world is terrified. But we can't let that stop us from *living*. One day, when Al takes over for me, I want you to have something more." Papa's words are quiet, but they twist like a knife in my heart.

"When Al takes over?" I ask.

"It's the way things are done, you know that." Papa's

hand shifts toward mine, but I scoot back so he can't reach me.

"He doesn't know Rhyme like I do. That it prefers Mondays to Fridays, and nail-biting puts it on edge." Words bubble up inside me, and once I say them, there will be no going back. "He—he still wants to use the shop to save Carl."

What little color is left in Papa's face drains from his cheeks.

"He said he gave that up." Papa shuts his eyes. "Just this morning, he sat here and promised me he was done thinking about that."

"He lied." I lean forward, begging, pleading for him to believe me. I am not about to let them take the shop away from me and give it to Al when Al still wants to use it for all the wrong reasons.

"He promised me he wouldn't," Papa whispers.

I lean into him, searching the tired lines of his face. "What happens if he tries?"

"Once he crosses that line, he won't be able to go back. There are consequences for breaking the rules, ones that can't be undone."

Papa winces as a cough builds in his chest.

I give him a moment, and then I press forward. "Consequences that have to do with the Dark?"

Papa's body jolts at the words. His eyes fly open,

filled with dismay. "How do you know about the Dark?"

I've never lied to Papa before, so I give him a half truth. "I read about it."

Papa reaches for my arm and pulls me close. "Whatever it is you read, wherever you got it, put it away."

"But what is it, Papa?" I'm desperate to have answers, to figure out what he's so afraid of.

"Forget you ever saw that word. Promise me." His grip tightens, and the fear on his face cuts through me.

"I'll try," I tell him, but I'm not sure I mean it.

Papa relaxes his grip as another hacking cough overtakes him. "Make Al see that he cannot break the rules. He'll listen to you."

Me? Papa wants *me* to stop Al?

"I'm just his kid sister."

"He trusts you, Poppy. He wouldn't have told you his intentions if he didn't. Convince him to stop. For the good of Rhyme and Reason." Papa fights to stay awake, his strength slipping away.

"But—"

The door opens, and James moves into the room for his turn with Papa.

I look at Papa and I am terrified I'm never going to see him again, that these are our last moments together. The terror takes my breath away, and I lunge toward him, burying my face in his shoulder.

"Papa," I whisper. The word *goodbye* sits on my tongue. I swallow it down. "I love you."

"And I love you." A shadow of a smile crosses his lips and then fades away. "Whatever happens to me, I want you to stop him, Poppy. Stop him before it's too late."

Chapter Ten

I sit, curled up in the empty space beneath the front counter. It was my safe place when I was little whenever things felt too big and scary. I haven't hidden down here in years. I pull my legs to my chest as the image of Papa in his hospital bed sticks in my head.

"They don't think he's going to get better, Rhyme," I whisper. "They didn't say that to us, of course. There was a lot of 'We're going to figure out what this is' and 'The doctors are going to run more tests,' but you should have seen Papa's face. He thinks he's going to die."

And I feel it then, something tugging at my mind.

The magic could save him. It could save Carl, make everything right.

The same voice I heard yesterday rises inside of me again. Maybe it's the part of me that wants to listen to Al and risk everything we have in order to save Carl and Papa.

"But I don't want to break the rules." I press a hand to my temple in frustration. There's no easy choice.

A cold gust of wind sweeps over me, bringing with

it a piece of old, yellowing paper. The petition our great-grandparents wrote that Al tried to show me earlier. Maybe he's right. Maybe it isn't wrong to want to change the past; clearly, we aren't the only Fulbrights who ever thought about it.

I can't let Papa die. I have to do something, anything.

I crawl out from under the counter and pull open the top drawer for a sheet of paper. I'm about to close it again when I see a bunch of envelopes stuffed at the back. They're addressed to Papa, with the word OVERDUE stamped across them.

Did Papa hide these? Or did Al?

I push them back into the drawer. I'll deal with them later; right now I have to do what I can for Papa. And the only thing I can do is petition the Council, just like Great-Grandmother Aggie did.

The pencil shakes in my hand as a surge of bravery courses through me, and I begin to write.

To: The Council of Shopkeepers

From: Poppy Fulbright, Rhyme and Reason

November 12, 1944

Dear Council,
My father is Shopkeeper at Rhyme and Reason in

Sutton, New York, and I am writing to you on his behalf. He has fallen ill with something the doctors can't diagnose. He's been very sick. The other day one of our regulars said that Papa is the heart of Rhyme and Reason, and they're right. We can't go on without him. We need him to get well.

I would like to submit a petition to use Rhyme and Reason to save his life. With your permission, and direction, we would like to obtain help from doctors in the future to treat him.

Sincerely,
Poppy Fulbright

P.S. If it's possible, could we also save the life of a dear family friend recently lost in the war? His name was Carl Miller. He loved to laugh. It isn't fair that he's gone.

The shop is our only hope for both of them.

I finish the letter and fold it in half, my hands shaking. If this petition gets approved, then Al can save Carl, and I can save Papa, and everything can get back to the way it was: all of us together and happy inside of Rhyme and Reason, and we won't ever think about breaking the rules again.

"It's *my* seat!" Katherine's voice rings through the mostly empty shop, and I startle.

The lights begin to flicker in fear above me.

"Move, right this instant, Whitney!"

I sigh and throw the petition into the top drawer behind the counter as I set out across the shop. I don't like dealing with conflict, but seeing as Al has disappeared again, it's up to me.

The arguing escalates, and I rush through the fiction section and burst into the reading area. Whitney and Katherine face off with one another. The chair with the needlepoint seat is firmly between them, both of them clutching the ornate walnut back.

"I don't know why over the last week you've decided this is yours, when it's so clearly mine!" Katherine shouts at him, her Edwardian hat bobbing up and down.

The anger in her voice catches me off guard. Katherine usually has some snark, of course, but I've never seen her yell like this.

"Is—is everything all right here?" I try to sound calm, but stumble over my words.

Katherine looks at me. "I went to use the powder room and when I returned, he'd taken my chair. Don't you see my books here?"

Whitney peers at them. "I didn't realize you were coming back."

"Of course you didn't." She rolls her eyes.

The hanging lights above us flicker and go out.

"I know you're used to getting your way because you own a newspaper, but the world doesn't revolve around you."

"That chair doesn't belong to you. I don't see your name on it!" he snaps at her.

Whitney and Katherine have always been competitive, their banter sharp, but still friendly. I've never seen them fight like this, and I don't know how to stop it. What would Papa do?

"There are plenty of seats," I tell Whitney. "Katherine was here before you. First come, first served. That's the rule."

"Yes, but I want that one," Whitney growls, and itches the side of his face. He pulls his hand away and stares down at his fingers. They're covered in a thin black coating.

"What is that?" Katherine snaps at him.

"It feels cold, like ice, and—" He raises it to his nose and sniffs, accidently inhaling some. He lets out a cry. "It burns!" He glances at Katherine. "What have you poisoned me with?"

Katherine laughs, high-pitched and unlike herself.

"That's what you get." She pulls out the chair and plops into it, her arms crossed over her chest. "This seat is mine, Whitney."

He wipes his nose on a handkerchief. "I was leaving anyway. Miss Fulbright, I would like to purchase these."

Katherine sticks out her tongue at him. I start to say something about the way she's acting when I notice a line of dark frost along the edge of her hat.

"He makes my blood boil." She lets out a sigh, and her breath is visible in the air for the briefest of moments.

"Miss Fulbright, are you coming?" Whitney calls for me, and I rush after him, a knot in my stomach. What's happening here? Is Rhyme and Reason so sad about Papa that it's influencing our customers?

I watch Whitney warily while he uses the currency exchanger. The gears twist and turn, gleaming as it accepts his money and spits out the 1944 equivalent. We stand in silence for a moment, and I watch the anger drain from his face, the muscles in his jaw relax, and his eyes soften.

"W-what's really going on, Mr. Rivera?" I ask, my stomach all nerves.

He looks up, confusion on his face for a moment. "I—I don't know." He shakes his head as if he's trying to clear it. "Do you ever get irritated at people for no reason?"

"Sometimes," I admit. "School *always* make me irritated."

"Really?" He raises his eyebrows. "An education is a marvelous thing."

"Of course," I agree. "But the other kids are . . . Let's just say I don't fit in. They think I'm strange because I like to read and I have a big imagination."

Whitney leans in. "No! Imagination is the most important thing a person can have. It gives you the chance to believe in the possibility of impossibility." He lowers his voice. "I was a poor factory boy, and the world wanted me to stay that way. But I believed, and now look at me." He waves a hand over his expensive suit. "Let me tell you a secret. Everybody has magic inside of them, you know. All you have to do is find it."

I stare at him. Magic inside of me? I've never thought about it like that. It's always been in the shop, but maybe Whitney is right. Maybe everybody has a little bit of magic inside too.

Some of the uneasiness inside of me begins to loosen. "Thanks."

"Anytime." He picks up his hat and puts it on. "Tell your father to get well, and that we miss him."

"I will."

He moves toward the door and tries to open it, but it sticks shut. He frowns and pushes harder, but it doesn't budge.

"That's strange," he says.

I glance at the ceiling. "Let him go, please."

Whitney gives it another try. Still nothing.

"Oh dear, is Rhyme and Reason displeased with me as well?" He nervously looks up at the ceiling. "I'm sorry if I have offended you."

I move around the counter and give it a try myself. He isn't kidding, it really is sealed up tight. Like twisting a lid off a jar, I manage to turn the knob to the right. With a good deal of force, and with Whitney's help, I finally manage to shove it open.

Whitney looks at me, his brow furrowed. "Maybe it just needs some grease?"

It's the same advice I gave Theo, and it echoes in my head.

"Have a good evening, Poppy." He tips his hat and then rushes down the sidewalk, where he hails a taxi and disappears.

A gust of freezing wind washes over me, pushing my hair off my shoulders as I stare out onto a dark cobblestone street. It takes me a moment to realize I'm looking at New York City, 1913. Tall business buildings and apartment complexes stand in the distance, all of them pinched in tightly together. A high-pitched horn honks as square automobiles shoot past.

I've never stared out the front door into a customer's

timeline. We have so many people moving in and out every day, there's never really a spare moment to stop and see the places they're coming from.

You could go out there, really explore 1913 for yourself.

The voice whispers inside of me again, and I don't want to hear it anymore.

All you have to do is step out there, and anything you desire can be yours.

And for the briefest of moments, I want to do it. To follow Whitney and explore 1913 New York for myself. My body sways forward from the wanting.

I'm about to take a step out when I stop, my foot hanging in midair.

"What am I doing?" Somehow, this strange voice has gotten into my head, urging me to break the rules and I—I willingly followed it.

The lights flicker frantically overhead as I pull back in horror and slam the door shut.

Papa asked me to stop Al from doing this very thing. I'm supposed to keep Rhyme and Reason together, not cost us everything we have. My pulse races, and I shut my eyes as the voice speaks again.

They don't want you to know about me.

I fall back against the door, and it's cold through the fabric of my sweater. My eyes fly open, and I turn around to see glittering black frost spread across the wood. It crackles as it forms faster and faster over the emerald surface.

If you listened to me, you could fix everything.

"What's happening, Rhyme?" I call out in desperation. "Make it stop!"

I'm afraid your shop can't hear you right now.

The voice grows so loud, it's like someone is standing next to me, and I throw my hands over my ears. "Leave me alone!"

All at once, the floor beneath me begins to tremble, quaking as if the shop is in pain.

"Rhyme!" I stumble forward, and that's when I see it. A dark figure standing a few feet in front of me. Not quite a person, it hovers in the air, reaching toward me.

"Poppy?" Al bursts from the fiction section and freezes when he sees the shadow looming there. The figure pauses at the sight of my brother, and then all at once it disappears.

The lights stop flickering and the world goes suddenly still. I take a breath.

"What's happening? What was that *thing*?" I grab Al's arm like he can protect me. He shrugs me off. "You saw it, Al, tell me you saw it."

Al's eyes flutter, and he turns away from me. "What are you talking about, Poppy? I didn't see anything. I think you're just tired; you need some sleep."

"But I keep hearing a voice in my head that's telling me to—"

"I said forget it, Poppy!" Al growls at me. "Why do you always have to go sticking your nose in places it doesn't belong? Always messing with everything around here. Did you ever stop to think that not everything is your business?"

My eyes well with tears. "All I've ever done is try to help *you*."

He stops, his back to me, shoulders tense. "I don't need your help."

That's news to me. "You wanted it a few days ago."

"Well, I changed my mind."

My head spins. He's been begging me to join him in his quest to save Carl for days; for him to suddenly change his mind doesn't make any sense. And then it hits me. He hasn't wanted my help since the Handbook went missing.

"Where's the Handbook, Al?" My voice rings out stronger than I feel.

He stiffens. "I don't know what you're talking about."

"I—I left it at the repair desk, and then it was gone."

"Go to bed, Poppy." His voice is hard and cold, and it leaves me feeling hollow and alone.

"Al," I say. "I'm scared."

His head turns just enough for me to see his profile.

In the low light of the shop, I make out the angles of his face, his nose with the bend from where it was broken, the sharp line of this jaw. His dark hair spills onto his forehead, and the sudden sense that I don't know him anymore washes through me.

"Get some sleep. You'll feel better in the morning."

I want him to tell me everything will be fine. That it's safe here, even with Papa gone. I want him to be the brother he was before Carl died. I look up at the ceiling and I swear the shadows shift around us, threatening to swallow everything I love.

I swallow down the fear and look back at my brother, but he's gone. I hear light footfalls as he slips down an aisle, hurrying away from me.

"Rhyme?" I whisper, my voice shaking. "Are you here?"

The shop doesn't answer.

"Poppy?" Katherine stands at the mouth of the fiction section, one hand on her chest. "What's going on?"

"Just a misunderstanding." I turn so she can't see my tears.

"Poppy—" she starts.

I give her a weak smile. "We decided we're closing up early today. You can come back tomorrow. I'll save your chair."

She nods, and I walk her to the door. When she's gone, I lock up behind her, my limbs heavy with exhaustion. I turn to go upstairs, and notice a new quote, written at an angle down the chalkboard.

"No matter how fast light travels, it finds the darkness has always got there first, and is waiting for it."—Reaper Man, *Terry Pratchett*

"What are you trying to tell me, Rhyme?" I stand in the empty, silent shop, feeling like everything is crumbling around me and no matter how hard I try to hold it all together, I can't stop it.

Chapter Eleven

To: Poppy Fulbright, Rhyme and Reason

From: Theo Devlin, The Woodland Winds

November 13, 1944

Dear Poppy,

Turns out, the Woodland Winds and Rhyme and Reason aren't the only bookshops where strange things are happening. My mother heard from a friend in Maine who said their shop keeps slamming curtains closed every time they open them to let light in. I heard my parents talking about it when they thought I'd gone to bed. My mother said she's never heard of something like this happening before. She's going to write to the Council about it.

I bet Granddad would have a theory about what's going on. It always seemed like he knew everything about the shop world.

Is Rhyme and Reason still having problems?

I'm sorry about what's happening with your father. My mother caught me writing this, and I told her that we've been sending letters and that your father is sick. She sent Ollie with these orange drop cookies. She says she won't be offended if they taste like concrete; war rationing sure makes food taste less good.

Sincerely,
Theo

Ollie takes a bite of a cookie, and I glance up from Theo's letter.

"These aren't half bad." She pushes the plate toward me. "Want one?"

But my stomach feels unsettled after last night, and I shake my head no.

When I woke up the morning after I saw the shadow figure, I hoped Rhyme and Reason would be fine, that everything would be normal, like nothing happened. But it feels like the magic has been ripped out of the shop.

Ollie dusts crumbs from her hands onto the floor, and I wait for Rhyme to react because it hates crumbs. Usually the lights flicker overhead, the vines and the flowers shrivel at the sight of them. But today there's no reaction, and my heart sinks.

Your shop can't hear you right now, the voice told me. What if that thing has taken Rhyme and Reason away from us forever?

"Poppy?" Ollie leans toward me, and I blink.

"What? Did you say something?"

"I asked you if I could take my break here." She frowns. "Are you all right?"

I debate telling her about the shadow and the voice in my head, but I can't imagine how she would react to it.

"In this letter, Theo says strange things are happening in some of the other shops. Have you heard anything about it?" She mentioned that her parents knew some of the Council, and she visits seven or eight shops on her route every day. Maybe she's seen something.

The concerned look on her face deepens, worry heavy in her eyes. "I've heard some of the shops have been acting strange. The magic isn't letting customers in or out, that type of thing. You haven't had problems here, have you?"

I bite my bottom lip. "Rhyme isn't itself today. It's like—like the magic is gone."

Ollie looks around, as if she's seeing the place for the first time. She reaches for the white jasmine that blooms along the front counter and the petals shrivel beneath her touch instead of rising up to greet her.

"Something is happening out there," she whispers. "It's almost like the shops are infected with a sickness."

Infected with a sickness? I've never heard of that happening.

"My mother says the Council is worried, that they're trying to keep it quiet." She looks at her satchel, weighed down with letters. "I don't think they're succeeding. I've had more mail the past few days than the entire time I've been training as a courier." She takes a breath. "You could write to the Council. Maybe they'll be able to tell you what to do."

"Maybe." I think about the petition tucked away in the top drawer of the front counter, feeling relieved I never sent it.

"If you want to write Theo back, I can get your letter after my break." Ollie looks around Rhyme and Reason. "Don't tell the other shops, but this one is my favorite."

I smile. "I won't tell a soul."

"Great." She grins and starts to leave.

"Oh, wait! A customer sold us a stack of poetry books yesterday, and I thought you might like first pick." I pull out a box and push it toward her. "If you find something you want, it's on the house."

Papa does that for people from time to time. He says a book is the greatest gift a person can get.

"Really?" Her face lights up, and she takes the box off the counter. "Thanks, Poppy! I can't wait to dig in."

I start to pull out a fresh sheet of paper when James and his friend Arthur come through the back door, both of them filthy from playing baseball in the snow.

"You take that back right now!" James shouts at him, and my eyes widen. They're best friends, so of course they get into fights from time to time, but James sounds furious.

"I won't. You're off your rocker."

"Am not!" James yells.

And before I know what's happening, James has lunged at Arthur and they're throwing punches at one another. I stand frozen in horror, and then I run.

By the time I reach them, James has Arthur on the floor, his face pressed into the wood.

"What are you doing?" I haul him off his friend, who has clearly taken a punch right to the eye. "What's going on here?"

"He started it!" James shouts, his bottom lip trembling.

"Gonna go cry to your mommy?" Arthur wipes a hand over a bloody lip, and I see red.

"Arthur Clarke, you get yourself home this minute!" I growl.

Arthur looks at me and smirks. "You can't tell me what to do."

I reach for his ear and twist as hard as I can, like I know Mama would do. He yowls and stumbles out the door.

Once he's gone, I look back at James. "What on earth happened?"

He straightens his sweater vest, still refusing to meet my eyes. "We were arguing about baseball cards, and I just got so angry." He stares down at his hand, the knuckles bleeding. "I know—I know—it's bad. I just . . ." He sighs the heavy sigh of a boy carrying too much. "I can't get rid of this feeling." He presses a hand to his temple, and Al doing the same thing echoes in my memory.

His fine brown hair sticks up at odd angles. There are tears in his blue eyes, and a trickle of blood trails down his cheek.

"Things are really hard right now, but it's going to be okay, James." I sound more confident than I feel.

His shoulders slump forward. "Poppy? I'm sorry."

"It's okay." I pull him in for a hug, resting my chin on his head.

I stare up at the ceiling, missing Rhyme. If it were here, it would have intervened and protected James. I want the fireflies to glow around us, for the magic to give us strength.

But Rhyme and Reason is silent.

To: Theo Devlin, The Woodland Winds

From: Poppy Fulbright, Rhyme and Reason

November 13, 1944

Dear Theo,
Things at Rhyme and Reason seem to be worse.
Last night something strange happened with the shop.
I—I thought about telling Ollie what happened,
but I didn't know how she would react. Honestly,
I don't know how you will either. I saw a shadow
standing in the entryway. It felt like it was goading
me into breaking the rules, like it wanted something
from me, and today Rhyme and Reason feels empty,
like the magic is gone.

You said your granddad knew everything about
the shops; that's how I feel about Papa. He grew up
here, an only child who dedicated his life to learning
everything there is to know about the magic. Mama
grew up in the shop world too, but she was the youngest of five daughters raised by a single dad. He
didn't always have time to teach them everything.

I should tell them both about what happened with

the shadow figure, but I don't want to add to their worries. Papa asked me to watch out for Rhyme and for my brothers. I can't tell him I'm failing.

If you hear anything else about the other shops, write to me about it?

I don't know what to do to bring the magic back, but I'm going to try my best.

Sincerely,
Poppy

———

To: Poppy Fulbright, Rhyme and Reason

From: Theo Devlin, The Woodland Winds

November 14, 1944

Dear Poppy,
Shouldn't your brother be the one taking care of you? Where is he in all of this? Does the Council know what's happening at Rhyme and Reason? Sorry for all of the questions, I just—I don't think your father expected you to handle all of this completely on your own.

I won't tell anyone about the shadow figure, but, Poppy, if you haven't written the Council yet, will you think about it? Whatever this is—I've never heard of anything like it happening in a shop. No wonder you're scared. If I could, I would come over there myself.

The Woodland Winds has been about the same. No reply from the Council yet on the situation here. My mother is angry she hasn't heard back. It's almost like they aren't answering on purpose, as if they don't want us to know what's happening.

Your father sounds a lot like my mother. She's also an only child. I wonder if it's how they became friends. She was the apple of Granddad's eye. She's trying to hide how much she misses him from me, but I still see it. I get it. I miss him too.

Little things remind me of him. Like today, I found a stack of his favorite books. You ever heard of Estefan Gonzalez? Boy adventurer! World traveler! Granddad loved reading about Estefan treasure-hunting in the Yukon or battling pirates off the Ivory Coast. There's a whole series of them. The ones we have are in rough shape from being read so much. I remember

Granddad tucked away in his chair by the fire, a grin on his face as he turned page after page. I think they reminded him what it was like to be young.

I picked up one of those Estefan Gonzalez books this morning, and I could almost feel Granddad through the words. It's funny, isn't it? How books can make you feel like you aren't so alone.

Well, I better go. I just got home from school and the shop is starting to get busy. We're in the middle of our winter book sale. We let our customers fill a bag with books for a dime. It used to be one of my favorite promotions. But it was Granddad's favorite time of year too, and I can't seem to find any joy in it now.

Things used to have color when he was alive, but now everything seems so gray.

Sincerely,
Theo

P.S. I'm sending you book one of the Estefan Gonzalez series. Since I can't come to Rhyme and Reason, I'll just have to send Estefan instead.

Chapter Twelve

I sit at the front counter, reading Theo's letter, warmth spreading through me as I take in his words. He sent me a book so I would feel less alone. I stare at the Estefan Gonzalez book. Nobody has ever done anything like that for me before.

The *scritch-scratch* of the quote changing on the chalkboard echoes through the shop and I glance back.

"I had not thought of violets late, the wild, shy kind that spring beneath your feet in wistful April days." —"Sonnet," Alice Dunbar-Nelson

I watch the words form and my heart leaps. Is the magic back?

"Poppy?" Al's voice reaches me from the other side of the fiction section, and the momentary hope fades. I hastily fold Theo's letter and stuff it in the pocket of my sweater just as he emerges from an aisle.

"What was that?" He looks at me suspiciously.

"Nothing." I get to my feet and dust off the back of my skirt. "What is it?"

"Have you noticed how strange the shop has been acting? It's like the magic is . . ."

"Gone?" I finish for him.

He runs a hand through his hair. "Yeah, that's it."

Anger flashes through me, that it's taken him so long to notice what I knew immediately. "It's been like this for days. If you didn't disappear so much, you would know that."

"I'm right here, aren't I?" he asks, adjusting his glasses with an annoyed sigh.

"No, you're not." I shake my head and move past him through the fantasy section.

"Prosper, that's mine! Give it back right this instant!" Kosma shouts at her brother just as they burst through the lilac hedge. Prosper laughs and swings a wooden sword in his arms.

"Bet you can't catch me," he taunts her.

"It's my turn to be the knight today, you're being unfair!" Kosma charges toward him, but Prosper spins out of her reach.

"Enough of this nonsense!" Bibine hobbles after them, wincing as she tries to keep up.

"Slowpoke!" Prosper, who doesn't usually torment his sister, seems to be enjoying it. He sticks his tongue out at Kosma and then dives down the aisle, plowing right into Al, who falls off-balance and cries out in pain as the tip of the sword catches him in the side.

Something in Al seems to snap, his face turning to rage. "You rat!"

There is real fear in Prosper's eyes as Al charges after him.

"Al!" I hurry to stop him, just as Katherine bursts from the reading area, her great big hat bobbing with anger.

"Whitney Rivera must be banned from this shop immediately! He's just insulted me for the last time, and I will not stand for it!"

Prosper slips past her, dashing away from Al, who is tight on his heels. Katherine presses a hand to her chest and blinks in surprise as Kosma nearly knocks her over in the rush to catch her brother.

"Kosma! Prosper! I demand you stop this at once!" Bibine growls.

A few browsing customers cower in the stacks, watching the whole ordeal unfold. I rush past Katherine and burst into the reading area, where Prosper winds in and out of the tables, screaming in terror as Al lunges for him. Al nearly snags his pant leg, but Prosper manages to escape.

"What on earth is happening?" Whitney jumps to his feet and backs into the fireplace, knocking a picture from the mantel that shatters when it hits the floor.

"That chair is mine!" Katherine screeches, and vaults over the table in an attempt to get at the seat Whitney has vacated.

Suddenly a great tremor goes through the shop. The ground shaking beneath my feet, I grab hold of the nearest table as the hanging lightbulbs sway overhead and books spill off the shelves around us. Kosma screams for her grandmother as Whitney ducks beneath a table.

And then, as quickly as it started, it stops.

Everyone stands, frozen. Al has a hold on Prosper's arm, and Kosma is attached to Al's waist. Bibine cowers beside a bookshelf, her hands clasped over her ears. Katherine is somehow sitting in Whitney's lap, both of them in the needlepoint chair.

Sunlight streams through the front windows, and from the angle I'm at, crouching on the ground, I see dark particles falling through the air like snow. They float toward the regulars, coating their hair and their eyelashes. A swarm of them gathers around my brother.

I reach out a hand to swipe at them in horror, just as the hanging light above me begins to flicker.

"Rhyme?" I jump to my feet, hope flooding through me that the magic has, in fact, returned.

"You should've just let me have that seat," Katherine growls.

"Give me the sword, Prosper!" Kosma reaches around Al.

"You two, stop it right now!" Bibine scolds.

An entire set of dictionaries smashes to the floor,

and the lights surge brighter than they have in days.

"Rhyme?" I call out.

The hanging light above me flickers twice. *Yes.*

Rhyme is back!

Now if I could just get everyone under control. I climb on top of the nearest table, and they all fall silent, their eyes fixed on me. I clear my throat and try to speak, but nothing comes out at first. Heat spreads up my neck in embarrassment. "If—if everyone could please calm down. You all know that kindness is mandatory here. I think the shop wants you to apologize to each other."

No one speaks. I catch Al's gaze and glare at him; setting this kind of example for the regulars, Papa would be ashamed. He drops his hold on Prosper and takes a step back.

"I'm sorry I hurt you with the sword." Prosper hangs his head. "I don't know what came over me."

Al doesn't say anything.

"I'm sorry to you too, Kosma." Prosper hands her the toy.

Whitney looks at Katherine. "You can have the chair. For now, anyway. I haven't been feeling myself lately." He rubs the side of his forehead.

The tension eases around us, the chill of the last few days beginning to melt as the wisteria vines start to bloom again, fresh buds pushing up through wilted layers. The roses on the mantel burst into a bright, glittering white, and the wallpaper, which has been hovering around a sad-looking purple, shifts to a soft lavender. The fireflies rise in the air, and gentle warmth sweeps through the shop, wrapping us in a cocoon.

I look at the window, at the light pouring through, to see if the particles are still visible, but there's nothing there. Maybe I imagined them.

Whitney and Katherine begin to pick up some of the books that slid off the shelves. I turn to ask Al a question, but he's slipped away when I wasn't paying attention.

And that's when I see a new quote has appeared on the chalkboard in the distance.

"The townspeople had grown up with tales of the monster in the lake. They had long hoped that with the right plan they could defeat it. But deep down they feared the truth: no matter what they did, the monster would always be stronger than they were. And one day soon, it would come for them." —The Monster of Obsidian Lake, Marco Moreno

A shiver runs through me as I read it twice through. It's sending a warning.

Who is our monster? What am I not seeing?

Chapter Thirteen

To: Theo Devlin, The Woodland Winds

From: Poppy Fulbright, Rhyme and Reason

November 14, 1944

Dear Theo,

I'll think about writing to the Council if I can't handle things here. But not yet. I want to show Papa I can be a good Shopkeeper, that I can take care of the magic.

Have you had any problems with your regulars acting strangely? Ours seem to be at one another's throats. I can't help but wonder if Papa's absence is the cloud hanging over Rhyme and Reason.

Speaking of Papa, we talked to Mama on the phone last night. They've been at the city hospital for two days, but none of the new medicine they've given him has made a difference. She says he hasn't gotten worse though, and I suppose that's something.

I spent the whole day at school thinking about the magic and why the shop doors are malfunctioning. I got called on to answer a question in science and I didn't even know what the teacher had asked, ha!

Back to the door—what if the shops are reacting in fear? I know when I'm afraid of a thing, I try to keep it away from me. Could the doors be sealing shut in order to keep something out?

Sincerely,
Poppy

P.S. You wrote that the color is gone from your life. Maybe you can borrow some from the world around you. Yellow and orange from the fading sunlight spilling into the shop at the end of a long day. Velvety red from a well-worn reading chair. Deep brown from a rich leather-bound copy of your favorite book.

The color is there, Theo. Please don't give up looking.

P.P.S. Thank you for the book, they make the best gifts, don't you think?

To: Poppy Fulbright, Rhyme and Reason

From: Theo Devlin, The Woodland Winds

November 15, 1944

Dear Poppy,

Jiminy Cricket, your idea about the shops is scary. All of this time, I thought maybe the Woodland Winds has been trying to keep us inside, but what if it is trying to keep something out? I think you're onto something, Poppy.

The question is, what's the shop trying to protect us from?

Sincerely,
Theo

I stare at the front book display, which shifted sometime in the night. Usually full of bright colors and happy titles, today they're all bleak. Dark greens, dreary purples, harsh grays.

"*Run While You Can.*" I read the titles out loud. "*The Dark Is Rising*. What are these, Rhyme?"

The books shift, new ones appearing with even darker covers. Rhyme shuffles them into a line.

In the Fading of the Light. The Dark Is Rising. Run While You Can. A Storm on the Horizon. My vision goes blurry as the titles sink into me. They're not titles, they're sentences. "In the fading of the light, the dark is rising, run while you can, a storm on the horizon." I stumble back in fear.

The question is, what's the shop trying to protect us from? Theo wrote in his last letter, and maybe here, Rhyme is giving me the answer. The Dark is rising.

"Poppy?" James calls out from the back of the shop. "I can't find Al anywhere, but we're going to be late for school."

The clock on the wall says it's almost eight. Al should be here to take charge of the shop for the day.

"You go on ahead, I'll watch the counter until Al shows up."

James stares at me uncertainly, then, with a sigh, heads out the door.

I need answers about what's happening, about the Dark. I move behind the front counter and pull out the drawer that holds all of Papa's Shopkeeper's logs. Taking them out, I begin to search for anything that might help.

Papa's notebooks are categorized by month and year, but when I search for his most recent log, I can't find it. November and October are both missing. Maybe Al has already gotten to them. Just as I'm about to pull out September, I find a folded-up piece of paper along the side of the drawer. I pull it open and see the tight font of the Shopkeeper's Handbook.

History of the Rift as Known, the title at the top reads. Someone has ripped it from the binding and scribbled notes across the page. It's Al's handwriting.

The shops have always existed to collect and share the healing books have to offer. In the beginning, the magic was one. Like people, it had both dark and light inside of itself. As the magic was used for good, the Light began to grow, but as the Light grew, so too did the Dark. When a keeper decided to use it for his own selfishness and greed, he caused the Rift.

The Rift tore the magic in two, creating the Light and the Dark. The magical world was changed forever. After the Rift, the Light was left weak and wandering, while the Dark grew. All it wanted was to destroy the keepers, to destroy the Light. It hunted our ancestors down, one by one. Those who were left fled across the ocean and eventually established the bookshops as a last line of defense, a wall against the Dark.

Al has circled the part about the keeper who caused the Rift. His writing says: *What classifies as selfishness or greed?*

The bell above the door rings, and I fold the paper back up, feeling like I'm about to be caught with something I shouldn't have. As I stuff it in the drawer, Ollie steps inside.

"Why are you here so early?" I call out to her, and she turns. Her eyes look worried, her usual cheeriness absent.

"I've been sent by the Council directly." She hands me a brown envelope, and I turn it to see who it's from. *Euphemia Adley, Council Leader* is written in a flourishing script at the top.

"What's this about?" I suddenly feel like I'm being called to the principal's office.

Ollie bites her lip. "I don't know."

My thoughts are racing as I read the rest of the address on the envelope. It's written to Papa directly.

"Maybe they're writing to everyone . . ." She trails off.

"Do you have letters from the Council for any of the other shops on your route?"

"No," Ollie admits.

Hands shaking, I slide my finger beneath the seal.

To: Vincent Fulbright, Rhyme and Reason

From: Euphemia Adley

November 15, 1944

Dear Vincent Fulbright,
We received a petition written by your daughter,

requesting permission to use the shop for her own gain. While we're sorry to hear you have not been well, we can't help but be alarmed. Such a petition has never been presented to us before. It is highly irregular, and somewhat distressing that you would allow her to send such a request. You've been Shopkeeper of Rhyme and Reason for nearly twenty years. In that time, the rules have never changed.

I am sending this letter to inform you that you are under inquiry.

We will be in touch.

Euphemia Adley

"Poppy?" Ollie asks, her brow creasing with concern.

I fumble for the top drawer, where I stored the petition I wrote to the Council the night we said goodbye to Papa. Writing it was a mistake; I never should have done it. I was desperate and sad and—

I stare down into the open drawer.

The petition is gone.

Chapter Fourteen

The phone receiver feels sweaty in my hand as I listen to the sound of Mama breathing on the other end. The letter from the Council, which Ollie brought yesterday, sits in front of me.

"Poppy, are you there?" Mama seems so far away.

I lean into the counter. I should tell her about the inquiry, but I can't deliver more bad news.

"Yes, sorry, what did you ask?"

"I asked if you would put Al on."

The truth is, today is the second day of school I've missed to take care of the shop, and I don't know where Al is.

"He went to visit the Millers." I almost mention that he hasn't been himself, that he's been disappearing for long periods of time, but I can't bear to add to her worries.

She sighs, and I hear her exhaustion. "How has he been?"

"He's okay." The jasmine vines on the front counter tap against my arm in protest of my lie. I turn away, facing the back wall.

A sentence appears on the chalkboard above me.

"Oh, what a tangled web we weave, when first we practice to deceive!"—"Marmion," Sir Walter Scott

I glare up at the ceiling.

"Tell him to call me at Aunt Lina's when he gets in."

I promise I will, and then we hang up.

"I'm not lying to her," I tell Rhyme and Reason. "I just don't think she needs to know everything."

The light above me flickers twice. *Yes.*

"No, it's not a lie. I—" A strange noise stops me, a sniffling sound. Someone is crying. I move out from behind the counter to find the source.

A few customers mill about in the fiction section, but they all seem fine. There are regulars in the reading area, Whitney among them, sitting in the needlepoint seat. I follow the sound to the lilac hedge and slip through.

The enchanted forest mural on the back wall looks strange today. The trees, always a vibrant green, are gray. The fairy hovels are missing completely. Katherine sits in front of it, her big Edwardian hat on the ground next to her, knees pulled up to her chest. The climbing hydrangea behind her has cocooned her in a hug.

"Katherine?" I ask, my stomach full of nerves as I tiptoe toward her.

She looks up at me, and there's dirt on her face, a small cut above her eyebrow. My heart drops.

"What happened?"

"W-Whitney is in my chair again."

"Is that all?" I ask with a sigh.

"Well, not exactly." Her green and purple *Votes for Women* sash droops off her shoulder. She sniffs and looks down at it. "The suffragist group I'm a part of marched in a parade today. Some of the onlookers were angry at us. They started to throw rocks, and a skirmish broke out." She takes a breath. "I needed somewhere to go, somewhere to get out of the street, and Rhyme and Reason appeared for me."

She brushes a stray strand of hair out of the way.

"I'm so sorry that happened." I crouch next to her, wanting to tell her that women *will* get the vote, but of course I can't divulge that kind of historical information.

"It's all part of the cause, I'm afraid. I believe in fighting for what's right, even when there are people telling you it's wrong."

"How do you manage to keep going?" I ask.

Katherine levels a look at me. "Because I refuse to give up. No matter how bad things get." She reaches into her pocket for a handkerchief with tiny apple blossoms stitched along the bottom corner. "My great-aunt Patricia was an early pioneer in the campaign for the vote. She has dementia now, I'm afraid. She'll never really see it come to fruition. She doesn't remember my name or my face, but I have to carry on the flame. For her." She runs her finger over the needlepoint.

"That chair Whitney and I have been fighting over . . . it has this exact same pattern. It—it reminds me of her determination, on the bad days, when I feel like giving up."

I wish I had known sooner why she loved that chair so much. I should've asked.

"It's such a small thing to be upset over. But when I got here and saw him sitting in it, I crumpled. I needed her strength today." She wipes her nose. "Whitney and I used to be friends, but these past few weeks everything he does sets my teeth on edge. This heavy feeling washes over me, and I—I just get so angry." She pushes a hand to her temple.

It reminds me of the way I've been feeling about Al lately.

"Well," I say. "Let me see what I can do."

I help Katherine to her feet, and together we wade through the lilac hedge.

Whitney looks up from the piece of paper he's been writing on, his dark curls falling over his eyes. "Oh no. I got here first, ladies."

I gently curl my hands into fists to stop them from shaking with fear. I can do this. I can handle this problem on my own.

"What is it about this chair, specifically, that you like?" I ask.

He frowns and stares down at the glossy walnut

armrests, then up at the shop. "It has a great view of everything, the way it lines up perfectly with the aisle between the fiction section shelves. I can always see who is coming in."

His eyes slide to Katherine, and something like embarrassment crosses his face.

"You like the way the seat lines up with the shop?" I say the words slowly, making sure I understand him correctly.

"This view reminds me that the impossible is possible every day." He waves his hand at Rhyme and Reason. "Well, that, and I enjoy the armrests."

I follow his gaze, and for a moment the shop seems to sparkle beneath his praise.

"Will you stand for a moment? I think I have a solution." I look at the various seats around the reading space while Whitney gets to his feet. The green with the floral cushion? No. Or the pink with the gold trim? Not Whitney's style. My eyes settle on the ebony with a velvet cream fabric and gold-accented armrests.

Carefully, I pick up the chair with the needlepoint apple blossoms and shift it to the left. Then I grab the ebony one and place it exactly where Whitney likes it. With the new chair in the old spot, I motion for Whitney to try it.

He pops the lapels on his jacket, and with a lot of pomp and circumstance, takes a seat.

"I have to say . . . this is far more comfortable than the other one."

Katherine sits next to Whitney with a happy smile on her face. Warmth seems to thread its way between the three of us as the fireflies flutter in the air around me.

"Thanks, Poppy," Katherine says.

"Yes, thank you! Finally, some peace." Whitney gives Katherine a wink. And I turn away from the reading area, a spring in my step. I can't believe I did it! I solved the feud that has been going on for days.

As I emerge from the fiction shelves, the calendar begins to change, landing on November 16, 1944. Today's date. The bell above the door rings out as a man and a woman sweep into the shop. The fireflies around me disappear instantly.

The woman wears a long gray coat with a high collar. She looks to be in her thirties, with sharp cheekbones and brown skin. Her dark hair is swept up in the latest victory roll fashion. The man is older. In his seventies, perhaps. He has pale wrinkled skin, silver hair, and a pronounced bump on the bridge of his nose.

They pause in the entryway, looking around the shop, at the lemon tree and the vines and flowers dripping from the shelves and the walls.

"Hello," the woman says, her voice smooth as syrup. "Is Vincent Fulbright here?"

I try to stand taller, to seem confident. "I'm Poppy Fulbright. My parents aren't here right now. I am in charge of the shop if there is something you need help with."

The man tilts his head to one side. "Why, you're nothing but a child."

I take offense to that, but I know better than to protest. "What can I help you with? Are you here for a specific book? We carry used books that—"

"My name is Euphemia Adley," the woman says.

It feels as if the air has been sucked out of the room, and I can't remember how to breathe. Euphemia Adley. Council Leader.

"Poppy Fulbright, you're the one who wrote to us. We found your petition quite—irregular. I decided it was best to pay a visit to Rhyme and Reason myself. This is Cyrus Finch, head of Shopkeeper Affairs. He deals in family dramas, rule violations, and other such incidents. Think of him as a liaison between the shops and the Shopkeepers."

They're here about the petition. I still don't know how it got sent to them, but I can only assume it was Al who did it. I can't tell them that or things will seem even more out of hand than they already are. I'm going to have to take the fall for him. Anger rushes down my shoulders and into my arms.

"You said that your parents aren't here. When will they be back?" Cyrus Finch looks around as if that will make them appear.

"M-my father isn't well, as I wrote in the petition. He was recently admitted to the hospital." My voice shakes as I speak, deciding not to tell them he's in New York City and not Sutton. "Mama is with him."

"Vincent isn't well enough to be in the shop himself?" Euphemia asks.

"No." I try to remain calm beneath her unwavering gaze. "The doctors aren't sure what's wrong with him."

"That's why Vincent hasn't been responding to our mail. His Shopkeeper's logs are weeks overdue." Cyrus focuses on me. His eyes are such a light shade of gray, I can't look away. "They left you in charge?"

"No, my brother Allan, he's eighteen, he's in charge."

"Ah, I see." Something like understanding crosses Euphemia's face. "Is Allan here?"

"He's out as well, but I'll tell him you came by." The vines along the front counter curl around my wrist, the shop lending me support.

Euphemia and Cyrus exchange a glance that I cannot read.

"I take it your father did not know you sent the petition?" Euphemia says.

"It wasn't supposed to be sent. It was a mistake." I

can't meet her eyes. I should never have left the letter in that drawer. I should've destroyed it. "I'm sorry if it broke any of the rules. I didn't mean to."

"Mistakes happen." There is kindness in her that calms me. "These are difficult times we're living in. I understand why you wrote it. Your father being ill, not to mention the loss of a loved one to the war, is a difficult burden to bear." There is sadness in her eyes.

Heavy silence sits between us.

"May we look around?" Euphemia finally asks.

"Of course." I nod. "I can give you a tour."

Cyrus turns away from me in disinterest. "That won't be necessary. I've been here many times for Rhyme and Reason's annual evaluation. We'll fare just fine on our own."

Cyrus starts toward the fiction section, Euphemia just behind him.

I pace behind the counter, trying not to panic as I watch them walk away. What if they find something they don't like?

"What do I do?" I ask the shop.

The quote on the chalkboard changes.

"All human wisdom is contained in these two words,—'Wait and hope.'" —The Count of Monte Cristo, *Alexandre Dumas*

"That's helpful," I mumble.

After what seems an eternity, Cyrus and Euphemia emerge from the lilac hedge. I clasp my hands together to stop them from shaking as they approach.

Cyrus tucks his arms behind his back. "It's clear the shop is under some stress. I imagine with your father off the premises, it's feeling a little uncertain about the future. That's to be expected. Shops have a special relationship with Shopkeepers."

I nod.

"We hoped your brother would have returned by now so we could discuss the running of Rhyme and Reason. Vincent should have sent a letter informing us of his condition and the fact that his son would be taking over in his absence. Under the circumstances, we may recommend Rhyme and Reason close until Vincent can return."

Rhyme and Reason close?

"But Al and I have been running it just fine."

Cyrus sets my petition on the desk. "This suggests otherwise."

I stare at the paper, panic rushing through me. "Please, we're trying to keep things normal for our customers. They depend on us."

"I understand you want to keep things going, but the magic is delicate," Euphemia says. Her words make me think of the other shops and the way the magic has been malfunctioning there, but I'm not brave enough to ask her about it.

Euphemia's gaze is strong and steady, impossible to read as she surveys me. Heat creeps up my neck beneath her scrutiny. "We will return in two days. That should be sufficient time to notify your mother and father that we would like to speak with them. I expect one of them to be present when we arrive. I trust you to deliver the message?"

"I will."

"Very good." She starts to turn away from me.

"Are we in trouble? Because I wrote the petition?"

Euphemia pauses, and when she looks back, some of her mask has melted away. "It isn't a crime to want things to be different. But we must follow the rules. Without order, without law, the results would be catastrophic."

"How do you know?" The question pops out before I can stop it. Fear winds its way through me as I realize I've questioned her, the Council Leader.

"Because I've seen what happens when someone uses the magic for their own gain." Half turned toward the door, she lingers, the soft glow of the shop illuminating her profile. When she speaks again, her words seem to shimmer in the air. "The rules keep the Light, Poppy Fulbright."

Chapter Fifteen

Cyrus reaches for the door just as it bursts open from the other side, the bell ringing as Ollie rushes in.

"Gee whiz, Poppy, I have a story for—" Ollie stops short when she sees Euphemia Adley and Cyrus Finch. Her eyes grow wide.

"Courier Bell." Euphemia nods in her direction.

For some strange reason, Ollie decides to curtsy. Euphemia fights a smile, while Cyrus seems to stiffen.

"Ollie," he says in greeting.

Ollie, who has been looking everywhere except at him, finally meets his gaze.

"Grandfather," she says.

Did she just call him Grandfather? My mind spins as I try to remember if she's ever mentioned that before. How did I not know her family is Council?

"How are your parents?" Cyrus asks.

"Fine." Ollie focuses on the ceiling. "Just fine."

"And you? How is the apprenticeship going?"

She raises her shoulders in half a shrug. "Fine. Just fine."

The air between them feels tense and cold.

"Good," he finally says. "Well . . . we were just leaving."

"Oh." Ollie glances at the door and realizes she's blocking it. She practically jumps to get out of their way. "Right. Have a good one, then."

Euphemia gives Ollie a smile and then glances back at me. "Two days, Miss Fulbright. Don't forget."

Two days. Dread settles against me. I'm going to have to tell Mama and Papa everything that has gone wrong here. All I've wanted since Papa got sick is to take care of the shop the way he does, to show him that I need the magic of Rhyme and Reason, and that it needs me.

She waits for my response.

I set my shoulders back, mustering up my courage. "Two days," I agree.

And then Euphemia pulls the front door open, and she and Cyrus step out.

When they're gone, Ollie groans, and takes a staggering step forward. Halfway to the front counter she just gives up, plopping onto the ground.

"What was my grandfather doing here?" Her words are muffled, her face buried in the burgundy rug.

"I can't believe he's on the Council—why didn't you ever say anything?" Though now I recall she told me her parents knew some of the members pretty well.

She sighs and rolls onto her back, staring up at the

ceiling. "Because we're not on the best of terms."

I press a hand to my forehead. "Holy mackerel. If your grandfather is on the Council, that makes you . . ."

"A future member of the Council?" She sighs. "Only if I accept the responsibility."

"Ollie." I take a seat next to her. "That's—"

"Ridiculous."

"I was going to say incredible."

She sits up. "I wasn't trying to hide it from you. It's just not something I've come to grips with yet."

"I can see why."

She rubs her forehead. "My mother and father met at a shop event, fell in love, got married, that whole thing. My mother had already become Shopkeeper at Copper and Ink, and my father, who never really got along with Cyrus, decided to move in with her, and together they'd make the shop grow. However, my father was supposed to take over Cyrus's seat on the Council someday; that was always the plan for his life. The problem is he didn't want it. When I was a kid, he told Cyrus he wasn't ever going to take that place. So, the opportunity falls to me." She unwinds the turquoise scarf from around her neck and takes a deep breath. "My grandfather has been pushing me my whole life to follow in his footsteps, and I'm just not sure it's something I want. It's part of the reason I'm apprenticing as courier. To get a better view of what the Council is about."

"I'm glad you told me."

She leans toward me. "What was he doing here?"

The shock about Ollie's secret fades to the background as the details of the visit return.

"I wrote a petition to the Council, requesting to use the shop in order to save my father. I wasn't going to send it, but somehow it got to them. Did you deliver a letter from Rhyme and Reason to Euphemia Adley?"

Ollie nods. "A few days ago, Al gave me your mail, and there was a letter. I thought you'd decided to take my advice and write them about what's been happening at Rhyme and Reason."

I shut my eyes. So, it *was* Al's doing.

"Euphemia wants to talk to my parents. The Council is upset about the petition. I've—I've messed everything up." I press my hands to my eyes. "There was something she said: 'The rules keep the Light.' I don't know what she meant."

"That's the Council's motto."

"They have a motto?" I look up at her.

She nods. "It goes all the way back to the first Council."

And I think of the story I found concerning the Rift, and the Light and the Dark. It said selfishness and greed caused the divide in the magic. So the rules, then, keep the Dark away? I start to ask Ollie if she knows about the Rift when the twins burst through the lilac hedge.

"Ollie! I thought I heard you!" Kosma has a red cape tied about her shoulders. She plops down next to me. "Why are we sitting on the floor?"

Ollie looks around. "It felt right."

Kosma accepts this answer and grabs Ollie's hand. "Will you come play pretend with us? We're going to storm a castle."

Ollie glances at her wristwatch. "I'm overdue for my break . . . so, sure! I'd love to. Can I be the knight in shining armor?"

Kosma shouts with joy and yanks Ollie to her feet. "You too, Poppy?"

I need a second to clear my head.

"I'll be there in a minute."

Kosma tugs Ollie through the lilac hedge, and then I'm alone.

Once they're gone, I stare out at the shop. I've seen the signs for days. The dying flowers, the angry regulars, the shadow figure, the frost.

"If the rules keep the Light, then it means it's all true," I say to Rhyme. "The Dark really does exist."

The flip calendar begins to shuffle through dates as if in response, and I jump, startled by the sound. July 10,

2024. Someone is coming from the future. I get to my feet as the door creaks open a crack. I wait, but no one comes into the shop. A moment passes, and then the bell rings as Al sets foot inside.

A tremor runs deep through Rhyme and Reason, the ground shaking beneath me. The hanging lights begin to flicker on and off in terror around us.

"What are you doing?"

James's voice comes from behind me. I glance back and see he's just come in from playing with his friends, coat zipped up to his chin, his baseball mitt in one hand.

Al whirls around and blinks in surprise at the sight of me and James. He wears a jacket and a pair of denim pants, both cut shockingly tight to his body. A sleek black baseball cap is pulled down over his eyes.

"You went out the front door!" James stares at Al in horror.

My head spins as I piece it together. All of the times I haven't been able to find Al . . . he's been using the magic, breaking the rules, traveling through time.

"I can explain," Al says.

"What is there to explain?" I say between clenched teeth.

The lights keep flickering, and Al glares up at them, his eyes full of rage. "Would you cut it out?" he shouts at Rhyme, and the shop goes completely dark.

Courage ignites inside of me. "Don't talk to the shop like that."

Al moves forward, his leather boots thudding against the hardwood. "Yes, I've been using the door. So what. Nothing has happened. I've been to the future multiple times and the world hasn't ended. It's exactly like I told you, Poppy. The rules are antiquated, made by the Council, who want to control us."

"You can't do this, Al."

His eyes meet mine, and there's a shadow in the blue I've never seen before.

"Papa is going to be so mad," James says, his face full of fear.

Al steps toward us. "You don't understand what I'm trying to do. Great-Grandmother Aggie understood. She petitioned the Council to save her daughter because she believed using the shop for such a purpose was possible."

"They never even sent that to the Council! Because no matter how much they wanted to save their daughter, they knew it wasn't possible. They knew that doing so would cost them Rhyme and Reason, the magic, everything."

"That letter is proof a petition can be presented. You agreed, Poppy, or you wouldn't have written your own petition."

"You had no right to send that," I snap.

"What are you talking about?" James looks back and forth between us.

"I knew you didn't have the guts to. You're so scared of everything. You hide out here, tucked away from the outside world, because you're afraid. I did what you couldn't."

It's the meanest thing he's ever said to me, and tears spring to my eyes as anger pushes past my fear. "If you're so brave, then why didn't you write a petition yourself? You sent the one I wrote so that if anyone got in trouble for it, it wouldn't be you."

"Of course that's why I did it!" he snarls.

And I see that I could never have stopped Al the way Papa wanted me to. I can't force Al to back away from the cliff when he's already jumped from the edge.

" 'The rules keep the Light.' " My voice shakes with desperation. "The Council has already given us a warning. If they find out you've traveled to the future, we'll lose the shop."

Al takes another step toward me, and his shoulder brushes against a hanging wisteria vine. A shiver goes through all of the plants and the flowers around us. They seem to emit a hiss as they shrivel down to nothing, like they've been burned by his touch.

"Al?" James asks, his voice quivering.

"If we lose everything, then we lose everything." Al ignores him. "Whatever it takes to bring Carl back will be worth the cost."

"What are you saying?" I whisper. "Carl's life for the life of the shop?"

"So much has gone wrong. With the magic we can save them both, Papa and Carl. You and I together can fix everything, Poppy."

I've thought about it too, haven't I? I researched the Dark, trying to find out what the cost would be if we alter the past. I want Papa back in the shop with his big booming laugh filling every empty space. I want to hear Carl call me by the wrong name one more time.

The pain fills me up, a pulsing ball that rises and falls with each breath. I want it to stop. I want to give Al what he wants and save everyone all at once. My heart aches from wanting it. But Rhyme and Reason, the magic it has—it's the best part of us. We would trade it for Carl and Papa, and all the good the shop does, all the light it spreads would be extinguished. We would be letting the Dark win.

Al levels a cold gaze at me. "You're either with me or you're not."

He's asking me to choose between him and Rhyme and Reason. The impossible choice I'm facing cuts through me, and my body shakes as I hold back tears.

"We can't lose Rhyme," I whisper.

He rakes his hands down his face. "You don't understand! No one understands! Everything is wrong! *I'm* wrong. And I have to do this."

He turns away from me and James, and I catch sight of the veins on his neck, bulging underneath the skin. They're black and splintered into a dozen different lines.

"There's a-a voice on the other side of the door. I started hearing it the night Carl died. It knows things about the magic." Al's eyes flutter as they dart to one side. "You saw it that night, the shadow figure in the shop. If you listen to it, you'll understand. Just hear it out."

A crackling sound grabs my attention from Al for a moment. I look up at the wisteria vines hanging from the ceiling. Thick black frost crawls over them, stiffening at the edges. When I glance back at Al, I see it on the lenses of his glasses.

"What's happening?" James reaches for my arm and holds on tight.

"Al," I start.

Al holds out his hand. "Take a walk through the front door with me, Poppy. Rhyme and Reason doesn't matter anymore. All that matters is what we want."

James presses tight into my side. I look down at him

and feel his fear, mixing with mine. When I glance back at Al, I see that this is not my older brother anymore. Something has taken over him, has been taking over him for weeks.

"No." I don't think I can help him now; he's gone too far, and the realization hurts so much I press a hand to my stomach.

"*Please*, Poppy."

"You can't do this, Al. The shop, the magic, this is home."

Al stares at me, desperation on his face. "It doesn't look like home anymore, not to me."

And then he reaches for the knob and yanks, but the door sticks shut. The lights come back on, flickering frantically in panic.

Al tries again, and when it doesn't yield, he kicks the emerald wood with his heavy boot just as one of the arms of the lemon tree takes a swipe at him. Al stands stunned, and then suddenly the branches begin to pummel him, trying to push him back.

"You can't keep me here!" Al wrestles with the tree, struggling to escape its reach. I lose sight of my brother as he disappears in a scuffle of leaves and is pelted again and again, then suddenly a loud snap echoes through the shop. Al drops to the floor as the tree goes still, a broken branch clutched in his arms.

"What did you do?" I rush toward him, but Al springs to his feet and lunges for the door. This time it swings open. A burst of icy air rushes inside, and I grab hold of Al's arm in one last desperate attempt to stop him.

His eyes meet mine, but they're not blue anymore, they're dark and murky and lost.

There is a war going on inside of him. Hate and anger and fear all mixed up in one. The pain of being left behind has broken him, and Carl's death has shattered any of the pieces that were left.

Al stares down at me. "I'm tired," he says between gritted teeth, "of sitting back and doing nothing."

"Al." I say his name one more time. "Please."

He starts to speak, then changes his mind. He yanks himself out of my grasp, the force knocking me off-balance as the door slams shut behind him.

Chapter Sixteen

The dark green drapes burst to life, throwing themselves shut over the windows, leaving us in complete darkness.

"Poppy!" James cries.

The regulars' voices rise from deeper inside the shop.

"Amona?" Prosper shouts.

"I'm right here!" Bibine replies.

"What's going on?" Anna Rose calls out.

"I can't see my hands in front of my face!" Whitney says in panic. "Katherine? Where are you?"

"I'm holding your arm, Whitney."

"Everyone, cool down, it's just a little bit of darkness." Ollie tries to keep the group calm.

I hear them all as they stumble to the front of the shop, using their hands to guide their way.

"I'm so sorry, everyone. Let me get the lights." I can't remember the last time I had to switch them on myself. I move forward, taking a deep breath, trying not to lose it.

My fingers make contact with the switch on the wall. Nothing happens. The shop stays pitch-dark. I flip it again, but still nothing. I try to stay calm, to shove down the feeling that everything is falling apart. What would Papa do?

"I think there's a flashlight in the front counter," I tell James. "Can you find it?"

"I'll try," James says.

"Amona, I'm scared," Kosma whimpers.

"I'll open the curtains." That should at least get natural light in here until I can figure out what the problem is. With my arms out in front of me, I stumble around the lemon tree.

"I'm at the counter!" James calls out.

"Good, the flashlight should be in the second drawer on the right." My fingers find the velvet curtains, smooth and soft against my skin. The braided cord is on the left, and I manage to find it, giving it a quick tug. The curtains stay shut tight.

"They won't open." I try again. They don't budge.

"Poppy?" A hand brushes up against my arm.

"Ollie, is that you?" It's so dark, I can't make out anyone.

"I'm on your right. Maybe we can force them. On three, let's both pull."

I grab one side of the curtains and Ollie grabs the other.

"Got it," I say. "One,"

"Two, three!" Ollie finishes, and I yank for all I'm worth.

A loud bang rips through the shop, and Ollie and I are blown backward. I fall to the floor, my head thwacking into the display case near the front door.

The world spins above me as a wave of pain reverberates through my skull. I reach a hand into my hair and come away with blood.

Someone is screaming. The light directly above me flickers to life, and in its beam, I see a dark mist hovering above us in the air. I stare at it in a daze, feeling the sudden urge to reach out and touch it.

"Poppy!" James calls my name, and it pulls me from the trance. I roll over and see Ollie lying a few feet away from me. She shifts in my direction. Something black coats the side of her face. She screams as she tries to brush it away.

"It's burning!" she growls. "Help me!"

James grabs the water pitcher in the window and tosses it at her, rinsing the black film from her skin. Ollie goes still, and I crawl toward her.

"Ollie!" Her name is a sob on my lips.

The lights flicker and go out around us.

"What can I do? I'm right here." Bibine's hands find my shoulders in the icy darkness.

"I—I don't know." I'm shaking all over, and I can't seem to stop.

James manages to get the flashlight on, and he points

the beam down at Ollie, who is groaning now, clutching her face.

"It's going to be okay," Bibine coos at her, in the way only a grandmother can. She pulls back Ollie's hands so we can survey the damage.

Ollie blinks up at us, and her eyes—they're black. Her veins are visible beneath her skin, thin tendrils of darkness that seem to pulse under the surface. I reach out to touch her.

"Wait!" James cries from behind me, but it's too late. A cold so intense it burns spreads over the tip of my fingers the moment I touch Ollie's wounds, and then all at once pain shoots up my hand and into my arm. I jerk back in surprise.

"Look." Kosma points toward the window, her eyes wide with fear. I glance up, and the sight tears the breath from my lungs. The velvet curtains hang open, revealing a massive crack that runs diagonally from left to right across the window, with jagged fractures splintering off at odd angles. Behind the glass a shimmering black mist writhes, tendrils of it slipping through the fissure, leaking into Rhyme and Reason.

James is standing closest to the window, and he begins to cough. The sound is loud and hollow, and he can't seem to stop.

"It hurts to breathe, Poppy," he gasps.

It's then I realize the curtains were shut tight because the shop was trying to keep the mist out, to protect us.

"Stand back!" I tell James as I clamber to my feet, my head pounding from where I hit the display case. I shift around Ollie and draw the thick velvet fabric shut.

Ollie moans and tries to sit up. The side of her face is burned. It runs down her neck and along one arm. Bibine gently holds on to her, patting her back.

My whole body shakes as I stare at her. I'm in over my head, and I don't know what to do.

"She needs a doctor," Bibine whispers. "Someone from your world."

I look at the front door. None of the regulars can take Ollie to Copper and Ink in Chicago, 1944. Only I can. That means breaking the rules for her.

"We need to get her home. Ollie, can we help you up?"

She blinks and nods her head. "I—I think so."

"I need help," I say.

Whitney shoulders his way through the crowd, Katherine on his heels. The three of us gently and carefully help Ollie to her feet. I lead her toward the door.

"No, Poppy," Ollie says when she realizes my intentions. "You can't go through it. Your shop will already be in violation of the rules after what Al did."

I ignore her protests. "Will your parents be able to help you?"

Ollie winces as we take another step forward. "Not my parents. My grandfather will know what to do. I have to go to the Council."

"You have a pin that can get us there?"

"In my bag."

I look around and find her satchel on the floor under the window. I snatch it and settle it over Ollie's shoulder, and then she opens the door. Salty air tickles my nose. On the other side of the street sits a sagging building. I can barely make out a sign that says THE LIGHTHOUSE BOOKSHOP.

"You can't come with me." Ollie pulls away. "I can make it on my own. It's not far."

"Ollie." I don't want to let her go, not after what's happened. "Please."

But she doesn't stop. "I can make it."

I wish I believed her. I watch as she hobbles down the front steps, her head tucked low, arms folded into her chest. She stumbles, then rights herself and disappears into the Lighthouse.

Once she's gone, we all stand in silence.

"Poppy, that black mist hurt." James rubs his chest. "And it made me feel so—so angry."

I tilt my head to one side. "What did you say?"

"It made me feel angry," he repeats, a dazed look on his face.

And I remember that day when the shop erupted

in chaos. Everyone seemed so agitated, even Kosma and Prosper. These last few weeks, we have all been on edge. It wasn't because Papa is gone and the shop is upset.

It's been the Dark the whole time.

I turn toward the others. Kosma and Prosper cling to each other. Anna Rose stands behind them, her face pale and afraid. Bibine clutches the neck of her dress, worry in her eyes. Katherine holds on to Whitney.

"We're going to lose Rhyme and Reason, aren't we?" James reaches for my hand.

I take in the shop around us. The mist that leaked inside seems to be gone. The hanging lights try to come to life, flickering at odd intervals. The wallpaper is a murky shade of brown. A chill wraps around us, and everything here feels different now.

I clear my throat. "I'm sorry you had to—to witness this. You should all get out of here while you still can."

"Oh, Poppy," Bibine whispers.

"After a bad day, my mother always tells us that things will be better when the sun comes up." I look at the regulars. "I have to believe that's true."

Bibine moves forward, her steps slow and unsteady. Her permanent hunch makes her much shorter than me. She reaches up and places both hands on either side of my face. She may be Prosper and Kosma's grandmother, but sometimes it feels as if she's mine too.

"Go to your father. Tell him what has happened. You cannot do this all on your own."

Bibine is right. It's time to tell him the truth. I nod, and she gives me a kiss on both cheeks before she backs away and gathers a grandchild under each arm. They leave the shop in solemn silence. Anna Rose gives me a sympathetic look and follows behind them. Then Katherine and Whitney go out together.

Once they've used the door to return to their respective times, James's shoulders droop.

"Let's go upstairs," I tell him, because what I want more than anything is to get away from the shop, and the cold empty feeling that is burrowing into my stomach.

I reach for the lock, and the metal is cold against my fingers. I take a deep breath and turn it shut with a heavy click that seems to echo around us.

"Al is out there," James whispers. "Shouldn't we leave it open for him to come back?"

I rest my hand against the chipped emerald wood. James is right, it *is* cutting off Al's only way back. He'll be stuck wherever he is now. If I leave it open, he'll just come back and abuse the magic again. Al's made his choice, now I'm making mine.

"It's not forever," I say, reaching for James. "Come on."

As we move through the shop, I don't feel safe here,

for the first time in my life. The chalkboard cycles through quotes, pulling random phrases and letters, nothing that makes any sense. The vines and flowers shrivel around us.

Al's words burn in my stomach. *You're so scared of everything. You hide out here, tucked away from the outside world, because you're afraid.*

He's right. I *am* afraid. I should have stood up to him. I should have told Mama and Papa days ago that things haven't been right with him. Maybe then none of this would have happened.

James starts up the steep stairs that lead to our apartment, but I glance back at the shop. Empty and dark and silent, so unlike its normal self.

"Poppy? Are you coming up?" James calls.

I give him a nod. And as I turn to follow my brother, I make a decision. I need answers about the magic. About the Dark and the Light. I can't wait for the Dark to come back and destroy us all forever. If I can't get them from Papa, then I will go to Euphemia Adley herself. I have to defend the shop and the magic and the place that I call home, no matter what. Because I am nothing without it.

Chapter Seventeen

In the morning, I stand on the stairs, my heart in my throat. The black, shimmering frost has spread overnight. It coats the climbing hydrangea, the wisteria, and the jasmine on the front counter in fuzzy-looking crystals. The walls are covered in it, so thick I can't see the paper underneath. And the door, it's almost disappeared completely beneath a layer of ice.

"Rhyme?" I call out, my breath a visible cloud in the air. A single firefly glows in front of me. It zooms off between the fiction stacks and I hurry after it. Bursting into the shop, I nearly knock James over. He stands, staring at the quote on the chalkboard. A single sentence scrawled across it, angling down the slate.

"The nightmare is coming. The nightmare is here. The nightmare is now. The nightmare is real."
—Red Like Crimson, *Kanna Sato*

"We should go," I say.

"It's hoarfrost." His breath is a white puff in the air.

"What?" I ask.

"That's what they call this type of ice." He touches a jasmine vine and it crunches beneath his fingers. "Did you see the tree?" Before I can answer, he's dragging me over to it, and shows me that the leaves are heavy with frost. He cups a fruit in his hand. The lemon is completely black, as if it's rotten. But that shouldn't be possible; this tree grows perfect fruit, it always has.

"Pick it," I say. "So it doesn't spread to the others."

James pulls and there's a brittle snap as the lemon comes free. It withers in James's hand, right before our eyes. I brush a finger across the skin, and it disintegrates. We stare down at the black dust it leaves behind.

"What's happening, Poppy?" James whispers. I could tell him my theory, that it's the Dark and it has come here, but I don't want to frighten him.

A knock pierces the silence that has fallen around us. James looks up at me, his fine hair flopping into his eyes.

"Al?" he whispers hopefully.

I move around James and pull back the white gauzy curtain from the small window in the door. An old man stands on the step. He waves for me to open it, and I do.

"Miss Poppy Fulbright?" he asks.

"Yes?" I say.

"Letter for you." He places a brown envelope in my hand and turns to leave.

"Who are you?" I call after him.

"Courier to the Council!" he calls as he hobbles down a cobblestone street.

My heart sinks. I tuck it into the pocket of my coat, feeling too tired to read it now.

James and I lock up the shop, leaving a sign for our customers explaining that we'll be closed for an unspecified amount of time and we're sorry for the inconvenience.

"We'll be back as soon as we can. Hang on, Rhyme," I say, and we step out into the back alley.

The bus station is busier than I imagined it would be. There are men, women, and children clogging the terminal. Boys in brown army uniforms linger near the buses kissing loved ones goodbye. They'll ride into the city, or maybe farther still to boot camps. Then in a few weeks, they will go to war.

"I'll write as often as I can, Ma, I promise." I recognize Adam Weiss fending off his mother's fierce farewell. He was in Al's grade at school.

Would things have been different if Al had been allowed to go? I imagine him and Carl telling all of us goodbye like this.

"Do you think that'll be me someday?" James asks as we drop our cases in the pile of luggage waiting to be put under the bus.

I freeze, horrified by James's question.

"No," I answer. "The war will be over by then."

"Oh," James replies, and I can't tell if he's relieved or a little bit disappointed.

It takes five hours to get to the city by bus. I try to sleep, but every time I close my eyes, the weight of yesterday sinks into me. Al has been using the door and it has changed the shop. If I tell Papa everything, can we still set things right?

I pull the letter from the Council out of my coat pocket. Taking a deep breath, I slip my finger beneath the seal and brace myself for the worst.

To: Allan Fulbright, Rhyme and Reason

From: Euphemia Adley, Lead Counselor

November 17, 1944

Dear Mr. Allan Fulbright,
We have received detailed eyewitness accounts of an incident which occurred at Rhyme and Reason. Ollie Bell is currently in our care receiving treatment for her injuries.

We are aware of the current condition of your father. When we visited your shop, your sister informed us that you have been left in charge of Rhyme and Reason. We hereby summon you to attend a tribunal to explain yourself before the Council tomorrow, ten o'clock a.m. local time. Enclosed in this envelope is the proper pin, which will lead you to the Lighthouse.

Sincerely,
Euphemia Adley

Chapter Eighteen

November 17, 1944
New York City, New York

I'm relieved when the city comes into view outside our window. New York stands in the distance, the buildings tall and tightly packed together. We used to come here every few years to visit Mama's sister, but since the war began, we haven't made the trip.

The bus pulls into the station, and I usher James out into the cold. He bounces on his toes with excitement, taking everything in.

I nervously start toward the line of yellow automobiles. I've never hired a taxi on my own before, and as we walk toward them, my palms grow sweaty.

"We need a ride?" I ask nervously.

"You got money, kid?" The driver, an older man with slicked-back hair, barely spares me a glance.

I nod and he motions for us to get in.

Aunt Lina lives in a brownstone apartment, twenty minutes from the bus station. We pull up to the dark brick front, but I don't make a move to get out.

"Is this the place or what?" the driver calls back to us. James reaches for the door handle.

"Just my little brother."

James's brow furrows. "You aren't coming in?"

I look at him, his eyes wide and blue and innocent. I want him to stay that way.

I make a split-second decision. "Tell Mama that I'm sorry. That I have to talk to Papa and then I'm going home to take care of the shop."

"You're not coming to Aunt Lina's at all? No!" His hand twists the fabric of my coat sleeve.

"Mama needs you, James. Right now, more than ever."

"Me?" he asks.

"Yes, you," I say, looking down at him. "You're full of energy and life. You're our hope and she needs that right now."

His eyes shine with unshed tears.

"Be brave, Poppy," he says. I want to ask him what he means, but he steps out of the car.

I wait until he climbs the front porch and knocks on the door. Uncle Will answers, surprise on his face when he sees James. He glances at the taxi, and I tell the driver to take me to the city hospital before anyone can stop me.

———

From the doorway of his room, I watch Papa sleep. At the nurses' station in the hallway behind me, a radio pours out the latest news from the war. "General Eisenhower has hurled six American armies at the Siegfried Line, in an attempt to overtake the German stronghold. Experts say the war—" Someone changes the station.

Papa has declined in the days since I last saw him. Somehow, he's lost weight, and his hair is almost white. How could he have gotten so much worse so quickly?

Staring in at him, I falter, worried about telling him what's happened.

Be brave, James said, and his words lead me forward.

Papa's eyes open, and he sees me here. "Poppy?"

I step into the room, easing myself into the chair beside his bed.

I reach out for his hand, and his skin feels papery and breakable against mine. He's cold, as if the life has already begun to leave him, and seeing him here like this, it hits me. Papa is *dying*.

My vision blurs with tears. "I'm here, Papa."

He takes a deep breath, and the corners of his mouth turn up in the shadow of a smile. His hand moves to my face, and he cups my cheek. "You're a sight for sore eyes."

I've missed him so much it aches as I lean into his touch.

"I'm glad you've come for a visit," he says.

I pinch my lips together. I wish I were here just to see him, to tell him I miss him and that nothing is the same without him.

His face pulls into a frown. "What is it? What's wrong?"

I take a deep breath. "I've been running the shop, just the way you taught me, but things haven't gone as I'd hoped." And then it all comes pouring out. I tell him about Al's long absences, the malfunctions, the Council visit, about last night and the crack across the window.

Papa says nothing through all of it; he listens, squeezes my hand every once in a while, but stays silent.

"The Council wants Al to appear at a tribunal; they think he's still running the shop." The tears wash over me. I bury my face in his bedsheets, too ashamed to look at him. "I'm sorry, Papa. You asked me to stop Al, and I couldn't do it."

He touches the top of my head. "None of this is your fault."

I look up at him. "But—"

"None of it." He doesn't let me finish.

"Al—"

"His mistakes have nothing to do with you. I never should have put the pressure on you to stop him." Papa sighs, and his eyes drift away from mine. "Poppy, the shop is a burden to bear. I know you love it, that you want to run it someday, of course I see that. You have a bond with Rhyme and Reason none of the rest of us have. But there are things you do not know."

I think about Ollie getting hurt, and the black mist leaking through the shop window. This is my chance to ask him. "Things I don't know about the Dark?"

Papa nods. "Yes."

"Will you tell me?"

Papa tries to sit up, and I help him adjust his pillows.

"There is power in the magic. My father taught me that, like his mother before him. As Shopkeepers, we use that power for good. To bring hope to the world; it's what we've always done. But there are two sides to that power."

"The Light and the Dark," I say.

"We work in the Light, it's our reason for being."

I nod—this is what I read about in the Handbook.

"But the Dark is still out there." His words are heavy as they fall over me. "And while the bookshops exist, we stand in its way of getting what it wants."

"What does it want?" I whisper.

"To put out the Light forever, because as long as the Light exists, the Dark can't have full control of the magic." There is fear in his eyes. "The bookshops stop it from having that power. We have for generations. But the Dark has always waited and watched for a crack, an open door that will let it in. And once it's inside, it will destroy the world of the bookshops." Papa takes my hand. "It waits for when we're most vulnerable and broken, and then it tries to worm its way in. My father told me there would come a day when I heard the Dark, and that I would have to be strong enough to evade its call."

I think of that night in the shop when I saw the shadow figure. *I* was vulnerable and broken. That pressure in my head, those rapid thoughts—the Dark saw *me*.

"The magic can be a burden, one that I never wanted you to bear."

"Because I'm a girl?" I ask.

He shuts his eyes. "Because I want more for you than a lifetime hiding from the Dark."

"Can't we destroy it? Get rid of it forever?" It seems the only choice to me.

"The Council doesn't believe it's possible to destroy the Dark because it's as much a part of the magic as the Light is. Therefore, the rules are the only way to keep the Dark in check. We must not use the magic for our own gain; if we do, we let it in."

I've heard the voice of the Dark and withstood it. Papa has underestimated me. "What if I can handle it? Didn't you ever think I might be stronger than Al?"

Silence settles around us. I listen to the ragged sound of Papa's breathing as he thinks over what I've said.

"When you were a baby and Rhyme created the fireflies for you, you did whatever it took to follow their light across the shop, even though it was hard." A faint smile crosses his face at the familiar story. "I knew that day you would be stronger than I have ever been."

I picture myself, toddling through Rhyme and Reason, stumbling after the magic. "But why?"

"Because you knew the Light when you saw it."

I stare down at my shoes, Mama's hand-me-down oxfords, the toes worn and scuffed.

"I wasn't strong enough to stop Al." My vision blurs as tears spring to my eyes, and I bury my face in my hands.

Papa reaches for me. "Al gets to make his own choices. Perhaps if I weren't sick, things would be different, but perhaps not. Al has always been strong-willed—it's a strength, but also a weakness."

"We can still save him," I whisper. We can't let him ruin his life—ruin the shop. I lean forward. "What do I do, Papa? What about the tribunal?"

His eyelids seem heavy as he fights to keep them open. "The Council has been around since the beginning. If anyone will know what to do, it will be them. I—I have to go speak with them."

I stare at him, so small and fragile in this stark white

room. He doesn't have the strength to do it, and we both know it.

There's only one thing to do. Fear fills my chest, but I manage to get the words out. "I'll go."

"Poppy," he says. "This is bigger than—"

"I've been in the shop. I know what's been going on. I can represent us. I know I can."

My hands shake at the thought, but I won't let my courage fail me, not now. I have to step up and do whatever it takes to protect the magic.

Papa nods, his eyes starting to slip closed. "All right, Poppy. All right."

I hold on tight to Papa's hand. "Do I tell them everything?"

"Protect Al if you can." A tear trails down his face. "But tell them whatever you have to."

I lean into him, pressing my cheek to his. It's scratchy against my skin, but as I breathe him in, I still smell paper and ink.

I start to leave, but his grip on my hand tightens for the briefest moment. "Mind your mother." He takes a gasping breath. "Tell James to spend time with his friends as often as he likes. Rhyme will understand." The realization that he's saying goodbye shakes me to my core, but I let him finish.

"What else, Papa?" My vision blurs and I can't hold back the tears anymore.

"Tell Al the past will ruin him, unless he lets it go." Papa's eyes are closed now, his hold slipping from mine.

"Poppy?"

"I'm here, Papa, right here."

He fights to stay awake. "Don't lose the girl who chases the light."

I watch his chest rise and fall, long after he's gone to sleep. A nurse comes and tells me visiting hours are over, and I lean into him.

"I won't lose that girl, Papa." I close my eyes, his hand still in mine. "I promise."

Chapter Nineteen

I burst out of the hospital, my heart heavy. A gust of icy wind sweeps over me, and I tuck my hands into my coat pockets. There are taxis parked along the street, waiting for customers, but I walk past them, my head spinning with worry. After a block or so the sidewalk grows crowded with people for some sort of fundraiser being held for our boys overseas.

A family walks past me, a little girl in a bright yellow coat riding on a man's shoulders.

"Grandpa, if we buy a cookie, the money will help Daddy?" the little girl asks.

"That's the idea," her grandfather says. "It'll help our boys win the war."

"Let's buy a whole dozen!" she shouts, and he laughs a deep booming laugh that sounds like Papa's.

Fresh tears flood my eyes and I feel myself starting to break. The exhaustion of the past twenty-four hours slams into me, and my steps falter. I sit down on the closest bench to catch my breath.

I'm overwhelmed at the idea of going to the tribunal alone. I wish I could talk to Theo now, not just in a letter, but face-to-face. I want to tell him all that's happened since I last wrote. How the shop seems out of control, how everything feels so big. If only I could go visit the Woodland Winds, I—

I stop, my mind racing. Shops appear for those who need them most. It takes desire, or desperation, or hopelessness, or fear. Once a customer visits, they get a pin as a conduit to find their way back. But in the beginning, it's the shop that finds them first.

If ever I've felt desperation, hopelessness, or fear, it's now.

I squeeze my eyes shut and call out with everything in me. *Theo, I need you. The Woodland Winds, are you there?*

A cold breeze gusts around me, pushing the curly ends of my hair into my face, and I look up. The street is jam-packed with cars honking and shifting lanes. On the other side of the block, there is a little café on the corner, and a shoe store, and an antique silverware store. And there squished in the middle is a bookshop with a dark wooden front. A white sign hangs over the door, THE WOODLAND WINDS.

I'm on my feet in an instant. It worked!

I look around to see if anyone else notices the Woodland Winds, but of course they don't; it's only shown itself to me. This must be what it's like for customers when they see Rhyme and Reason for the first time.

My hands shake as I rush to the crosswalk. I step into the street before it's my turn, and a car honks as it slams on its brakes. I'm half afraid the shop is going to disappear before I reach it, but of course, it doesn't. The door is a glossy white, the front window filled with children's books. Dr. Seuss, *Peter Pan*, *Grimm's Fairy Tales*. The tarnished gold handle is cold to the touch as I pull it open and step inside.

A sense of cheerful calm engulfs me, and it instantly feels like being hugged by a well-loved grandfather. The smell of pine needles and wood hangs heavy in the air, mixed with the scent of books, old pages, and worn leather. A massive stone fireplace sits at the center of the shop, emanating waves of heat.

Towering shelves line the walls. I crane my neck and see that the Woodland Winds has an open second floor, and there are books all the way to the ceiling. Long ladders on wheels shift about the room so that customers can find what they need. One of them moves, rolling quickly to a woman who stretches to reach a book on a tall shelf.

"Yes, Mr. Altman, I promise I have sent a request out and I will let you know as soon as it comes in. Oh—" Theo Devlin moves around the fireplace, a stack of books in one arm.

He wears a dark blue sweater, pulled over a white collared shirt and a striped tie. He's taller than I expected, with wide shoulders and a round face. His ears stick out a bit, but the ends of his slicked-back brown hair curl outward and are almost able to hide them. It's then that I notice his left eye, which is milky and drooping at the edge, the skin scarred above and beneath it.

He turns, and when he sees me, he drops the books he's holding. He fumbles awkwardly, trying to catch them before they hit the ground with an enormous plop.

"Oh, let me help." I spring forward and kneel at the same time he does. We nearly knock heads. I pick up a copy of *The Secret Garden* as he scrambles for the rest.

He stares at me in wonder. "Poppy?"

"Hello." Sudden nerves sweep through me. "Sorry to startle you."

"What are you—how are you—" His ears burn red. "You're here." He puts a hand to the side of his face as if to cover his eye so I can't see it.

"I—I needed to see you, and I thought about the Woodland Winds and it heard me," I try to explain.

His cheeks seem to flush. "You needed to see me?"

"Something horrible has happened at our shop, and I—I just needed a friend." I hand him the book and take a step back.

He slowly lowers his hand from his face. "I heard something happened at another shop—a replacement courier told me Ollie was hurt. I didn't know it was

Rhyme and Reason. Are you—is everything all right?"

"Not really." I anxiously tuck a loose strand of hair behind one ear.

He nods and glances down at the books gathered in his arms. I steal another look at his face. His skin is burned beneath his eye. It's red and glossy, like it happened recently and it's still healing.

"Granddad and I, we got in an auto accident. That's how he died. We were hit by a driver going the wrong way. It was dark and Granddad was driving and . . . I tried to write to you about it, but I couldn't figure out what to say."

I think about the letter I wrote, telling him to look for color in the world around him. I wish I had known what he's been through.

He clears his throat. "Can I give you a tour of the Woodland Winds?"

"A tour would be great." I give him a smile. I can't believe I'm here in the Woodland Winds. Friendly warmth seems to bloom around me.

"It's pretty simple. Granddad used to say our shop isn't as big as some of the other ones he'd heard of, but it has just as good of a selection." He sets the books in his arms down on the closest table. "Granddad loved children's books. That's our entire first floor. Upstairs we've got fiction, and a little bit of nonfiction."

The Woodland Winds feels open and airy. We move closer to the bookshelves, and I notice they have forest animals carved into them, deer and wolves and other creatures. I lean in for a better look at a bear with her cub and they begin to move, lumbering up and across the edge of one of the shelves.

"They're walking," I whisper.

Theo watches with a grin. "The Woodland Winds must like you. My great-granddad carved all of those."

I'm about to ask how long they've been established when the ground beneath my feet begins to tremble. I reach out and grab Theo's arm for balance.

"Not again," he mutters.

"What's happening?" I look at Theo, eyes wide.

"Technology," he says, starting toward the front door. I follow him to the entrance, where a girl stands with wires in her ears and one of those flat square phones from the future in her hand. I've seen cell phones in Rhyme and Reason; the customers who have them always ask for Wi-Fi, which apparently is a type of communication system in the future.

"Millie, modern devices frighten the Woodland Winds, you know that."

"Sorry, Theo." She takes the wires out of her ears and stuffs everything into her bag.

Theo moves behind the front counter and reaches

for a record player. He adjusts the needle and ragtime music comes pouring out. The shivering beneath my feet goes still.

Millie leaves her bag by the front door and moves deeper into the shop.

Music still on, Theo comes back to me. "Old music always calms the shop down." He takes a breath. "Let's continue the tour. Over here are the picture books, my favorite section. The artwork in them is incredible. If I wasn't destined to be a Shopkeeper, I think I'd want to be an illustrator or something."

The shelves throughout are a deep cherry wood, polished and gleaming. Lining the tops of them are candles with flickering flames that crackle all in time with one another.

"You like to draw?" I ask.

"Little things, here and there." He pulls a blue-covered book off the shelf. "This is one of my favorites from when I was a kid." The gold-foil title gleams as he tilts it toward me. *The Tale of Little Bluebird.*

I smile and reach for it. "My family loved this one too. My older brother used to read this to me when we were supposed to be asleep. You know, the flashlight-under-the-covers trick?"

Theo laughs. "I may have used that a time or two myself."

He moves around the shelf, but I stay where I am,

staring down at the picture book. Seeing it reminds me of Al reading us fairy tales as kids. And then I think of what he's done, and the tribunal, and some of the warmth the Woodland Winds has brought to me fades away.

"Rhyme and Reason has been summoned for a tribunal tomorrow." I say the words so quietly I'm not sure he'll hear. I see him through the shelves, standing one aisle in front of me. He's still as he considers what I've said.

"It makes sense that the Council would want to interview you. Determine what happened and all."

"I don't know what to expect." For some reason, it's easier to talk to him when I can't see his face. Maybe because that's how we began, as words on a page. "I'm scared, Theo."

"After Granddad died, he left the shop to my mother and she had to go to a ceremony where they passed ownership to her. I saw them for just a minute."

"What were they like?"

"A little intimidating," he admits.

My stomach is in knots already, and it isn't even tomorrow yet. I press my forehead against the shelf in front of me and close my eyes.

"I think you'll do just fine, Poppy."

"Why do you think that?"

He's quiet for a moment, then he presses forward.

"Because you care about everything and everyone. You want to protect your shop and your family and your customers, not for selfish reasons, but because it's who you are. Follow that instinct, it won't fail you."

His words sink into me, and I'm not sure if any of those things are true, but maybe some of them are.

"Tomorrow at the tribunal, don't let them treat you like some kid. Show them the real Poppy Fulbright and you'll—" He stops. "You'll do swell."

I push away from the shelf and move around to the aisle he's been standing in. Theo adjusts books, making sure they're neat and tidy. I stare at him, and he glances sideways at me.

"What?"

"Nothing. I'm glad we're friends, is all."

Theo nods and silence falls around us. I'm about to ask him if his mother is here and if I can meet her when the front door opens.

"Let me see who it is. I'll be right back." Theo shifts past me. "Hello," he calls. "Welcome to the Woodland Winds."

I walk down the aisle after him, emerge into the open space of the shop, and stop cold.

Standing in the entryway, soaking wet, in the same clothes he was wearing when he left Rhyme and Reason yesterday, is Al.

Chapter Twenty

"What are you doing here?" I ask him, curling my hands into fists.

Al's head shoots in my direction, his eyes filling with confusion. "You—you used the magic for yourself?"

"No, I didn't. The Woodland Winds appeared for me when I needed it."

"Interesting development. I didn't know that was possible." He glances at Theo. "What, you write a couple of letters to your old pal Theo, and suddenly his shop wants to help you?"

I narrow my eyes at Al. He's been going through my mail. It shouldn't surprise me, but it does. "Why are you here?"

He backs away, ignoring my question. Ragtime music plays, energetic and loud, through the Woodland Winds.

"You locked me out of Rhyme and Reason. I was just trying to find a way back home." Al's eyes are dark, his jaw tense. I'm not sorry for what I did.

Theo glances back and forth between us. "Hi, nice to see you again, Al. I've heard a lot about you recently."

"Stay out of this," Al snaps at him. "You had no right, Poppy."

I am done with Al's blame, done giving him the benefit of the doubt. He betrayed us, and he betrayed the shop.

"Do you have any idea what you've done to Rhyme and Reason?" I don't know how to make him see. "Everything is a mess there."

Al looks tired and ragged, and after what happened to Ollie, I wish he looked worse. "I don't have time for this." He turns to leave. "I've got to save Carl."

"Isn't that where you've been?" I ask. "Saving Carl?"

"I can't figure out how to get the door to take me where I want to go. I've read the Handbook ten times, but I keep ending up in the future." He spins toward me. "Poppy, it's unlike anything I've ever seen. They have inventions there we could never even dream of. It keeps distracting me, and I—I forget what it is I'm trying to do in the first place."

The way he says it sounds like he's seen it a lot. "How many times have you used the magic?"

He stares at me, and his eyes are glassy and empty and dark. "Dozens."

The word reverberates in my head. How could he have done that?

"The Council have called you to a tribunal tomorrow." I fumble for the letter in my coat and hold it out to him as proof of the chaos he has caused. "They want to talk to you about what you've done."

Al tugs the envelope from my hands and tears it open, his eyes skimming the words. Once he's finished, he shoves it back at me.

"I'm not going. I have nothing to say to them." Al waits for me to take the letter, and when I don't, he lets it fall to the floor.

"Carl wouldn't have wanted you to become this," I whisper.

Al's eyes grow wide. "Don't say his name! You had a chance to try to help him, and you did nothing. Just like everyone else, you left him out there to die."

"Hey, meatball, lay off." Theo moves to stand beside me.

Al scowls at Theo.

"This has nothing to do with you!" Al gives Theo a shove. "Leave us alone!"

I step between them, pulling Al away before he can touch Theo again. "Get out of here right now." I point my brother to the door.

Al stumbles away from us. "Perfect Poppy, always-doing-the-right-thing Poppy. You ever think about climbing down from that high horse?"

Anger courses through me. "The shop is dying because of what you've done. Carl wouldn't have wanted that."

"He would have wanted a life! And I'm going to give it back to him." Al heads straight for the front door, and the ground beneath us begins to tremble again. It starts small and then grows up into the walls, the whole shop shaking as Al reaches for the knob and rips it open. He looks back at me, his face scared and confused before it shifts to rage.

And then quick as he came, he's gone.

I press a hand to my stomach as nausea rolls through me. I want the same thing he does. For Carl to be alive and Papa to be well and for Al to be the same brother who told me not to worry about fitting in at school because I'm one of a kind. I want him to call me firefly.

The Woodland Winds doesn't stop trembling. Theo rushes to the record player and throws on a new song. He pats the large wood counter, gently whispering to it. Slowly the shop begins to calm. When the shaking stops, he looks at me.

"Are you all right?"

I am embarrassed and horrified and exhausted. I can't look Theo in the eye. "I'm sorry. You didn't ask for any of this, I—I should go."

"How did he get in here?" Theo looks between me and the door. "The shop showed itself to you because you need it. But Al said he didn't know that could be done."

"I don't know." I press a hand to my forehead, and

then I see the basket of pins sitting on the right side of the counter. They're silver, with *The Woodland Winds* printed in a slanted script. A pine tree sits just behind the lettering, a fox peeking around the trunk.

"The pins," I say, realization crashing over me.

Theo glances at them, then back at me. "What?"

"Ollie lost the pins that belonged to the shops on her route. She thought she'd misplaced them. But what if Al stole them?" I never should have brought my problems here. "I—I have to go."

"Poppy," Theo calls for me as I reach for the doorknob. "Wait, I—" He pauses, at a loss for what to say. Then he looks at a piece of paper on the counter. "Just wait one second." He picks up a pencil and hastily scribbles something.

I spot the letter from the Council lying on the floor where Al dropped it. I retrieve it, my head aching from our confrontation.

Then Theo folds his note in half, slides it into an envelope, and hands it to me. "Bye, Poppy."

"Goodbye, Theo."

I step out into the day, my eyes set on the horizon as I think about the tribunal, and what I have to do.

Chapter Twenty-One

Once I'm on the bus, on the way back to Sutton, I pull Theo's scribbled note from my pocket.

Dear Poppy,

Granddad used to say that people think too much of courage. Some people spend their whole lives trying to get it. Granddad's theory was that most of us don't realize bravery is like a recipe. It's made up of lots of traits. We all have it somewhere, Poppy.

Theo Devlin's Recipe for Courage:

1 cup Self-confidence   *2 tbsp. Strength in Adversity*

1 cup Determination   *1 heaping tbsp. Compassion*

1/2 cup Urgency   *1 tsp. Hope*

A dash of Belief

Mix well in large bowl.

Sincerely,
Theo

I stand on the back porch, hoping beyond hope that when I open the door, Rhyme and Reason will somehow have returned to normal. I turn the knob and push. It doesn't open at first, I have to really put my shoulder into it. There's a loud crack and I fall inside.

The air is so cold it pricks my skin. I reach for the light switch, and as the bulbs flick on, the sight of the shop takes my breath away. Thick black frost has swept up over the counter, glittering icicles drip from the bookshelves and the hanging lights and the ceiling. There is not a surface left untouched by it.

"Rhyme?" My voice shakes as I slip forward on the icy floor. "Are you here?"

Rhyme and Reason doesn't respond.

"Please talk to me." My body shakes as I hold back a sob. I turn toward the chalkboard, hoping for comfort. There is a single sentence carved into the slate.

"Beware; for I am fearless, and therefore powerful." —Frankenstein, *Mary Shelley.*

"Rhyme? Please, don't leave me!" I call out.

A piece of paper drops from somewhere above and lands on the ground at my feet. I bend to pick it up. It's old, the page yellowed by time, with words written in ink on both sides. The signature at the bottom reads *Ada Elaine Fulbright*, and my blood goes cold. This was written by my great-aunt who disappeared, the one my great-grandparents petitioned the Council to save.

I flip the paper over and begin to read.

Dear Mother and Father,

I'm sure you're looking for me by now. I packed some of my things this morning and hope to catch the six a.m. bus out of Sutton. How long did it take you to notice I was gone? I suppose it doesn't really matter, but something tells me you were so wrapped up in the Grand Reopening for the bookshop expansion that you didn't notice my absence for at least a day.

First, I want to say I'm sorry I had to go. The shop and I have never gotten along, but I wouldn't wish it harm. It wasn't safe anymore, not with me there.

In order to explain, I have to go back to one of your stories, Father. Remember when I was little, I used to beg for you to tell me about the bookshops while we sat in front of the fire? Your tales always enchanted me. You were careful to tell me about the silly things, the happy things. But every now and again you'd mention the Rift and the Dark. I always pressed for more, but you never let me know the whole truth. But now that I do, let me refresh your memory, and tell you what I've learned.

Before the Rift, the Dark and the Light were one.

The keepers curated stories and books, spreading their hope and light and healing to all who needed it. Born with magic in their blood, they believed in one truth: stories are more precious than gold; they are the very soul of humanity.

However, the magic was not perfect. It had two parts, a Light and a Dark. They existed, side by side, two heads controlling the same body. As the keepers spread the Light, it began to flourish in strength and intensity. But there was a balance to the magic, and as the Light grew, so too did the Dark. And the Dark, which had been held back and restrained by the Light for so long, began to search for a way to cut itself free.

The Dark found a keeper, one willing to listen to its call, and slowly it started to poison his mind. He began to desire wealth and power, to be seen and admired for his own greatness. The keeper formed a plan, a way to use the magic to have everything he ever wanted. But when the moment came, when he attempted to use the magic for his own gain, a great rift tore through the magical world, shattering the magic as the Dark ripped itself free from the Light, dividing it forever in two.

On its own for the first time, the Dark spread like a virus to the other keepers, turning them against one another with one goal in mind: to kill everything that was left of the Light.

They began to disappear, extinguished one by one. And those who survived fled across the ocean, went into hiding, and for a generation they stayed there. But in hiding, the Light couldn't grow. So, the keepers gathered together and made a choice. They would put their magic into bookshops; they would create safe havens that would draw people in from across time and space, bonding them together with stories. They would not let the Dark win. They formed a Council, and over time they started to thrive.

But the Dark has watched and waited for the day it could return to power. It has searched for a crack in our defenses, for someone willing to use the magic for their own selfish gain.

I've heard its voice, Mother and Father. It has told me the truth, the one that none of the Council *want us to know. We as Shopkeepers have the power to wield the magic of the shops for ourselves because before it lived in the bookshops, it lived in us. The Dark has told me I can have so much power for myself, if I want it.*

The problem is, I'm starting to want it.

I tried to tell you about the voice, Father. You said I have an active imagination. But the Dark says it has called to you too. I see the fear in your eyes. You've heard it, you worry it's growing stronger.

All I know is that I have to run from it.

I suppose the shop will fall to Edmund now, when he gets old enough to take over. Tell him I'm sorry to give him that burden.

—Your Ada Elaine

P.S. I'm sorry about the fire; it was never my intention to start it. I wouldn't hurt Rhyme and Reason on purpose. So you see, it's safest for me to go while I still can.

I reread the letter twice, my head spinning. She ran away because she heard the Dark too.

I glance at the front door, and the feeling that I'm being watched washes over me.

It's not too late. You can still save him. The voice pushes into my mind, along with a sharp ache in my temple that makes me cry out.

You can learn to use the magic for yourself, Poppy Fulbright. You would never have to feel pain like this again. You could always protect the people you love.

And I feel myself almost agreeing with the voice. I do want to protect the people I love. My family, the shop, our friends.

Return to the past to save Carl Miller from death.

I can almost hear Carl's laugh.

Go to the future and find a way to heal your father.

I can save Papa. Things can go back to the way they should be.

Your father doesn't have to die, little firefly.

Little firefly. The words are like a bucket of cold water. I blink and realize I've somehow moved toward the door. The emerald green is covered in an inch of glittering frost.

Al needs you. He's going to die if you don't help him find the way.

I feel a tug at my center, as if the Dark is pulling me toward it.

"Stop!" I press my hands over my ears. I don't want it in my head anymore. "I know what you are, and what you're trying to do, and I'm not going to fall for it."

I look around at the shop, frozen and empty of the magic. The Dark has infiltrated so deep, what if the Light is gone forever?

Except it can't be. Because I'm here, and I won't let it die.

I rush away from the door, my head pounding as the voice tries to press in again. Behind the front counter, I fumble with the drawers, finally finding an old piece of chalk in the one on the bottom. Holding it in my hand, I spin toward the board on the wall. I begin to write one of Mama's favorite quotes, from *The Old Curiosity Shop*, by Charles Dickens.

The Sun himself is weak when he first rises, and gathers strength and courage as the day gets on.

A great tremble shakes the ground beneath me all at once, and I jump back as ice particles fall from the ceiling like snow, coating my eyelashes and hair.

"Rhyme! Are you there?" I call out as the pounding in my head leaves as quick as it came.

The hanging light above me weakly flickers twice. *Yes.*

I spin to look at the chalkboard for a message in return, and gasp. A great crack stretches across the slate.

A single firefly lands on my shoulder, it's glow flaring on and off.

I managed to fight off the Dark this time, but how much longer will I be able to do it on my own?

Chapter Twenty-Two

The clock behind the front counter reads nine thirty in the morning. It's time to go to the tribunal. I try to push down my nerves, but my hands tremble anyway.

Dressed in my nicest wool sweater, with one of Rhyme and Reason's pins attached at the collar, I slide the letter from the Council off the front counter. Inside is the Council pin; perfectly round and made out of copper, with an open book at its center. The words *The Rules Keep the Light* are written in script along the bottom.

I take a deep breath and open the front door.

The air is cold as I step out. The Lighthouse Bookshop stands tall and sagging in front of me. The memory of Ollie limping toward it fills my head, and I shake it away.

I move down the steps of Rhyme and Reason, my stomach a ball of nerves. When I reach the door of the Lighthouse, it swings open by itself. Inside everything is stark white, even the shelves anchored along the walls. A circular front counter sits directly in the center of the room. An old woman behind it looks up as I enter.

"Hello," she greets me.

I set my shoulders back. "M-my name is Poppy Fulbright, and I have an appointment."

"What, dear? You'll have to speak up." She adjusts her horn-rimmed glasses.

"I'm here for a tribunal," I say louder.

She gives me a look. "Aren't you a little young?"

I try to stand taller, but before I can respond, she turns her back on me.

"Hold on one second." She reaches to her left and pulls a lever. The grinding of gears fills the quiet of the shop, and one of the bookcases on the shelf behind her swings open.

"Well, go on then, don't keep them waiting." She motions for me to move. I hurry around the counter and step through the secret doorway into a dark passage. A dim light glows in the distance, and I follow it forward to the base of a glass staircase spiraling sharply upward.

"They couldn't have an elevator?" I mumble as I start to climb.

The journey is lit by small bulbs nestled into black wall tiles. And as I climb, there seems to be no end in sight. After what seems like forever, I hear voices as I near the top.

I gulp, searching for the courage I need to go on. I have to find the ingredients somehow.

Taking a deep breath, I step out of the dim stairwell and into sudden brightness. I raise a hand to shield my eyes as they adjust.

The room is circular and open. Floor-to-ceiling windows cover the walls and show a perfect view of the ocean on one side and a tiny town on the other. A giant glass light fixture hangs from the center of the ceiling.

A man in a bow tie greets me. "Hello. Rhoda called up. This is a bit awkward, but I was expecting an Allan Fulbright for this tribunal. You aren't Allan Fulbright, are you?"

"I'm Poppy Fulbright, here to represent our family."

The man sighs. "Very well then. I'm Thomas, assistant Council member. Please, follow me."

The room is situated like a stadium, two levels of seats descending lower and lower into a shallow bowl. At the center, six chairs sit on a raised platform, and in front of that there's a single seat. I suppose that's for me.

Men and women linger around the room.

"Who are these people?" I give a quick count. Eleven of them in all. "I didn't know there would be an audience."

"They're delegates from some of the other bookshops. They function like a congress, working with the Council to make decisions." Thomas motions for me to sit. "Wait here until the tribunal starts, please."

As he hastily retreats, I get the feeling he's happy he is not me.

I lower myself into the chair and press a hand to my throat as fear swells inside me. I can do this. I can be brave.

"You look like you're going to pass out," someone whispers behind me.

I glance over my shoulder. Seated in the front row is Ollie. I fight the urge to jump up and throw my arms around her.

"I've been so worried about you! Are you all right?" I whisper.

She wears a bandage on one side of her face and down her neck but manages to give me a weak smile. "The Council's magic is strong. I've been able to heal."

"I'm so sorry about what happened." Tears spring to my eyes.

"It wasn't your fault." She glances around the room. "Isn't your brother supposed to be here? He's the one I blame for this."

"He's not coming."

Her smile slides away. "Poppy, the Council are upset. They—"

But she doesn't finish. Silence falls over the delegates. I turn and see that all six Council members enter the room in a line. One at a time they step up onto the raised platform and take their seats.

I recognize Cyrus Finch and Euphemia Adley, but not the other four.

Euphemia stands at the center of the raised platform. Dressed in a white blouse with a colorful silk scarf and wide-leg navy blue slacks, she emits confidence and strength.

"We have called an emergency tribunal to discuss an event that took place at Rhyme and Reason two days ago. Courier Bell was wounded in the incident. Luckily, we were able to treat those wounds, and she is getting better day by day." Euphemia's eyes slip to my face. "Taking into account the circumstances with your father, we called your brother to appear at this tribunal. I see he is not here. Explain to the Council who you are and tell us why you have come instead."

I clear my throat. "My name is Poppy Fulbright. As you know, my father is ill, and he's left my brother in charge of our shop. However, my brother is currently not himself. He recently suffered the loss of a close friend and he's not handling it well. I have come to represent our shop instead."

Euphemia looks at the other Council members. "Shall we proceed?"

"She's a child," one of them says.

"I was in charge of Rhyme and Reason when the event happened." I speak up and immediately my cheeks flush with embarrassment. I take a deep breath. No one says anything as they consider. Cyrus studies me.

He clears his throat. "I vote we proceed."

"Agreed." The woman next to him, with black hair and a narrow face, nods.

Euphemia turns back to me. "I think it only fair we introduce ourselves to you. Me and Cyrus you've met, of course."

The woman to the left of Cyrus speaks again. "I'm Catalina Mathias."

The woman on Catalina's other side leans forward. She has long dark hair in tiny braids, and kind eyes. "Hanna Erasmus."

The last two introduce themselves as Dante DeGray and Sterling Wolfhart.

When introductions are finished, Euphemia turns back to me. "Today, we simply want to get to the bottom of the events that have occurred at Rhyme and Reason. Can you describe what happened in your shop two nights ago?"

My feet and hands suddenly feel numb with apprehension. I wrap my ankles around the legs of the cold metal chair.

"Allan and I were in Rhyme and Reason that night. We had an argument. Al—" I pause, not wanting to get Al in trouble. "He stormed out of the shop. The minute he left, Rhyme and Reason went dark. When

Ollie and I tried to open the curtains, there was some kind of explosion, and a strange black mist on the other side of the windows leaked through where the glass had cracked. It was ice cold and burned to the touch."

Euphemia Adley stares at me, her brow pulled low in a frown. The other Council members are silent on either side of her, and then Hanna Erasmus leans forward.

"The Dark," Hanna says. "We feared a shop was responsible for the havoc the Dark has caused. Now we know which one."

"The question is, what has been done that invited it in? And how long has it been going on for?" Sterling Wolfhart asks.

The others look at me, waiting.

"You were the one who sent the petition asking permission to use the magic, were you not?" Dante DeGray asks, his voice deep and rich.

My mouth goes dry. "I was never going to send that petition. There was a mix-up, I—"

"Writing a petition questioning the rules isn't enough to let it in. Whatever was done at Rhyme and Reason must have been far worse than that." Hanna Erasmus levels a look at me.

"I believe I have something to offer." A woman in the audience stands. I recognize her from Shopkeeper's

Weekends. Her name is Alice Hawke. She and Mama write often.

Euphemia Adley stares at her. "You have the floor, Shopkeeper Hawke."

Alice takes a nervous breath. "A few nights ago, I was up late finishing a project. From behind the counter, I heard the door open, and seeing as we were closed, I stood up to tell the customer they'd have to come back later. But it wasn't a customer . . ." Her face pales.

"Do get to the point," Euphemia says, trying to keep her patience. "If it wasn't a customer, who was it?"

"It's been a few years since I saw him at our last Shopkeeper's Weekend, but I would've recognized him anywhere. It was Allan Fulbright."

My head snaps in her direction.

"He stepped inside, shut the front door behind him, and then began to open it again. I asked what he was doing. Poor kid seemed half out of his mind. Kept talking about making everything right, whatever that means. He had a lapel full of shop pins. I pressed him on why he had them and he ran for it."

The Council looks at me one by one, their eyes seeming to bore into my soul.

"I believe he was using those pins on his lapel to gain entry into shops. That's all I wanted to say." Alice sits down.

I sink back against my chair, everything shaking inside of me.

Euphemia's eyes are full of fire as she turns to me. "Poppy Fulbright, can you refute this?"

I cannot cover this up anymore, no matter how much I want to.

"I—"

"She doesn't need to say anything," Dante DeGray scoffs. "This story is all the proof we need."

"The Shopkeepers at Rhyme and Reason have violated the rules of our world," Hanna Erasmus says. "They must be punished."

"What really happened the night of the incident?" Cyrus asks me. "Part of your story is clearly missing. Think things over very carefully, Miss Fulbright. We do not have patience for lying."

Al has created a mess and left me to lie in it, and the realization slams into me that I can't protect him anymore. "I—I—" My shoulders fall. "I caught my brother coming through the front door. He confessed he'd been out of it before, trying to go back in time to save his friend's life."

A chorus of judgment surges around me. I hear the words *oath*, and *Rhyme and Reason*, and *Vincent*.

"My brother is not himself." I try to speak for Al. "Something is wrong with him. He said he . . ." I trail off, my words lost in a chorus of arguments among the

Council members, and in the crowd surrounding us. My head starts to spin; the numbness in my hands and feet creeps up into my limbs as the panic inside of me grows. My voice is being drowned out. I told Papa I could come here and represent us, I have to be brave now. I push myself to my feet, heart pounding.

"Something is controlling him!" I shout, and the room falls silent. "A voice has been calling out to him for weeks. He can't stop hearing it. I—I've heard it too."

Euphemia takes in a single, sharp breath. The others sit in stunned silence.

"It's worse than we feared," she says.

Catalina Mathias scoots to the edge of her chair. She's the oldest of the Council, and the room pays attention as she begins to speak. "Nearly a hundred years ago, the first Council put the magic into the bookshops to preserve the Light against the Dark. When they did it, they didn't consider that the Dark and the Light, though severed, still share an origin, and that by creating a host for the Light, a host was also needed for the Dark. It has been trying to find a host ever since. It's come close once before; this time the Dark has learned from its past failure and hidden itself from the Council, hoping that by the time we saw it, there would be no time to stop it." Her dark eyes meet mine. "If what you say is true, and your brother is not acting of his own accord, it means the Dark has already chosen him as its host."

Euphemia Adley gets to her feet, panic in her eyes. "Where is your brother now?"

My hands are shaking so hard I tuck them into the pockets of my coat. "I don't know."

An outcry crescendos around me, a rising tide of panic and fear. Euphemia Adley calls out, "There is no telling the damage he has already done. I want a watch placed in every shop. He must be found, immediately."

Chapter Twenty-Three

The Council springs into action, making plans to block Al from entering other shops and spreading the Dark more than he already has. I look for an exit, wondering if I can make a run for it.

"What about the girl? We cannot allow her to go back to Rhyme and Reason and run it alone. The Fulbrights have caused enough trouble as it is." Hanna Erasmus motions toward me.

"She must stay here." Dante DeGray's words settle into my stomach. "We cannot allow her to interfere on her brother's behalf."

Euphemia Adley doesn't spare me a glance. "Rhyme and Reason will be placed under our control immediately. Dante, I'll leave that up to you. Cyrus, Hanna, check in with the other shops, see if anyone else has seen him. In order to contain the damage, we have to find out exactly where he's been. Catalina, call in every courier we have."

Euphemia turns toward the door they used to enter the room. She pauses and glances back. "Poppy, Ollie, come with me."

I glance over my shoulder and exchange a glance with Ollie.

"Now," Euphemia commands, and I jump to my feet, rushing after her, wondering what my fate will be.

Euphemia hurries down a long hall to a glossy oak door at the very end of it. After pulling a key from her pocket, she unlocks it and motions us inside.

"Quickly," she says.

The room has windows along the far wall, all of them overlooking the ocean. There's floor-to-ceiling book-shelves, a worn sofa, and nothing else. Is this where they're going to lock me up?

Euphemia closes the door behind us and spins to face me. "Do you have any idea which shops your brother may have been using to travel?"

I blink.

"Poppy, we don't have much time. I'm trying to help you, but you have to be honest with me."

I search her face, not sure if I can trust her. I want to. She's the leader of this world, and she has only shown me kindness.

"He stole Ollie's pins, the ones that belonged to the shops on her route."

Euphemia looks at Ollie, her eyes wide. "Why didn't you report they were missing?"

Ollie swallows. "I reported to my supervisor. She gave me a replacement set and told me not to let it happen again. I—"

"Give me your route list, please." Euphemia cuts her off.

Ollie nods and quickly names them for Euphemia.

"That's a start for us, thank you. Now, let's get you both out of here." Euphemia Adley turns and begins to search the bookshelf. Her fingers caress the spines of several books, stopping on a Jane Austen. She pulls it out, and the case swings open, revealing a wrought-iron staircase.

"You're letting me go?" I ask. The rest of the Council were so angry, so intent on keeping me here. "I don't understand."

"The Council thinks we can find Al and stop the Dark, but I am not that hopeful. If the Dark is using Al as its host, then it has a strength we've never seen before. I'm not sure we can win this time."

She's talking about my brother, and it doesn't seem real or true. Fear is icy in my blood at the thought that the Dark has taken him when he was most vulnerable.

"So, what are you suggesting?"

"Run. Find your parents and tell them to lie low until this is sorted out. We have Rhyme and Reason in our control. We'll save it if we can."

If they can? Horror rolls through me. I can't accept what she's saying.

"You too, Ollie. Tell your family to get out. I'm going to begin evacuation plans for the other shops."

"But—"

"Al has taken the Dark everywhere he's been." Terror emanates off Euphemia Adley in waves. "Which means it has been rooting itself in the other shops for weeks now. It will attach itself to our customers, who will then take it back through time to their homes, where it will spread further and further. The Dark wants pain and misery and chaos. It wants to destroy the Light so that it can have full control of the magic itself. The only thing that has stood in its path until now is us. There's a chance we can stop that spread before it happens, but the only way I know how to do that is to shut down the shops and evacuate. Now, will you please—"

"What about Al?" I ask.

Euphemia blinks at me, but I don't back down.

"In this plan of yours, what happens to my brother?"

She takes me by the shoulders. "There's nothing we can do for him, Poppy. Not now."

It feels like a punch in the gut, and I can't breathe as I stare at her.

"No." I shake my head, horror crashing against me in waves. "No! I haven't given up on him yet, I won't give up on him now."

"Your brother made his choice when he broke the rules." Euphemia's words sound cold and empty of emotion.

It's true, Al made his choices, but so have I. All of this time I've been angry at him, but I never once stopped to listen as he told me over and over that something was wrong. He's right, something *is* wrong. The Dark has been using him, and driven by desperation, he listened.

He made one mistake and they're giving up on him? It's not right. I turn away from her, my mind moving, running, leaping as it tries to find a way to save him. "If having a host makes the Dark stronger, can't we just remove Al as the host?"

"Separate the Dark from its host." Euphemia thinks it over. "If you could break the bond the Dark has fused with your brother, it might lose its strength. The pieces of itself that have spread wherever Al has been would be severed. But I doubt it can be done."

"Leader Adley?" Someone knocks on the door, and Euphemia frantically waves us into the stairwell.

"Why can't it be done?" I press as I step past her.

"If the Dark has chosen your brother as host, there is likely not much of Al left at all. It doesn't need his mind, just his body. There will be no reaching him, Poppy. It's too late. The brother you knew is already gone."

"Leader Adley, are you in there?"

The doorknob rattles, and Euphemia gives us one last look. "Run while you still can."

Then she closes the hidden doorway, leaving us in darkness.

A shiver jerks through me, and my teeth chatter so hard, I clamp down my jaw to stop it. I barely make out Ollie's features in the dim light of the wall fixture.

"What do we do now, Poppy?" she whispers.

I curl my hands into fists. "I have to save Al."

"You heard Leader Adley, it can't be done."

"I can get through to him," I insist.

"How? You've already tried."

Ollie is right. I have tried. Over and over as Al has spiraled into the Dark. Nothing I've said has made a bit of difference. But I think of Rhyme and Reason, of all the books on the shelves, all of the bindings that hold pages and pages of stories. I've read so many tales about heroes and heroines slaying the dragon, breaking the curse, rescuing the kingdom from destruction. They've taught me that there is one thing in this world stronger than anything else.

"Love," I whisper. "I can use love, Ollie."

"That's only in books," Ollie whispers. "You can't guarantee that will work."

I take a breath. "I have to try."

Ollie grabs my shoulders, holding me steady. "You realize what you're saying."

"That I'm going to go against the Council?" I should stop this train of thought before it's too late for me to turn back. But there is a roar in my heart far louder telling me that it's not too late. "Yes."

She swallows. "I suppose Al has already done the worst. You really can't go any further down from here."

"Exactly." I try to reassure myself. "You should do what Euphemia said. Go home, warn your parents. In case I can't save Al, you can still get out."

Ollie shakes her head. "You don't have a chance without me. Now come on, if we're going to find Al, we need something important to him, something he cares about. And we better do it fast, before Dante DeGray shuts down Rhyme and Reason."

Chapter Twenty-Four

"**D**id you find something?" Ollie stands watch by the front door, both of us anxious that Council members will swoop into Rhyme and Reason at any moment.

"Yes." I hold up a half-dollar coin. It belonged to Carl and Al. They found it in the gutter when they were younger and swore it was lucky, passing it back and forth whenever they needed to win a game or ace a test. Carl had it with him in the war, and Mrs. Miller brought it by the shop last week; it had been shipped home with his other effects. I meant to give it back to Al, but with everything going on here, I never had the chance.

Ollie nods at it. "Objects are powerful tools in this line of work. Most of the Shopkeepers don't realize that the magic of the door works in reverse. Shops bring people here, but they can take us somewhere too. All you need is a conduit." She points to the coin. "Are you ready?"

"What about the Dark?" I say. "We're breaking the rules."

"Yes, except that the rules say *never use the magic for your own gain*. We're doing this to stop the Dark from using your brother to destroy the bookshop world."

I stare at her. "A loophole."

"A loophole," she agrees.

"Rhyme?" I want the shop to know that I'm not doing this for selfish reasons. "I'm breaking the rules to set things right. You understand, don't you?"

The light above us flickers twice. *Yes.*

I give Ollie a nod.

"Very well, then." She reaches for my arm. "Focus on that coin and finding Al." She turns the knob and opens the door.

The street we step out on is—Marigold. It's our street.

"What the—" Ollie glances back at the shop, then in front of us. "We didn't go anywhere."

"No, that's not true. The season is different." I point at the street. There isn't any snow, not to mention the air is sticky with humidity. It feels like summer.

"He went to your town in another time?" Ollie shakes her head. "That doesn't make any sense; why would he do that?"

"Because he's trying to find Carl before he went to war." I pull off my coat and start down the sidewalk.

It's a busy afternoon in Sutton. As we head down

the street, I see the Saturday market set up in the town square and all sorts of posters advertising war bonds and fundraisers for our boys.

We reach the crosswalk where Marigold and Rose Hill meet. I stop to look down Rose Hill when someone bumps into me from behind.

"Oh! I'm real sorry." Louie Miller, Carl's little brother, grabs my arm to steady me. "Not watching where I was going. I didn't see you, Poppy."

"Hi." I give him a smile. "I'm actually looking for Al—have you seen him anywhere?"

"I'm sure he's off with Carl." Louie glances down at his watch. "They might be at the station already. I'm headed there now if you want to come?"

"The bus station?"

"Carl's leaving today." Louie stares at me. "For the war. Didn't Al tell your family?"

"Oh. Yes," I say. It must be just a few months ago. If I remember right, Carl shipped out in August. Carl and Al both turned eighteen and tried to join up together. Carl was shipped off to training camp shortly after Al was denied.

"I gotta get going." Louie frowns. "I don't want to miss my last chance to say goodbye."

And then he's off.

I remember this day, this horrible goodbye we had to say to Carl.

"We should go with him." If we're going to find Al, that's where he'll be.

I trail behind Louie all the way to the station and spot our group off to one side. The Millers are all there, trying to be strong for Carl. Then there's me and James and Mama and Papa, and last is Carl's girlfriend of the month, Lucy Morgan. She's tucked under Carl's arm as he entertains his well-wishers with a joke, in usual Carl fashion. My heart leaps at the sight of him, alive and well.

"Where's your brother?" Ollie stops just behind me. "Shouldn't he be here?"

"He was late that day," I recall.

Carl steps back from his parents, his eyes narrowing as he surveys the station. And then all at once, Al is walking through the door, his hands in the pockets of his tweed jacket, his hair in the shorter army-style cut he got just before he found out he was disqualified. I step back into the shadows as he passes.

"For half a minute I thought you weren't coming," Carl calls out.

"Of course I was coming." Al shakes his head. "I was trying to find something." He reaches into his pocket and pulls out a large silver coin.

"You son of a gun! It's our lucky half dollar. I thought we lost that last year." Carl laughs again as Al drops it into his palm. I look down at it now, clutched in my hand.

The edges are black, and I wonder if it's from blood or battlefield dirt. My stomach turns at the thought.

"I spent all night looking for it. Found it at the bottom of my closet." Al runs a hand under his nose. "Funny thing is, I can't remember why it was special."

"Because you had it that day you asked Martha Freberg to go steady in the eighth grade, and against all odds she said yes. Then I took it when I tried out for varsity baseball, and I made it, youngest guy on the team. This thing is magic." He flips it in the air.

They're both so innocent. Touched by the war, but full of hope that things will end soon.

The smile on Al's face falters. "Should've taken it to the recruitment office with me."

"Listen here." Carl pulls his rucksack higher on his shoulder. "You're gonna be all right, you hear me? I know you're disappointed you can't go, but there's plenty to do for the war effort at home." Carl glances at all of us standing to the side. "Watch out for my family? For Louie? Don't let him do something brainless like joining up before he's eighteen."

Al nods. "Listen, I know it's gonna be hard for you, with that fat head of yours, but don't try to be the hero out there."

Carl gives him another grin, and it's then I see he's got tears in his eyes. "We've always done everything together. This feels wrong, doesn't it?"

Al doesn't say anything.

"Come on, Carl! Don't want to miss the bus!" Mr. Miller shouts.

Carl and Al shake hands, then at the last minute, Carl pulls him into a hug. "See you on the other side, brother."

Carl kisses his mother, hugs his father and his brother. His girlfriend walks with him to the bus and he plants one on her in front of everybody, just before he hops on board. I want to stop him, to tell him not to go. To stay, no matter the consequences, just stay.

Carl leans out the window, waving to his family and his friends as the bus pulls away. Everyone stands there, watching until it's no longer visible in the distance. And just like that, he's gone.

The hole Carl left in our lives has never felt so big to me, so unfillable.

Ollie clears her throat. "Carl seemed like a lovely guy."

"He is," I say, and the words sink down inside me. "He was."

Mama holds on tight to Mrs. Miller. Al claps a hand on Louie's shoulder and says something in his ear I can't hear. Louie laughs and nods as they make their way out of the station. Papa and James trail behind everyone else as they leave. Past Poppy links her arm through Mrs. Miller's and heads toward the exit.

"No."

I glance over my shoulder, and Al, dressed in the same tight-fitting clothes from the future, stands behind me. He doesn't seem to see me. Instead, he watches as the bus disappears from view. He scans the station and spots our group heading up the stairs toward the double doors. Realization washes over his face.

"I missed him," he hisses, slamming a fist against his temple. "I was *this* close, and I—I screwed it up again."

His eyes flutter and then focus on my face. "What are you doing here?"

"Looking for you." I hold out a hand, palm up, trying not to scare him off. "There's something I have to tell you. I—"

Al backs away from me. "Get out of here! Go home!" A thin dark mist secretes from him, as if it's seeping out of his skin. The fog lingers in the air, and I reach out a hand to touch it. The minute it brushes my skin, it burns just like the stuff that came in through the crack in the window the night Ollie got hurt.

Ollie calls out to me and backs away, her eyes wide with the horror of remembering. "Let's go."

Al shuts his eyes, and when he opens them again, his gaze is hard and cold. "How did you get here? How did you find this moment in time?"

He takes a step toward me, but I move back.

"Tell me how you did it!" Rage pours out of him, and the fog seems to thicken in the air. My courage starts to falter, and I stumble away. I thought I could save him, but maybe Euphemia Adley is right, maybe my brother *is* gone.

"Poppy!" Ollie turns back just as Al lunges for me. I manage to dodge him and dash up the stairs after her.

We run. Out of the bus station, back down Rose Hill and Marigold, through Sutton.

We stumble inside Rhyme and Reason and slam the door shut behind us.

"Why did the Dark choose your brother?" Ollie asks, doubling over as she tries to catch her breath. "And why the fixation on his friend Carl? What does that matter to the Dark?"

"B-because Carl's death destroyed him." I lean into the wall, taking gasping breaths, my heart racing. "It opened the door for the Dark, and Al let it in." And now Al is gone. I don't say the words, but they hang in the air between us. Except. If Al was completely gone, he wouldn't be so set on saving his best friend. "Maybe . . . maybe the part of Al that's still alive in there is the part of him obsessed with finding Carl."

"But the fog," Ollie says.

I stare at her, a heavy realization flooding through me. "It's the Dark trying to put that light in him out."

Which means Al is running out of time.

Ollie's eyes grow wide.

"I see your brother isn't the only one breaking the rules in this shop." A deep voice comes from behind us, and I whirl around. Dante DeGray stands at the front counter, his arms crossed over his chest.

"How long have you been here?" I growl at him.

"Long enough." His eyes are cold and steely as he stares us down. "Clearly, your parents have let everything spiral out of control."

Anger cuts through me. "Everything was fine, until—"

"Rhyme and Reason is now under the authority of the Council." He looks around the frosty main floor. "Though I suspect the magic here is almost dead already. The Council demands you turn over all Shopkeeper's logs, and I'll be taking possession of your pins."

I stare at him in horror. "But this is *our* shop."

"Not anymore."

I want to be brave, to stand up to him and scream at him to leave. But what good will that do? I look sideways at Ollie, and she nods for me to do what he says.

It takes all the strength I have to move around the counter and pull out the drawer where Papa keeps his logs. Then I collect our basket of pins and hand both over.

"Courier Bell needs to get home," I tell him.

He glances sideways at her and shakes his head. "All travel from Rhyme and Reason is suspended. I'm afraid you're stuck here for the time being."

"Excuse me?" she says. "I don't know if you realize who my—"

The phone rings out behind the counter, high-pitched and shrill. Before Dante can stop me, I reach for it, the receiver freezing against my fingers.

"Hello?"

"Poppy?" Mama sounds distant and hollow from the other end of the line. "I've been calling for an hour."

"I'm here now. What is it? How's Papa?"

"Your father is—he's getting worse. The hospital says they don't know how to help him. He wants to come home, Poppy."

I don't understand what she's saying. I try to feel shock or horror, but there's a loud rushing in my ears. I stare at the chalkboard, where Rhyme tries to form a sentence but only manages to produce gibberish.

"Are you there? Can you hear me?"

I press a hand to my forehead. "There has to be—"

"It won't be long now. Poppy. He doesn't have much time left."

No, no, no. My knees go weak and I lean into the counter to keep myself standing.

"James and Aunt Lina are coming with us. Our transport back to Sutton leaves in about an hour. I expect we'll be home by tonight."

It's such a long journey for someone so ill. And I'm angry that this is how the doctors are handling it. They sent him to the city to help him, and now they're giving up?

"I've got to go, sweetheart. See you soon."

I slam the receiver down, my anger overflowing.

"Poppy?" Ollie asks.

I had forgotten Ollie and Dante were here. When Papa gets home, he's going to find out that the shop has been taken from us, that everything is in shambles.

"It's my father—they—he—" But I can't finish the words. All I want is to be alone, somewhere safe. I back away from the counter and Dante calls out my name, but I run from them. I reach the lilac hedge first, or what should be the lilac hedge. But it's gone, the vines reduced to a frozen pile of twigs on the ground. I jump over the debris and move around the picture books. The climbing hydrangea and white wisteria have crumbled to nothing, and the enchanted forest mural on the back wall is blank.

"Rhyme?" I call out, tears blurring my vision as I spot our flock of paper birds frozen on the floor. "I need you."

I wait for the fireflies to appear, for the lights to flicker. But the shop is silent.

Rhyme and Reason has been fighting the Dark off for days now, and it has nothing left to give.

My chest burns. "Why can't you save us?" I whisper, and I don't care at all that I sound James's age. "You're supposed to protect us from the bad things—isn't that what you're here for? If you can't do that, then what good are you?"

I scream and reach for a book, yanking it off the shelf. I pull off another, and another, and another, throwing them against the wall. I fall to my knees, my heart in pieces. I was supposed to keep everything together, but I can't do it all alone, and now the magic is gone, Rhyme is gone, and I'll never be the same without it.

Chapter Twenty-Five

The bell above the door rings, and I hear raised voices in the distance.

I stumble to my feet and rush back to the shop entrance.

"As I said, Rhyme and Reason is closed." Dante DeGray stares down at Bibine and the twins. He's not a large man, but in a crisp tweed suit he has a commanding air. Bibine doesn't shrink back from him.

"We just want to make sure everything is all right." Bibine sees me over his shoulder, and her brow pulls down in concern. Before Dante DeGray can stop her, she brushes past him and has me in her arms, her hand on my back. I bury my face in her shoulder, the tears rolling down my cheeks.

The door opens again, and Katherine steps inside, Whitney right behind her.

"Poppy! We've been trying to get in the shop all day." Katherine looks around Rhyme and Reason in horror. "Why is it so cold in here?"

Whitney steps forward. "How can we help?"

The door opens one more time, and there is Anna

Rose, her face pale. "I've been frantic to get back here. I've been so worried about you."

They all stare at me, and I feel a shadow of Rhyme and Reason's warmth return.

"Thank you all for coming—" I start.

"But Rhyme and Reason is closed until further notice." Dante sizes them all up. "We have an ongoing crisis we're handling, and I must ask you all to leave immediately."

Nobody moves.

"Things aren't stable here, and we're trying to ensure the safety of all Rhyme and Reason's customers." Dante tries again, clearly not used to being ignored.

"It really would be best if you return home," I say weakly.

Anna Rose sets her shoulders back. "This shop is my family. And family doesn't leave when things get scary. They stay."

At her words the hanging bulb above the door flickers to life, followed by the two over the front counter, as Rhyme and Reason fights the Dark.

"This isn't up for discussion." Dante's voice is firmer as he stares them all down.

Bibine crosses her arms over her chest in a defiant stance. "I am not going to leave Poppy here alone like this."

"Same with me," Katherine says, locking eyes with Whitney.

"I'm with her." Whitney points his thumb at Katherine.

My chin trembles as a fresh wave of tears threatens to spill over. The shop knew I needed them here, so I wouldn't be alone.

"I'm afraid she doesn't have the authority to let you stay. Rhyme and Reason is no longer under the control of the Fulbrights."

"My father is dying," I tell him. "He's on the way home from the hospital, and I—I don't know what to do."

Dante's face seems to soften then. I wonder if he knows my father very well.

"Fine. But I'm not leaving." He pulls a chair close to the front door and sits. "And no one else is allowed in or out of these doors."

"Well, then," Bibine says, ignoring Dante. "Let's see if we can't tidy this mess."

Before Dante can protest further, the regulars surround me, and we move into the shop, ready to get to work.

When Papa is wheeled into Rhyme and Reason late that evening, his face is gray. It's almost more than I can bear. Two orderlies carry him in on a medical bed with wheels, Mama and Aunt Lina and James trailing just behind.

"Papa," I whisper as they push him past. His eyes meet mine, but he doesn't say anything.

"Hello, darling." Mama gives me an exhausted attempt at a smile and wraps her arms around me.

I have missed her hugs, and the smell of her perfume, and how she sings to me when I'm sick or sad or afraid.

"Where's Al?" she asks.

"He'll be back soon," I say, and she's so tired she doesn't press for a further explanation.

The regulars stand behind me, all of them watching solemnly. For the past few hours, they swept and polished while the shop managed to heat itself up, melting most of the frost. It doesn't look like normal, but it's better.

Dante DeGray sits at the door, his arms crossed, his mouth set in a line. Mama doesn't even notice him.

"I've missed you all," Mama tells them as she looks around Rhyme and Reason. "The shop too." When she takes in the wallpaper and the dying flowers, she frowns. "What's happened?"

I search for a way to explain it all. "It's—"

But the sound of Aunt Lina arguing with the orderlies interrupts me. "Their apartment is on the third floor. You can't just leave him down here. This is a bookshop."

"Oh, dear." Mama hurries past me.

"I'm sorry," the orderly near Papa's feet says. "But the stairs are too narrow. We'll never get him up there."

Mama's chin trembles. "But—he—he wants to be home."

Papa reaches for Mama's hand. "The shop is home."

Mama sets her shoulders back. "Then let's move some of these tables and chairs out of the way. You can stay by the fire."

The regulars don't ask if they can help, they spring into action around us, moving things to the side. When it's finished, the orderlies settle Papa in close to the mantel. Aunt Lina speaks with them in low tones, and then they leave us.

Papa turns his head, looking out at the regulars. "Hello, everyone." His voice is so weak they have to move in closer to hear.

Prosper and Kosma stick to their grandmother's side, frightened by the way Papa looks. Bibine gives Papa an affectionate smile. Katherine has tears in her eyes, and Whitney passes her a handkerchief. Anna Rose nods at him.

Prosper drops his grandmother's hand and moves forward.

"I finished reading the chapter book you gave me. I didn't believe you, but you were right about what you said. Maybe the end *can* be both sad and happy at the same time."

Papa's eyes glisten as Prosper reaches for his hand and gives it a squeeze.

"Thank you," Papa says, tears running down his cheeks. "Thank you all for being here." A cough rises in his throat, and it takes him a moment to speak. "It was a long trip, and I just need some . . . sleep . . ." And even though he fights it, his eyes slip closed, and he drifts off.

"I don't know what we would do without you all." Mama takes a step toward Papa, and her feet seem to give way beneath her because suddenly she's falling. Whitney just manages to catch her, and Aunt Lina rushes forward.

"You need rest, Evi," she says. "You haven't slept in days. You can't keep going like this."

Mama is crying now as she gets to her feet. She looks so broken, her hair hanging in stringy clumps, her eyes puffy from stress and worry.

"We'll sit with him." Katherine steps forward. "We can take shifts. He won't ever be alone."

Mama blinks at us in the dim light. Her eyes fall on me.

"All right," she whispers after a moment. Aunt Lina helps Mama up the stairs, and I look back at the regulars.

"You all have done so much. I can stay with him for now," I say.

But Bibine won't hear of it. "It's late. You need your rest too. You don't have to be alone here, Poppy."

A soft peace spreads up my throat and down into my stomach. Rhyme and Reason brought us all together, and that's kind of magic too. Proof that even in the midst of darkness, there is hope.

Chapter Twenty-Six

Nightmares haunt my sleep. Flashes of Al and Carl, both in uniform, stepping on that bus together. Al waving at us as it pulls away. Then Al is dead, buried in the snow somewhere in Germany, and Carl comes home from the war with medals on his chest and sorrow on his lips.

I wake with a jolt, realizing I've fallen asleep on the floor in the children's section. I roll over and find Prosper and Kosma curled up in a pile of blankets. Bibine and Anna Rose sleep on cots pushed against the picture books.

The clock on the wall says it's just after two a.m. Papa has been home for four hours.

I roll over to go back to sleep when I hear the calendar shuffling through dates. Someone is coming, and I'm up in an instant. As I near the front of the shop, I see Dante, dozing in the chair between the display and the window. The door creaks open and a person falls inside, landing on the rug with a dull thud. I wait to see if Dante will wake, but he doesn't.

The figure moans lightly and rolls over on the floor. The light above him flickers to life, and it's Al lying there, staring up at the ceiling in a daze. Steam pours off of him, black and thin.

"Al?" My voice is barely a whisper.

He tries to sit up but can't quite manage it.

"Poppy?" His voice is brittle, as if he doesn't have the strength to speak.

I rush forward and fall to my knees at his side, keeping my distance from the wispy fog lingering in the air around him. "I'm here, it's me."

His eyes roam my face, wide and wild. Deep black veins run around his mouth. One snakes its way up his jaw to his ear. But when he looks at me, his eyes are clear and blue.

"Poppy." A faint smile finds its way to his lips.

"Al?" I'm careful not to touch him, afraid of the Dark inside him.

"I can't find Carl, no matter how hard I try. Time keeps slipping through my fingers. I—I just want to save him. There has to be a way!" The blue in his eyes wavers, black creeping in. "Poppy, I don't feel right."

"It's the Dark inside of you, Al." I glance over at Dante, and he's starting to stir, his eyelids flickering.

"But the Dark wants to help me." Confusion crosses his face as Dante shifts in his chair. We're running out of time.

"We have to get you out of here, you're not safe." I debate whether or not I can touch him without getting burned. Before I can make a decision, he grabs my arm.

"I just want things to be the way they used to be. You and me and Carl. Remember when we were kids, we used to play comic book heroes?" His eyes flutter rapidly, but a distant smile forms on his lips. "Carl always wanted to be Flash Gordon and the rest of us had to be sidekicks or villains."

"You need some rest." I reach across him and take his other hand, relieved we can touch safely.

"I never wanted to be the villain." A tear escapes the corner of his eye and trails down his cheek.

"You can sleep on the cot in the storeroom." I'll sneak him past Dante and lock Al inside the room. In the morning, his mind might be clearer, and I can try to get through to him again before the Council finds him.

"How did you do it, Poppy? How did you find Carl that day at the bus station?" The sadness on his face gives way to desperation, and his grip hardens, his fingers digging into my shoulder.

"Al!" I hiss, and then frantically look up at Dante, whose eyes are opening now. "The Council is after you, one of the members is here, and—you're hurting me!" I cry out, and Dante startles awake.

"Al, run!" I grab hold of my brother and try to pull him to his feet.

"You!" Dante jumps from the chair and charges straight for my brother just as Al yanks himself out of my grasp and rushes for the door. Seeing that he's going to leave again, Dante pivots, throwing himself in Al's path just as the Dark's fog explodes out of Al. It hisses as it fills the air around Dante, who screams and throws a hand over his face, falling to his knees. Al jumps over the top of him, grabs the knob, and turns back once.

"They will not win this war," he says, his voice deep and heavy and not like him at all, and then he nearly jumps out the door. Right before it can close behind him, Dante manages to grab it and stumbles to his feet, flinging himself after Al, leaving me standing alone in the empty entryway, my heart pounding out of my chest.

"What's going on?"

I look over and there, standing against one of the bookcases, is Papa.

He tries to take a step forward, but his legs give out, and he falls to his knees.

"Papa!" I rush toward him and manage to wedge my arm under his shoulder. With most of his weight on me, I try to get him back to bed, but realize I can't do it on my own. Together we stumble toward the chair where Dante DeGray was sleeping. Papa collapses into it, his breathing labored and raspy.

"W-what's happening to Al?" he gasps, eyes wide. "The fog coming from him, the look in his eyes?"

"It's the—"

"What have I done?" Papa buries his face in one hand.

"You didn't do anything." I shake my head and start to reach for him.

"Poppy." He looks at me, and his eyes are clearer than I've seen in weeks.

"What?" I smell antiseptic and hospital on his skin. His labored breathing is hot against my cheek.

"I made a mistake." He winces at the words. "I should've told your mother, but now—" He stops to breathe, as if he's been running a marathon instead of walking a few steps. "Now it's too late."

You're scaring me, Papa. The words are on my lips, but I don't say them out loud.

"I couldn't lose him, you must understand, you must see that." He pauses to cough into his elbow, and I wait for it to subside.

"Lose who?" I say, thinking of Carl.

"Al." His eyes meet mine and the guilt pools in his eyes.

"Al? I don't know what you mean. Lose him?"

"There was never any childhood asthma. Al didn't have a problem with his lungs."

I listen to Papa's words, but they don't make sense. I remember it, remember Papa telling Al to be careful, to never push too hard or his lungs wouldn't be able to handle the strain. Papa always made sure Al sat on the sidelines while the other children played. He could never throw a baseball with his friends. There were visits to doctors. I remember it all. Papa was always there to handle it.

"But—you—he—Papa, that doesn't make sense."

"The war came, you see. After Pearl Harbor, Carl and Al, and all the boys their age—they couldn't wait to go off to fight, but they didn't—" He swallows, and then presses on. "They didn't know what war was like. I tried to tell Al, on more than one occasion, to convince him to wait until he was called up. But Al was never one to wait. He turned eighteen, and then so did Carl, and they went to the office to join up. Both of them were accepted. They left for training. It all happened so fast."

My mind races as his words send a chill through me. This isn't the way it happened.

"Al was sent overseas. He couldn't tell us where he was going, of course, and then two months after he left, we—" He shuts his eyes as he tries to compose himself. "We got a telegram that he was missing. Not long after, he was confirmed dead."

I pull back from him, curling my fingers around the arms of my chair. I shake my head. This can't be true.

"He was gone." Papa can't hold back the tears now. "Carl came home. He was injured, lost an arm, but he blamed himself for Al's death. We were—we were all devastated, and Carl, he—he could barely function.

I would sit every night in the shop, wondering what good Rhyme and Reason was if it couldn't fix the past. And the more despair I felt, the more I thought about using the shop to change what happened, and the more I heard a voice on the other side of the door that promised it could bring my boy back. After a while I started to listen. I could end our pain. I could change the past. It promised me."

I stare at Papa, a blanket of cold wrapping itself around me as he speaks.

"My father warned me my whole life that there was a force out there, waiting for us to choose it over the Light. He told me to stay away from it, but I—I was willing to do anything to save Al. You must understand."

"Papa, what have you done?" I whisper.

"I used the magic. I went back before Allan was born and found my younger self somewhere outside of Rhyme and Reason. I told myself everything that was going to come. Armed with the information that Al would die in the war one day, my younger self formed a plan. When he was born, I began the lie, threaded it into his life, convinced everyone that it was true, that he really had asthma. I explained his symptoms to the doctors, and Al believed he had them. It made him physically weaker than the other boys, but it was worth the cost. When he went to join up, already underweight for his age and height, he had to tell them about his asthma—my lie—

and they rejected him. I didn't know that it would twist him, change him—turn him into something else." Tears fill his eyes. "My son, what have I done to my son?"

The first night Al suggested we use the door to save Carl, he yelled at Papa. *What would you have done if it were me?* I shut my eyes, nausea washing over me. How did I not see it then?

"I broke the rules." Papa's chin quivers. "I didn't know I would be trading Al's life for Carl's. If I had known, I never would have done it." He pauses to catch his breath, his eyes shut tight. "When I returned home from talking with my younger self, everything had changed. Al believed he had asthma. He was denied entry into the military just the way I hoped he would be. New memories came to me, all the things I had done to ensure he would never have to fight. But . . ."

"But what, Papa?"

"But I realized quickly that the Dark had latched on to me. I was losing my temper with the regulars, my connection with Rhyme and Reason started to fade. When I tried to fight against it, I started to get sick." He pauses to take a shaky breath. "I opened the door and let the Dark in." He presses a hand to his mouth as if he can hardly stomach what he's done. "When we went to the hospital, I thought perhaps things would be better, that without me, the Dark would leave Rhyme and Reason alone."

"But it took Al instead." I search his face, realization washing over me. The Dark tried to make Papa its host first, but Papa refused. That refusal cost him his health, his strength. I remember the way his flecks of blood looked on my dress the night of Monday Favorites. They were black.

Papa's face collapses then. "My son, what have I done to my son?"

My body feels cold as I look at the door, picturing the Dark, desperately searching for a host, for someone broken enough to accept it. That person was Al.

"The magic is fragile, Poppy. So very fragile. We have a choice between the Light and the Dark. I chose the Dark, and now we're in this mess because of me." Papa presses a hand to his forehead. "I thought if I did the wrong thing for the right reason, we would be all right."

"Why haven't you told Al the truth?" I say.

"It would destroy him. Don't you see? If he knew I saved his life only to sacrifice Carl, it would kill whatever part of him is left."

"W-we can go back. We can undo it." Desperation overwhelms me. Papa has proved the past can be changed. Not without a cost, but we can deal with that when it happens.

Gently he shakes his head. "When does it end? The cycle repeats itself, would go on and on. Look at Al, at how my actions have led him to this." Papa takes a raspy breath. "And in the end, it would only make the Dark stronger."

"But Al—the Council thinks he has become the Dark's host. I don't know how to stop it from taking him."

"Let me die and—"

"No!" I cut him off, horrified.

"If I die, the Dark will lose the strength it has gained through me. Once it's weakened, the Council will be able to stop it."

Tears drip down my cheeks.

Papa takes a deep breath. "I have to ask you to do something for me, Poppy. I'm so sorry to place this on your shoulders. But you're the only one who can reach Al now."

"What is it?" My voice shakes.

"Once I'm gone, you'll have to get Al back to the shop, and then seal off his access to the door. There are directions in the Shopkeeper's Handbook. Close Rhyme and Reason, then take him away from here, somewhere he can breathe again free of the Dark. Do you understand?"

I don't understand anything anymore.

"You can't ask me to do that." I clasp trembling hands together. "Papa, you can't—"

"It's the only way to save him, Poppy."

Another coughing fit seizes him. I reach for his arm,

holding on as he tries to work through it.

"Papa?" James, bleary-eyed and barefoot, stands in the entryway behind me.

"Mr. Fulbright?" Katherine emerges from the fiction section. "Sorry, Poppy, I went to the powder room for one second, and came back to find him gone."

Papa's strength is fully exhausted now. He looks at Katherine like he can't remember who she is.

"Let's get him back to bed," I say.

Propping Papa up between us, we manage to move down the aisle to where they've set his bed up by the fire. Once he's settled, Papa looks at me. He tries to speak but can't manage it. I raise his hand to my lips.

"I'll do what you asked." Saying the words costs me every last bit of strength I have. "For you, Papa."

Peace crosses over his face, and then he can't keep his eyes open any longer, and he falls asleep. His hand relaxes in mine, and the handkerchief he's been holding falls onto the bed. It's coated in black blood. Katherine gasps, and then hastily picks it up and discards it.

James looks up at me, tears in his eyes. "What can I do?"

"Sit with me?" I pat the chair next to mine. "Just for a little bit."

James nods, his face grave, and settles in beside me. We sit in silence, staring at Papa, waiting, waiting, waiting for the worst to pass.

Chapter Twenty-Seven

Ollie shakes me awake, and it takes me a moment to realize it's morning.

I stare at her through blurry eyes. "What time is it?"

Ollie ignores me. "There's been an incident. When I got up this morning, Dante DeGray was gone, so I went home. But when I got there, my parents were in a panic. My grandfather has been hurt. I guess he was watching the door at the Woodland Winds, and at some point in the night, Al showed up there. When Cyrus tried to stop him, Al attacked him."

I sit up so fast my head spins. "Al attacked Cyrus?"

"There's more." She takes a breath. "Theo is missing. They don't know if Al took him, or—or what." She seems frantic.

I glance at Papa, who sleeps with James curled up next to him, and then I'm on my feet.

"We have to find them," I say, just as the bell over the front door rings. Muffled arguing fills the shop.

"I'm telling you, this isn't going to work," someone says. "She isn't going to give you what you want."

Theo.

"Just be quiet. Be quiet!" Al shouts.

At the same time, Ollie and I realize Theo and Al are together, and we're off, running down the aisle toward the front door. I burst out of the fiction stacks, just behind Ollie, and find Al holding Theo in a headlock. Al is ghostly pale. The black veins have spread down his neck, and up the sides of his face. Steam diffuses from his skin, filling the air with a thin cloud of smoke.

"Tell me how to use the door to find Carl, and I'll let him go," Al growls, glancing back and forth between me and Ollie.

"Why are you doing this?" I move closer to him, but the fog seeping out of him burns my skin, and I step back.

"You know how to use the door to get what you want. Tell me how to do it, and I'll let Theo go," he repeats, tightening his hold around Theo's neck. "Tell me now!"

I look at my brother, wild and uncontrollable and far from who he used to be. Is this what Papa's choices have done to him?

The veins beneath his skin pulse and blacken. Al howls in pain and scratches at them, as if whatever is coursing through them burns. Theo seizes the momentary distraction. He digs an elbow into Al's side and tries to pull out of his grasp, but Al reaches for him, raking his nails across Theo's neck. Theo screams and clutches at the wound, and Al jerks him back into the headlock.

"Al, please!" I move toward him. "This isn't you."

Al looks at me, and I can hardly see him beneath the pulsing black veins. His lips twist into a snarl, and for the first time, I only see the Dark.

"I am the Dark now," he says. "I will not be held back or restrained. The *Council* thinks they can control me, but those days are at an end. I have bided my time and waited for the right host."

"Carl wouldn't want you to do this," I say, trying to bring Al back.

He shakes his head, his eyes fluttering. The blue starts to creep into the black, mentioning Carl pushing back the Dark, the way I hoped it would.

Theo moans and reaches for the spot on his neck where Al scratched him. Blood soaks into the top of his shirt.

I hold up my hands, trying to keep everyone calm. "Let Theo go."

"You care about him, don't you? That day in his shop, I saw the look in your eyes. I think you have a little crush." Al laughs.

Heat floods into my face. "The Dark has been lying to you. You don't understand what it's doing."

"It's shown me everything. I've been to the past,

the future. There is power in the Dark, I've felt it. You could too if you were less of a coward."

Anger rushes through me, and I curl my hands into fists, my heart pounding. Following the rules doesn't make me a coward.

"You've seen everything, huh?" I say the words slowly, one at a time, because I know they're going to hurt him, just like I want them to. "Everything except for Carl."

"What did you just say?" Al snarls at me.

"I found Carl when I went through the door. *See you on the other side*, isn't that what he said to you?"

Al screams in rage and pulls Theo backward. Theo tries to fight him, but the Dark seeps into the wound at his neck, weakening him. "Tell me how to do it, or I swear I'll push him out the door and you'll never see him again."

I don't know this Al, what he's capable of, or what he'll do. I look at Theo. He is kind and good. He spends so much time trying to meet expectations that he misses the things he does that exceed expectation. He is not going to lose his life because of me.

"Wait." I put my hands up, trying to calm him. "Just—wait. Think of what you're doing."

Al reaches for the knob.

"Stop!" I beg him. "Please, I'll tell you. I—I—"

"Poppy, don't," Theo says.

"You can't!" Ollie growls. "Look at the damage he's already done."

But this is Theo's life in the balance.

"You need the coin." The words are little more than a whisper on my lips.

"Poppy!" Ollie screams. "What are you doing?"

Al looks back and forth between me and her. "What coin?"

I sidestep to the front counter, where I left the half dollar after Ollie and I used it last night. I hold it up, and it gleams in the light. When he sees it, the pain on Al's face is instant.

"Where did you get that?" He snarls. "That doesn't belong to you!"

"They sent it home with Carl's other effects. Mrs. Miller brought it by for you." I hold it out to Al. "Take it, and then think of him with everything you've got. The door will do the rest. It will take you where you need to go."

Al glances between me and Ollie. "Just like that?"

"She's lying," Ollie says, a last-ditch effort to conceal the truth.

Al snatches the coin from me. His eyes settle on mine for the briefest of seconds, and I see that the blue is already fading, the Dark pushing into him again.

He tucks the coin into his pocket, and then reaches back for the doorknob. He finds it and gives it a yank, Theo still in his grasp.

"Thank you for the directions, it has been a pleasure. Think I'll keep him, just in case you lied."

"No!" I scream and lunge forward, but it's too late. Al pushes out the front of the shop, yanking Theo after him.

As the door slams shut, a tremor rocks Rhyme and Reason and dark vines rip through the walls of the shop. They climb across the wallpaper, intertwining as they grow over the door in a giant, gnarled mass blocking our only way out after Al and Theo.

Chapter Twenty-Eight

The vines twist and squeeze, writhing like snakes over the door.

"What is this?" Ollie cries out, clinging to my arm.

"The shop can't keep the Dark out anymore." My legs shake as we back toward the front counter. "Rhyme?"

The shop doesn't answer.

"Why did you give Al what he wanted?" Ollie growls at me. "You just handed it to him!"

"Because Al is still in there." I shut my eyes. "I thought I could get through to him."

Ollie stares at the vines. "The Dark is going to destroy everything. Not just our world, but the ordinary world too, just like Euphemia Adley said it would. This is only the beginning."

I press a hand to my forehead, thinking about Papa's confession. He tried to save Al, but in using the magic, he turned Al into the perfect host. I don't know how to reverse what's been done.

"What's happening?" Katherine stumbles from the fiction section, her big hat askew on her head, Whitney tight on her heels.

"Was it an earthquake? We felt a tremor—" Whitney stops, his eyes widening in horror as he sees the walls, cracked in dozens of places, thick gnarled vines sprouting from floor to ceiling.

"Poppy?" James is right behind them. "What's going on? Why is the shop doing this?"

"It's not the shop," I say. "It's the Dark side of the magic."

Kosma and Prosper and Bibine emerge from the lilac hedge, with Anna Rose right behind them.

"What can we do?" Whitney asks.

"Let us help," Anna Rose agrees.

But I don't know what they can do. *I* don't even know what to do.

Another tremor shakes the ground beneath our feet as the vines burst from the walls, squeezing Rhyme and Reason tighter. The lights overhead flash bright and then go out, the shop crying out in pain, and my heart hammers in my chest, a scream building inside of me.

The magic is almost gone, I feel the last threads of it dying around us. There is no warmth or light left here. I look up at the ceiling. "Rhyme, what do I do?"

And it's then I see it. The chalkboard begins to flicker through letters of the alphabet, trying to find a quote, or a message. I move toward it as the words finally settle into place, so faint I can barely see them.

Theo Devlin's Recipe for Courage:

1 *cup Self-confidence*   2 *tbsp. Strength in Adversity*

1 *cup Determination*   1 *heaping tbsp. Compassion*

1/2 *cup Urgency*   1 *tsp. Hope*

A dash of Belief

I don't understand what it means. Of course I need courage, but I can't just pull it out of nowhere. I—

"If there's one thing I know, it's that determination can get you anything." Katherine's voice is clear and strong. "Whatever this is, we can beat it."

The gears in my head spin as it starts to come together, warmth rushing through me, pushing out the fear. The regulars—my friends—*they* make up the courage.

I spin, my gaze flicking over each of them. Anna Rose is the self-confidence, Katherine the determination. Kosma and Prosper are strength in adversity, Bibine the heaping spoon of compassion. Whitney is the belief, of course. James the hope, and Ollie—I almost laugh—is the urgency. They all play a part.

Rhyme and Reason knew I would get this far, and that when I did, I would need their light to go the rest of the way.

A firefly flickers to life in front of me, dim and weak. I watch as it bobs in the air, then lands on my shoulder.

"What's happening, Poppy?" James asks as fireflies

rise in the air all around us. They land on each of the regulars' shoulders. The shop giving us the light it has left.

Whitney's words come back to me, that we all have magic inside of ourselves, and I know what I have to do.

Setting my shoulders back, I turn toward the vines and rush at them, my hands reaching for their thick, thorny skin.

"Poppy!" Anna Rose cries out in warning as my fingers curl around them. A hissing sound fills the shop, dark steam rising up around me as the vine shrinks beneath my touch.

I turn to the regulars, hope reigniting inside of me. "I need your help, quickly!"

They spring into action, charging forward and using their hands the way I did, wielding the Light against the hold of the Dark. As they grab the plants, a chorus of hissing fills the air, along with a thick, humid steam that rises and then disappears.

I pull back my hand and bring it down again and again, and the vines shrivel beneath my touch, crumbling to dust at my feet.

Once the door is clear, I press my palm to the emerald surface. "Rhyme, I need your help to get to Al and Theo. I know that the Dark hurts and you must be exhausted. You've been fighting it off for weeks now, and I didn't see it. But I see you now." I take a deep breath. "I know you're frightened. I am too . . . desperately, but if I can just find Theo and Al, I can end this."

The ground trembles beneath us, books flying off the shelves as Rhyme and Reason pulls itself together, shaking off the grip of the Dark.

"We did it!" Katherine shouts.

The regulars cheer behind her, and I reach for the doorknob with trembling hands, desperate to follow my brother and get Theo back.

"Wait." Ollie stops me. "We need something Al or Theo cares about or it won't take us anywhere."

I'd forgotten that part. I shut my eyes, trying to think. "I could go up and look in Al's room . . ." But I'm not sure what I would find.

"Oh!" Ollie flips open her satchel and frantically searches through the letters inside. She pulls out a brown envelope. It's a letter from Theo to me. "He gave this to me the day the Dark burned me. I never had the chance to deliver it."

I stare at her. "That won't work, it's just a piece of paper. It—"

"It's you," she cuts me off.

"Me?"

"Theo cares about *you*, Poppy." She pushes the envelope into my hands. "This letter matters to him."

Her words hit me in the stomach, and warmth spreads through me. "You think it will work?"

"I think we should give it a try. Worst-case scenario, it doesn't take us anywhere." She shrugs.

"He's your friend too, you know," I say.

"Right." She grins, a mischievous glint in her eyes. "Well then, let's close our eyes and think about Theo."

I glance at James and the regulars. "Thank you," I tell them, tears in my throat. "Please, stay with Papa?"

They nod, one by one. James takes my hand. "Go find Al," he says.

I turn and reach for the knob, my hands sweaty and cold. I think of Theo with everything I have, of his letters, his shop, and his smile. My palm connects with the cool metal, and gently, ever so gently, I open it.

Chapter Twenty-Nine

⫷⫸

October 5, 1944
The Siegfried Line, Germany

A cobblestone street waits on the other side of the door. The buildings across the way press in tight together, most of them three stories tall with slanted roofs and large windows. A cold drizzling rain soaks into my skin. The air smells strange, sulfuric and sharp.

"Where are we?" Ollie whispers.

"I'm not—"

The sound of gunfire erupts somewhere in the distance. A series of quick pops all in a row. Ollie stands frozen beside me, but as return fire reverberates off the buildings around us, I drop to the ground, covering the back of my head as if my hands can protect me. Where are we?

Pop! Pop! Pop!

"We have to get out of the street!" Ollie shouts.

I look over my shoulder, and see that Rhyme and Reason is already disappearing behind us. There's no going back. I push myself to my feet, grab hold of Ollie, and we run for all we're worth to the nearest building.

Some sort of restaurant, with a broken window. I tug her through the door, and we both press against the wall, crouching down as a loud rumbling shakes the ground.

"This isn't right," Ollie hisses. "We have to go home, now!"

On the floor beneath my shoe, I recognize a newspaper. I pull it out and look at the front page. My blood runs cold. It's all in German.

Ollie glances at it. "There's the date."

5 Oktober 1944.

"The war," I whisper. We're someplace on the Siegfried Line in October. The same month Carl was listed as missing in action.

I look around the restaurant. Tables are strewn every which way, and menus lie among shattered plates and scattered silverware.

"We have to get back to Rhyme and Reason!" Ollie turns to leave, and I grab hold of her wrist.

"We can't go without Al and Theo," I say.

"We're in a war zone, Poppy! I'm not willing to risk our lives for your brother."

The sound of glass crunches behind us, and I flip around. Two American soldiers stand in a dark hallway, their guns pointed over our heads toward the street.

"We're Americans!" Ollie cries out.

They lower their weapons in confusion. "You've got

to get out of here! It isn't safe!" one of them shouts to be heard over the sounds of the battle. More gunfire erupts, closer than before. Ollie crouches back down to the floor, but I stand my ground.

"Have you seen two boys around here? I'm looking for my brother. He has brown hair and glasses, he's about this tall?" I motion with my hands.

The soldier blinks at me in confusion. "No. Now get out of here!" He motions to the hallway behind him.

Ollie doesn't wait; she springs up, grabs hold of my arm, and starts to pull me down the hall.

"Wait, Ollie, just—"

She doesn't listen, and I give in to her. We hurry through the back of the restaurant and out a door that leads to a closed-off courtyard.

"There's an alley over there." Ollie points to the building across from us.

"We have to find Al," I say.

"We have to stay alive!" she fires back.

Something explodes in the distance. She screams and covers her head with her hands. "I'm not about to die in this war! Now come on!"

She hurries to the alley and I follow behind her. It's narrow and so tight I have to squeeze my shoulders to fit. It smells like gunpowder and something rotten. At the end of it there's an open building, and Ollie starts toward it just as an explosion shakes the ground, knocking me to my knees. I look over my shoulder, and the building we've just left has been hit.

Ollie crawls through a doorway ahead of us, her eyes streaming from smoke or fear or both. I stay low to the ground and follow her inside what looks like a hat shop. We both crouch in a narrow hallway, and I stare down at my shaking hands. There's glass in them, from crawling over the debris outside, but I can't feel it, as if I'm not quite connected to my body.

"Go back to Rhyme—" I start, but Ollie's eyes go wide and she throws a hand over my mouth to silence me. Someone else is in the building.

"The Lighthouse brought us to this place for a reason. He's here somewhere, but we need to form a plan; it's not going to be easy to find him in a war zone." I'd recognize that voice anywhere. Dante DeGray.

Ollie drops her hand from my mouth and motions that we should leave. As I turn to follow her out the back door, someone else speaks.

"They're worried Cyrus isn't going to survive. That boy has practically killed a Council member. We can't bring him back alive, not if the Dark is still in him." Hanna Erasmus moves into view, stopping at the mouth of the hallway. Her eyes widen when she sees us. "Poppy Fulbright? Courier Bell?"

She stares at us, stunned, and I spin toward the back door, diving out after Ollie.

"Run!" Ollie shouts, as a string of gunfire explodes somewhere nearby. I clasp my hands over ringing ears, and we rush down an alley to our right. Buildings press in on either side of us, and we follow the path as it grows narrower and narrower with every turn until suddenly we hit a dead end.

"No." Ollie spins, searching for a way out, but there aren't any.

"Maybe we lost them," I say, but I hear their heavy footsteps in the distance.

Ollie surveys the wall blocking our escape. "I might be able to climb."

I look up at it, knowing I won't ever be able to make it. "I'll give you a boost."

"But you—"

I push down the fear rising inside me. "Run, Ollie, while you can. Get yourself home."

She pulls back. "Poppy, I—"

The Council is nearly to us now, their footsteps thundering, and I cup my hands.

Ollie hesitates for one moment, and then she steps into my interlocked fingers and I push her up. She manages to grab hold of the ledge and haul herself over. She peers at the other side.

"I can make it down."

I give her a nod.

"Poppy—" she starts.

"You can't run forever, young Fulbright!" Hanna Erasmus's voice rings out.

"Go!" I hiss, and then Ollie, with tears in her eyes, swings herself over and disappears.

Dante and Hanna appear in the alley. They both wear dark cloaks, a Lighthouse pin on the lapel. I tilt my chin back as Dante approaches.

"We have the right to detain you on behalf of the Council of Shopkeepers," Dante says, and I swear there's a gleam of joy in his eyes. He takes me by the arm and pushes me in front of him.

"We'll escort you to the Lighthouse immediately, where you will be held until this mess can be sorted out."

He forces me to walk ahead of him as we wind back through the narrow alley, and I feel any hope of saving Al slipping through my fingers.

If Rhyme were here, I would look at the chalkboard for help. This time I'll have to use my own words.

"The Dark is more than you can handle. Back at Rhyme and Reason you didn't have a chance against it," I say to Dante.

He pretends not to hear me.

"The harder you hunt Al, the farther he's going to run. You won't be able to stop him." I push away the fear and give it everything I've got.

"Stop talking." Dante's voice is hard and cold as we reach the street; he taps the pin on his lapel twice, and the front of the Lighthouse appears before us.

"I'm the only person he'll listen to right now, the only hope any of us have at getting through to him."

Hanna Erasmus trails behind us, and Dante shoves me in her direction. "Get her to Euphemia and let the Council know what she's been up to. I'll handle the boy and Courier Bell."

"The Dark will destroy you if you go alone!" I call out. "It'll destroy everything! Give me a chance to stop it. *Please.*"

Dante pauses, his shoulders tense.

"I can do this." My voice is softer now. "Just give me a chance."

Dante turns and starts to say something, but an explosion erupts at the end of the street. The ground quakes beneath us, and none of us manage to stay on our feet. Hanna loses her hold on me, and I scramble away from her, dragging myself over piles of loose brick.

I make a run for it, skirting around a street corner. Dante hollers behind me, and I spin, not sure where to go, when an arm reaches out and yanks me through a bombed-out storefront.

"Ollie!" I stare at her, my eyes wide as we crouch down, ducking for cover beneath the ledge of a broken front window.

"Did you really think I was going to leave you here?"

The ground rumbles beneath us again, and we lean into each other.

"I'll lead them off!" Ollie has to shout, and even then, I barely make out her words.

I pull back from her and shake my head. "No!"

"It'll buy you time. I'll run around the block and see if I can get them to follow. They won't be able to catch me. Once I've lost them, I'll get out of here." There is set determination on her face. "Take my coat, it'll confuse them."

"Ollie," I say.

"Give me your sweater!"

Hands shaking, I undo the buttons and slip my arms out of it. I hand it to her, and she helps me into her emerald-green coat. It's so tight in the shoulders I can hardly move. She shoves her arms into my cardigan and pulls the hood up over her hair. As a last touch she wraps the ends of her yellow scarf around my neck.

"Find Al and end this," she says, reaching for my hand. I hold tight to her for one moment.

"If I don't come back, tell my parents what happened. Tell them . . ." I swallow, unable to finish the sentence.

"You're coming back." She gives me a fierce nod.

"Picture the door when you're ready to leave. Picture your shop and all the things you've left behind, and it will reappear."

"Which way did they go?" I hear Hanna's voice in the distance.

"They can't have gotten far!" Dante shouts.

"Come back in one piece, Poppy." Ollie gives me a smile that doesn't disguise the terror in her eyes, and then she stands up and leaps from the building into the street. She takes off at a run, and when she's almost to the corner, she picks up a brick and throws it. I watch as it flies through the air and makes contact with an abandoned cart lying sideways in the road.

Dante and Hanna turn at the sound of stone crunching wood.

"Hey, geezers!" Ollie calls out to them. She turns before they can see that she's disguised herself as me. Hanna lets out a shout and pivots in her direction, Dante tight on her heels. I watch as Ollie and then the Council members disappear from view, leaving me alone.

Chapter Thirty

I get to my feet and creep toward the front door, peering out at the empty street. The fighting has shifted directions, the pops and bangs sounding farther in the distance. But I can hardly breathe as I slip out onto the sidewalk, keeping my eyes peeled for trouble. Debris covers the streets, glass and broken brick and wares from shattered stores scattered every which way.

Someone screams nearby and I shrink into the shadows, staying low as two soldiers move around the corner, carrying a limp comrade between them. They come to a stop a few feet in front of me and gently lay the third soldier on the ground.

"Roberts!" one of them shouts. "C'mon, Roberts, open your eyes."

"He's gone," the other soldier says. "Bullet went through his neck, there's nothing we can do for him."

They haven't looked up, haven't noticed me, crouching in the shadows so close.

"No—no—there has to be something we can do!"

The second soldier grabs hold of the first. "We have to go, Torres!"

"He was seventeen. Shouldn't'a been out here in the first place," the first soldier says.

The soldiers sit in silence for half a second.

"Torres, we gotta get out of here and find our way our back to the others!" the second soldier tries again.

I shift forward to peer at the men. They're covered in grime and smoke, and all I can make out are the whites of their eyes. As I move, debris on the sidewalk slides sideways beneath me, and the second soldier whirls around, rifle aimed at my head.

"Who's there? Stand up! Show yourself!"

The first soldier springs to his feet beside him, his weapon up in an instant.

And I realize that in the shadows, crouched low, I could be the enemy. I hold my hands where they can see them and move into the light.

The second soldier keeps his gun aimed at me. "What's your name? Wie heißen sie?"

His face is disguised beneath a mask of mud and grit, but when his green eyes meet mine, he is unmistakable.

"Poppy Fulbright?" He stares at me in horror and shock.

"Carl?" It's him, I found him. My heart leaps into my throat, tears flooding my vision. He's here, and he's alive, and I never thought I'd see him again.

He lowers the gun, rubbing a hand over his eyes as

if he's trying to convince himself this is real. He looks older than the last time I saw him, the boyish laughter gone from his face. He wears a helmet and a filthy uniform, a rifle tucked underneath one arm.

"I'm dreaming, I must be dreaming." He looks back at the other soldier. "You see a girl with blonde hair and brown eyes here, Torres?"

Torres glances from Carl to me. "I see her, Miller. What's going on?"

Carl moves instantly, pushing the gun Torres has aimed at me away. "I know her." He turns. "How are you here?" And then something like understanding crosses his face. "The shop."

It's my turn to be shocked. "You know about Rhyme and Reason?"

More gunfire sounds somewhere close by, and Carl moves. He grabs me by the arm and pulls me into the nearest bombed-out building.

"What are you doing?" Torres calls. "Leave her. We've got to get back to our squad."

"Watch the street, Torres," Carl growls. We take shelter in what looks to be an abandoned apartment. "I don't know why you're here, but you gotta go home, now!"

"You know about Rhyme and Reason?" I repeat.

He lets out a breath of air. "I grew up at your place,

of course I know. Al told me when we were seven. I didn't believe him at first, but . . ." He stops, shakes his head. "But then I saw it for myself."

"Al is here," I say.

Carl jerks back at those words. "Al is here? What? Why? Is something wrong? Is my family all right?"

"Your family is safe. The problem is Al." I look up at Carl and I can't do it. I can't tell him that a few weeks from now he's going to be killed. "He's lost his mind since you left. He's not the same Al you knew. He's changed. He thinks he has to find you, convince you to desert, to hide out in Rhyme and Reason until the war ends."

Carl presses a fist to his forehead as if he's trying to think. "I'll look for him. We'll figure it out, but you—you gotta get out of here. This is no place for a girl."

I bristle at his words.

Carl grabs hold of my shoulders. "Do you hear me? Go home."

I look at him, at his bright green eyes, and I want to tell him so many things. But there isn't time.

"The shop—the magic has done something to Al. He's taken my friend hostage. I can't just leave him here."

Carl tilts his head closer to mine. "This isn't a game. This is war. The things I've seen out here . . . you aren't safe."

I give him a firm gaze, trying to look braver than I feel.

"Tulip." A hint of a smile crosses his face and then fades. "Please."

"I—"

Another explosion rings out, and Carl throws me against the stairwell wall, tucking me underneath his arms. Dust from the ceiling falls around us, coating my hair and my shoulders.

"Miller!" Torres calls from the street. "Are you okay in there?"

Carl checks that I'm unhurt, then pulls back. "We're alive!"

I cough and brush the dust from Ollie's green coat. The ceiling creaks overhead as if it doesn't have the strength to keep standing.

"We've gotta move." Carl steps out of the building, into the street, his rifle raised. When he's satisfied that it's all clear, he motions for me to follow.

"I think we oughta head down—" Carl stops, his eyes set on the horizon.

"Jeez, oh man, what is that!" Torres backs up a step, and I turn my head to follow his gaze. A billowing black cloud fills the sky in the distance. It rises up thicker than smoke, wild, unlike anything I've seen before.

The Dark.

"Al," I say.

Carl's eyes widen. "What?"

"If we want to find Al, then that's where we have to go."

Carl shakes his head. "It could be a last-ditch effort to prevent us from taking the town. We don't know that the Germans—"

"I *do* know," I shout at him. "It's Al."

The Dark has been growing inside of my brother. Perhaps it formed the day he went through the front door for the first time, or the day Carl died, or the moment Papa traveled back in time to change Al's fate, history forever altered. Whatever the reason, he has taken it with him, everywhere he goes, and left a trail of destruction in its wake.

I step forward, my hands in fists at my sides, with all the courage I can muster.

"I'm going to find Al," I tell Carl. "Are you coming or not?"

Chapter Thirty-One

"You can't just charge out there!" Carl calls after me. "That's the center of town. The Germans have barricaded themselves inside a hotel that we've been trying to take for days. You get tangled in that mess and you'll get yourself killed."

I whirl on him. "Then what do we do, Carl?"

"The buildings in this place, they're all interconnected. We move through them toward that cloud."

Torres glances at Carl. "We can't cover ourselves that way. Too many windows and doors."

Carl nods, his face grim. "We do the best we can. It's our only option."

Torres's eyes shift to me. "How do you two know each other, again?"

"We grew up together," I say.

"There." Carl motions to an alley, and we start toward it, me behind Carl, Torres behind me.

Carl winds a path through the alley that weaves in and out of abandoned structures, hollow shells of the places they once were, testaments to the people who had to leave everything behind to find safety. We emerge from a bakery, and Carl stops me. The massive cloud is almost directly overhead. We must be close to Al.

"The hotel is just around the corner." Carl points in the direction, just as gunfire ignites close by.

"We can't just walk out there," Torres says. "They've got soldiers in every window."

Carl swallows and leans back against the brick bakery. "Let me think."

A gust of wind whips around us, and the Dark hovers closer overhead. It's thick and wild, a swirling vortex emitting a freezing cold.

Loud screams pierce the air, followed by an intense increase of firepower. Torres clasps a hand to his helmet and drops to the ground, body shaking.

"Get down!" Carl shouts at me, dropping beside Torres. I do as he says, falling next to him, as the wind rushes over us. The shooting begins to die out, and then goes silent altogether. I peer around the corner.

"What is she doing?" Torres hisses.

The hotel Carl described is across the street. Broken and bombed and barely standing. There are soldiers in the windows just like Torres said. I can see the tops of their round helmets.

But the Dark churning in the sky has them cowering in terror. Many of them abandon their posts, running for cover as it descends ever lower. Allied soldiers fighting in the street have already retreated as the Dark moves forward, filling all of the empty space.

And then I spot my brother. He stumbles along, dragging a limp Theo by the arm. Theo's face is a mix of dust and grime, black blood oozing from the wound at his neck.

"You weren't kidding." Carl leans over me. "Golly, it's really him."

The swirling black vortex pours out of Al. Streams of it seep from his body, thick and dark, filling the street more and more as he moves farther forward.

Before I know what I'm doing, I step out.

"Stop her!" Torres growls at Carl. Carl's fingertips graze my arm, but I'm faster than he is, and I move out of his reach.

"You can stay behind," I say. "But I have to do this."

Carl follows me, his rifle up and at the ready. He scans the street as I push forward. The block is silent now, as soldiers on both sides have taken cover. Theo squirms, landing a punch into Al's ribs. Al laughs at him, tightening his hold and saying something I can't hear.

"Allan!" I shout his name.

Al stops, his head low. Theo tries to pull free again, but can't manage it.

"Allan Fulbright!" Carl's voice, clear and strong, rings through the square.

Al freezes.

"C'mon, Al," Carl shouts again.

"C-Carl?" Al flips around. "Carl? Is that you?"

"It's me."

Al takes a step toward us, his eyes wide, mouth open as if he can't believe after all this time, he has made it here. He stops just feet from us, Theo clenched in a headlock under his arm, the wound on his neck spreading across his jaw.

"What are you doing here, Poppy?" Al asks, surprise at finding Carl giving way to suspicion.

"I brought Carl to you," I tell Al. "Now let Theo go."

Theo glances up at me, and I see scrapes and cuts along his face, as if Al has dragged him kicking and screaming through town.

"Do what she says. Let him go," Carl tries.

Al ignores this. "I've been looking for you. There are so many soldiers here. You all dress alike."

It's supposed to be a joke, but no one laughs.

Carl takes in Al's dark eyes and the black veins pulsing beneath his skin. "What are you doing, Al?"

Confusion crosses Al's face as if he can't remember, and then all at once it comes back to him. "I had to find you before it's too late." He drops his hold on Theo, and Theo falls to his knees, gasping for air.

Al takes a step closer to us, and the Dark seeping out of him dissipates in the air as if seeing Carl alive is enough to hold the monster at bay.

"Before it's too late?" Carl says.

"You die, Carl." Al reaches for Carl, but Carl steps backward out of his grasp. "The war—it's going to get you. That's how this ends."

The words don't seem to sink in to Carl, not at first. "Wh—when?" He takes a heavy breath.

"Soon."

Carl shuts his eyes as if he has been struck.

Al reaches into his pocket and pulls out a crumpled piece of paper. Hands shaking, he holds it out to Carl as he quotes the *Tribune* article from memory. " 'Carl is remembered as a kind boy, quick to lend a helping hand to others. He was much beloved by his high school teachers and classmates.' "

"Stop." Carl presses a hand to his mouth.

" 'Cut down in the prime of his life. He—' "

"I said shut up!" Carl shouts.

"It doesn't have to happen this way, don't you see? I can save you. *We* can save you." Al motions to me as if we are on the same side. "The shop will protect you; it can keep you hidden. Stay until the war is over if you have to—just—just come with me, Carl."

"No."

The word is so quick, so quiet, I'm not sure I heard Carl say it at all.

Al freezes, his eyes drawn wide in horror. "What?"

"I said no." Carl's stare is icy. "You have no right to come here—to ask me to desert and give up on everything we've been doing. I've worked too hard to leave now."

Al looks from Carl to me. "Did you not hear what I said? You're going to die if you stay in this war."

"Then I die." His face is laced with pain as he says it, but he doesn't back down. "That's what I signed up for. That's what I'm fighting for—what all of us here are fighting for. Wouldn't you do the same thing if it were reversed?"

Al opens his mouth, but words don't come to him, not right away.

"Wouldn't you?" Carl growls.

Al looks away, out over the rubble of the bombed-out city.

Carl stares down at the rifle in his hands. "I will not be a deserter. You can't ask that of me."

Al takes a shallow breath. "Fine, all right, I'll—" He's scrambling now; obviously this is not how he thought things would unfold. "I can tell you when and where it's going to happen. You can avoid it altogether or stop it from happening. Whatever you want."

Carl's jaw tenses. "You told me once you could never use the magic for yourself. That it was for the shop and the good of the people who came into it. What have you done, Al?" Carl's stance is rigid as he stares at my brother. "This isn't you."

"I—I came to save you," Al snarls between gritted teeth. "I was willing to do anything to save *you*." The Dark starts to pour out of him again.

"I volunteered to be a soldier. I knew the risks," Carl shouts to be heard over the sound of it.

Al shakes his head. "No! It wasn't supposed to be like this. You weren't supposed to die!"

Carl's eyes sweep over Al and what he has become. "Life doesn't always work out the way we want it to."

Al stumbles backward as if he has been struck. "I jeopardized everything for this. To get here, I—"

"I didn't ask you to do that." Carl cuts him off.

"You were—you were my brother." Al stares at him, empty and broken. And for one second, I forget everything he has done. I know his pain. Carl was my family too.

"We'll always be brothers, you and me," Carl says, just as the sound of gunfire reignites somewhere ahead of us. I search the horizon and find a lone German soldier has returned to a window on the second floor.

I duck low as Carl raises his rifle and fires in the soldier's direction. "I have to go now, Al. We have a war to win!"

"No! No, wait!" Al lunges for Carl, grabbing hold of his shoulder.

Carl looks at him, a sad smile on his lips. "See you on the other side." He pulls away from Al and his eyes shift to me. "Get your brother home, Poppy."

And then he's gone, charging toward the barricade, Torres tight on his heels.

Chapter Thirty-Two

Al falls to his knees, his body shaking with sobs, and then the Dark explodes out of him, a tornado, black as night, curling into the air above us.

More shots ring out, and I see Carl for one fleeting moment before he throws himself behind an abandoned truck and disappears from view.

"P-Poppy." Theo tries to get up but can't manage it. The wound at his neck has spread into his face. "Get out of here." He points toward the sky, at the monstrous cloud that swells over us, blocking out the sun, all of it pouring from Al.

"Allan!" I call for my brother.

"He didn't come with me. Why didn't he come with me?" Al weeps.

I swipe a hand across my face, mixing grit and sweat and tears. "Because Carl gets to choose. He gets to decide how his story ends."

The wind picks up around us, whipping my hair into my face.

"It should've been me who died here, not Carl." He takes a stuttering, gasping breath. "Nothing is right, Poppy."

Maybe all this time, some part of him knew the truth. *I was willing to do anything to save Al,* Papa's words come back to me. Al has said over and over that something was wrong. Al thought the feeling was because of Carl's death—and it is—but it's also because of Papa's choices. If I tell him what Papa did, maybe it will settle the storm inside of him; maybe it will bring him back from the Dark. The truth can set him free, can't it?

"We need you, Al. All of us, Mama and Papa and James."

"Need me?" He looks up. "No one needs me."

Tears drip down my chin, soaking into the neck of Ollie's coat. "That's not true."

Theo shouts my name as Al moves closer to me, the Dark around him almost engulfing me too. I back up, my heart pounding, blood rushing in my ears.

"It is true!" Al growls, and winces. "I'm just the disappointment. Everyone would be better off if I disappeared."

"Papa loves you so much, he risked everything for you!" I call out.

Al blinks, his eyes flickering between blue and black. "What are you talking about?"

"You died." The truth comes pouring out of me because Al deserves to know. And if I tell him now, he'll see that it's not his fault. Papa made so many mistakes because he loved Al so much. "You died, and Papa couldn't bear to lose you, so he broke the rules."

"What are you—what are you talking about, Poppy?"

"There was a different ending to this story." I have to shout to be heard above the sound of the storm overhead, and I fight against the building wind to stay on my feet. "You went to war with Carl and *you* died, not him. So, Papa went back, and he made the childhood asthma up. He made sure they would never let you be a soldier."

Al presses a hand to his forehead. "You're—you're lying."

"I'm not! He changed things so that we wouldn't have to lose you, but we lost Carl instead." And I see the way bad choices show us who we are more than the right ones can. Papa's choices, Al's choices, my choices.

Al looks off into the distance, realization dawning. "It was—it was supposed to be me?" He takes a gasping breath, and the agony he has been carrying seems to fade away, peace settling over him. "This is why it's not right, this is why everything feels wrong. Because it *is* wrong."

I'm nodding as I reach out my hand. "Come with me, Al. The shop will keep the Dark out, it can protect us." I say words that I know can't be true because the shop has nothing left to protect us with.

Al staggers sideways and barely manages to keep himself on his feet. "The Dark is inside of me now." He jams a fist into his temple. "I—I keep forgetting things. I can't remember Papa's face anymore."

"I can help you." I stretch my arm farther, just wanting to hold on to him, to make him see that he matters, that we love him.

"Help me?" He gasps as his eyes focus back on mine. "Why would you want to help me?"

"No matter what you've done, you're still my brother." I can hardly speak over the lump in my throat.

His eyelids flutter as he blinks over and over, trying to clear the Dark from his mind.

"I need you, Al!" I shout. "I need you to come back and be my big brother. We'll—we'll figure this out. There has to be a way we can make amends for what's happened. Take a walk through the door with me."

Something I've said must sway him because he reaches for my hand. I look into his face, hope rushing through me, but when our eyes connect, I see that his have gone completely black. There's a pause, a deep breath, and then the Dark erupts out of him stronger than before, raging around us.

He latches on to my hand, and the minute our skin touches, the Dark surges up my arm and bursts through my body. It flows out of Al and into me, a whirlwind of fear and pain that burns in my blood. Like a torrential downpour, it fills me with every bad feeling I've ever felt. *You're so scared of everything*, Al said. And I feel it, the fear and the terror of the outside world closing in. I see myself cowering inside the shop, too scared to ever leave. I hear Papa, *One day, when Al takes over for me, I want you to have something more.* And Mama, *There's more to life than the shop.* I see my classmates laugh when I read my poem in front of them, and I hate myself because Al's right, I am afraid, and it is going to hold me back forever. I try to wrench my hand out of Al's grasp, but his fingers dig into my wrist and I can't feel anything but the pain, and disappointment, and fear.

But then I hear a voice.

Everybody has magic inside of them, you know.

I open my eyes and look through the cloud of black toward my brother.

You're one of a kind, firefly.

You knew the Light when you saw it.

The Dark wants him to remember all of the pain, all of the bad things that have ever happened to him.

But I am the girl who chases the Light.

Memories rise inside of me, all of the moments with the Light living in us. Nights spent in front of the fire reading books about pirates and eating popcorn fresh off the stove. Long summer days of hide-and-seek with Rhyme and Reason. Staying up late and reading fairy tales beneath the covers until the sun came up.

He has to remember who he is. The Dark has pushed all of the good out of him, all of the love, all of the moments that make him Al. And I won't let it win. I won't let him forget.

I grit my teeth as the Dark tries to find its way back into my head, and I feel the Light swell in my chest. I grab hold of it and shove it against the Dark.

Heat surges down my arm, and the magic courses through me, flowing into our clasped hands. Al lets out a scream as the Light finds its way inside of him, and then it seems to explode around us, pushing back the wind and cold and the swirling vortex overhead. The Light grows until we are encased inside a golden sphere of it. The chaos of battle falling away, as a warm calm settles between me and Al, like waves evening out after a storm.

Al staggers forward, and then falls to his knees.

"Poppy?" His body sags with exhaustion. He looks up at me, and there is endless blue in his eyes, the Dark gone from him. Gently, he tilts his face upward. "I—I can feel the sun again." A faint smile forms on his grit-covered lips. "I'd forgotten what it was like."

The Light surges through me, pulsing with strength as the Dark slams against the sphere from the outside, trying to find a way back to its host.

"Let's go home," I tell Al. "While we still can."

"Home." Peace washes over his face.

"We can have an inventory race. Winner gets to do the front display for a month."

Al smiles, and then sways, barely able to keep himself upright. "I'm sorry—for everything I've put you through."

"It wasn't your fault, Al."

Al looks over his shoulder at the battle, at the hotel where the Germans have barricaded themselves. The Dark presses in around it, soldiers screaming as it rains down around them.

My body begins to shake. The Light is too powerful for me. I can't hold it up much longer.

"We have to go!" I shout at Al, as the Dark lashes against the sphere again. Al doesn't even flinch as it tries to fight its way back to him.

"The Dark has been in my head for weeks. Telling me I could have all the power I wanted." Al laughs bitterly. "I think I've heard it my whole life. Like it's always been watching me and waiting." He turns toward me. "But it's gone. You did that for me, Poppy." He takes a breath. "Now I know what I have to do."

"What?" My heart leaps at his words. "What are you talking about?"

"The Dark is still too strong. It's taken everything from me. I—" He barely manages to stay on his knees.

"The Dark hasn't left much of me in here . . . and it's not going to give up fighting. It'll come for the shop, for our family." He pushes himself to his feet as the gold sphere flickers around us, my strength fading fast. "Let's end this together, firefly. You and me."

"But—"

"You've done your part. You saved me. Now let me save you." Al curls his hands into fists. "The Dark and I are still tied together. It'll find me no matter where I go." His eyes are bright and strong as they look at me. "It's seen my weakness, but I've seen its too. If the host dies, then it can't survive."

"No!" I scream as my body gives out and the Light disappears from around us. The Dark rains down, and I cry out as it burns my skin. This isn't how it was supposed to happen. Al is supposed to come home with me.

"You want a host? Then come get me!" Al shouts, holding out his hand to the Dark. It surges into him again, and I stumble back in horror.

Theo shouts for me again as the Dark takes hold of my brother.

"Save him!" Al tells me. "While you still can!"

I crawl toward Theo. He lies writhing on the ground, his face covered in black veins. I brush his skin and the touch sears my fingertips.

"Theo, stay with me," I say.

He takes a raspy breath, his eyes cloudy and dark. "Poppy? I can't see anything."

"We're going to get you home, just—just hold on." I lean into him and try to pull him to his feet, but I can't manage it.

I glance back for Al. He stands facing the hotel, the black vortex rising out of him faster, and faster.

Al's eyes meet mine. "Get out of here!"

No! I won't leave him, I can't. I can still get them both home! I just—I need the door.

We're close to the sidewalk, lined by a row of bombed-out and abandoned shop fronts.

I shut my eyes. *Rhyme and Reason, I need you. Please, help us.*

When I open them, I want to cry in relief. The most beautiful thing I've ever seen appears: our shop front, the green door so bright amidst the gray.

"You have to help me," I beg Theo.

He takes a breath and tries to get to his feet, but he doesn't have the strength.

"Go without me," Theo mumbles, his head lolling to one side.

"No! Theo, I—"

"Poppy!" Ollie is here, emerging through a cloud of smoke, eyes wide. "I tried to lose the Council, but I couldn't. Hanna and Dante are coming!"

Together, we manage to get Theo to his feet. Most

of his weight drags against us as we struggle to move forward. I look back but can't find my brother in the chaos.

"Al!" My throat is hoarse from screaming, and every muscle in my body is on fire.

The wind gusts again, moving some of the black cloud, and I see Al standing a few feet from us. When he looks at me, he's changed. His eyes are completely black, the dark veins thick and pulsating beneath his skin.

My knees nearly give out at the sight of him, and I stumble sideways. Ollie pulls on Theo and manages to keep us all upright.

"They're here!" Ollie shouts. I follow her line of sight to the street corner. The Council have located us. Hanna and Dante stand, frozen in shock at the sight of what's happening to Al.

"Al!" I reach for him again, my vision blurring with tears.

But there is determination in his face. "I can end this."

"I love you!" I call out, the realization slamming into me that Al is going to sacrifice himself for everyone else.

I look back at the shop, but the front is flickering, beginning to fade from view. It doesn't have the strength to stay here much longer.

Al takes a step toward the hotel. "Tell them I'm sorry,

for everything. And tell Papa I forgive him."

"No, no, no," I sob. "Al, please."

"We're—out—time." He staggers to the left, trying to fight the rising Dark. Al looks at the town square, at the soldiers fighting their way toward the hotel. "I love you, firefly."

His eyes hold mine, for one last moment, and then with a growl he runs for all he is worth toward the battle.

"Poppy, the shop!" Ollie sounds far away.

I look back and see that Rhyme and Reason is hardly visible at all anymore. Half sobbing, half screaming, I move toward the door. Every step burns inside of me as we make our way forward.

We reach the step, Theo fading fast between us. I glance over my shoulder at the battle.

American soldiers charge forward, German soldiers shooting from the windows again. The Dark moves faster, closing over Al as he hurls himself toward the barricade. The Dark envelopes the entire hotel just as something metal flies into the fray.

"Grenade!" a scream calls out.

I watch in horror as it sails into the cloud. There's a pause, and then an explosion rips through the air around us, magnified tenfold by the Dark.

"No! Al!" I shout for him as the force of the bomb shakes Rhyme and Reason to its core.

Ollie shoves the door open just as my strength gives out. On my knees I drag Theo over the threshold.

"Get the door!" Ollie screams, and I do the only thing I can do. I lunge forward and pull it shut, leaving my brother—my troubled, stubborn, courageous brother—behind.

Chapter Thirty-Three

I press my face to my hands, sobbing for Al and for Carl, for all of it.

Ollie touches my shoulder. I glance up. There are tears on her cheeks as she kneels down beside me.

"I'm sorry," she whispers. "I'm so sorry."

Theo lies on the floor, taking heaving, gasping breaths. I crawl to him.

"Theo?" I touch his face and feel the heat of his fever as it begins to cool. He opens his eyes, and there is endless brown, the Dark already retreating.

"I can see you," he says. "Out of my good eye, that is."

Half of a laugh and a sob burst from my chest, and I bury my face in his shoulder.

After a second, one of Theo's arms wraps around me, and he hugs me back.

"He—he sacrificed himself," I whisper. "Why would he do that?"

"Because he loves you," Theo answers.

I pull away and look Theo over. The dark veins retreat from his face and down his jaw, fading faster and faster.

The deep black wound at his neck is already beginning to heal.

"It's leaving him," Ollie says, and when I glance up at her, I scc that her wounds are healing too.

"The Dark couldn't keep its strength without a host." I repeat what Al told me as I stare at Theo, my heart broken in so many pieces.

"Poppy!" James calls my name. "Where are you?"

And I realize the hard part isn't over yet. I'm going to have to tell Mama and Papa and James everything that has happened.

"Poppy!" James calls again, bursting through the fiction section. "Come quick!"

I feel weak and empty as my eyes meet his.

James bounces on his heels. "It's Papa. Hurry!"

"Papa?" I'm on my feet as fast as I am able. "What's happened?" Fresh terror rushes over me. He can't be gone too.

"C'mon!" He turns and runs back the way he came. And I hurry to catch up, my head pounding and a sour taste in mouth. The flowers and the vines along the bookshelves bloom as I pass, sunlight pouring through the front windows, illuminating the shelves in a soft glow.

James and I burst through the stacks. The regulars crowd around Papa's hospital bed. There's Katherine and Whitney, Bibine and the twins, and Anna Rose.

Bibine moves out of the way, and I see Mama and Aunt Lina huddled together, crying. My hands shake as I reach up to wipe tears from my cheeks.

Mama turns and reaches for me, a sob slipping from her lips as she pulls me in for a hug, and then she steps aside.

"Poppy?"

Papa sits up in bed. His eyes are bright and clear, and color fills his cheeks. He isn't coughing.

"It's a good surprise, right?" James laughs.

"I don't understand. What's happening?" I try to take it in.

"The cough is gone," Papa says, wonder on his face. "I can breathe again. I can—I—" He stops, and I think perhaps he's wrong and the cough isn't gone, but then I see that he's crying.

"He's feeling better," Mama says, wiping at her eyes.

"Much better," Papa agrees, and Mama laughs— really laughs, for the first time in months.

"That's wonderful . . ." I trail off.

The magic is fragile, Poppy. So very fragile. Al's sacrifice. It was enough to destroy the Dark. The truth sweeps over me, leaving me breathless. If Papa is better—it means Al really is gone.

"We need to find Al," Mama says. "Have any of you seen him?"

I shut my eyes, trying to gather the strength to tell

her. When I open them again, Papa is watching me from across the room. He knows that something is wrong. Silence stretches out around us.

"What is it?" Papa asks.

Mama turns and really looks at me. "Poppy, why are you covered in filth?" She touches my cheek, and her fingers come away with soot and grime.

Everything feels hazy around me.

"I have to tell you a story," I whisper.

Mama looks at Papa, her eyes wide with fear. She clutches the collar of her dress.

Pain rises inside of me as I search for the words. Tears trail down Papa's cheeks, and he must suspect what's coming. I sit at the end of his bed, and from the deep, broken place inside of me, I find the strength to begin.

Chapter Thirty-Four

"If you need anything, don't hesitate to ask." Katherine holds on to me. "We're with you, Poppy."

I give her a grateful smile. The others have all gone home now; Katherine is the last to leave.

"I will," I tell her, brushing away the tears that well up in my eyes.

She lets go and moves through the front door.

I sag against the counter, all of my emotion spent. Mama and Papa and James are upstairs waiting for me. They have the old family album and they're going through pictures, remembering our lives, grieving together over all that has been lost. I know they want me there with them, but I just need a second to breathe.

The wallpaper of the shop has shifted from solid black to a delicate white stripe, as if to say the worst has passed. I press my hand down on the rosewood counter, trying to soak in the heat of Rhyme and Reason as it melts the rest of the hoarfrost.

Theo emerges from the stacks, his hair a disheveled mess about his ears. "How much for this?" He holds out a thin book. I tilt my head to get a look at the title. *Prince Caspian: The Return to Narnia.*

I gasp. "What? Where did you get that?"

He pulls the book toward his chest. "After I cleaned myself up a bit in the bathroom, I was browsing in the westerns and there it was."

"Westerns? For Pete's sake, I've been trying to find a copy of that for months."

"Well, I suppose it's yours then." He sets it on the counter, and I reach for it. As I look at him, the smile fades from my lips. His face is beaten-up; cuts and bruises cover his forehead, his nose, and his chin. Not to mention the still-healing wound on his neck.

"You probably wish you never wrote to my father."

"Don't—don't say that. I'm glad I did."

"But—" I don't get a chance to finish the sentence.

Ollie emerges from the stacks, in a hurry per usual. "We've got to get you home to the Woodland Winds . . ." She trails off.

Theo runs a hand over the back of his neck, his eyes on mine. "Right, I guess this is where we say goodbye."

"I'll wait out front." Ollie moves through the door, giving me a wink as she goes.

Theo clears his throat. "I didn't get a chance to thank you."

"Thank me? For what?" For Al forcing him from his shop, dragging him here, and then pulling him through a war zone? He owes me nothing.

"You didn't leave me there," he says.

"I would never have left you, Theo." I look up at him and I don't want to say goodbye, not yet.

Theo tugs at one of his shirtsleeves. "Do you remember the letter I wrote to you about how the world seems so gray these days?" He pauses and takes a breath. "Ever since we started writing, it's different. It's as if— as if everything is painted gold."

Tears blur my vision and spill down my cheeks.

"Oh, I didn't mean to make you cry. I—I should go." He spins toward the front of the shop, his cheeks turning red.

"Theo, wait." I hurry after him. "Take this." I hand him the copy of *Prince Caspian*, and he tips his head at me in confusion. "You read it first. Then send it back with Ollie."

He grins and holds my gaze for a moment longer. One hand on the door, he starts out. Halfway through, he stops.

"Poppy." He turns back. "I—"

"Write me?" I ask.

A smile turns the corners of his lips and he nods. "Always."

Chapter Thirty-Five

To: Poppy Fulbright, Rhyme and Reason

From: Euphemia Adley, Council Leader

November 21, 1944

Dear Poppy,

I received the letter you sent explaining what happened between you and Al and the Dark. Dante DeGray and Hanna Erasmus have corroborated your story. Let me express how deeply sorry I am that you have lost your brother. You and Al showed me that even in the hardest moments, light can be found. Al gave his life to save our world. We wish it had not come at such an immeasurable cost.

I'm not sure if you are aware that I received a letter from your father detailing his part in what has occurred at Rhyme and Reason. The Council is placing him under inquiry; there will be a tribunal to determine how he will be dealt with. Though your father will have to live knowing he had a hand in everything that's happened, and there is no worse punishment than that.

As Council Leader, I must convey that I am very disappointed with what has occurred at Rhyme and Reason. To say that the unleashing of the Dark could have been catastrophic to all the shops—indeed, to our world—is an understatement.

As a friend of the Fulbright family, however, I am proud of all you and Al have done to protect the balance of our world.

In your letter you wrote about the Light that flowed through you, encasing you and Al in a sphere and beating back the Dark. You asked what could have been the cause of that event.

I'm going to divulge a little-known secret, I think I can trust you to keep it. Before the magic existed in the shops, it existed in our ancestors' blood. Though our ancestors gave up that magic after the Rift, I suspect remnants of it still remain in us. I believe you were able to access those remnants in a way no Shopkeeper has in generations. You wielded the Light, Poppy. And I believe you saved your brother, in the end.

Sincerely,
Euphemia Adley

———

To: Theo Devlin, The Woodland Winds

From: Poppy Fulbright, Rhyme and Reason

November 24, 1944

Dear Theo,
It has been five days since the "incident," as I've been calling it. Or four days, six hours and twelve minutes since Al left us, to be exact. I can't imagine that number getting bigger, growing to months, and then years. Someday, I worry, I won't remember the sound of his voice, or his laugh, or the way he always read the last page of a mystery first, because he couldn't wait for the end.

I love my brother. He saved us from the Dark and protected the Light, and there is hope in that.

Papa is recovering from his illness, but I'm not

sure he will ever recover from the loss of Al. He talks to him, when he thinks no one else is around to hear. It breaks my heart.

I know what you mean now, about the world being devoid of color. Nothing shines anymore.

I miss my brother.

I wish I could have saved him.

I'll try to write again soon,
Poppy

———

To: Poppy Fulbright, Rhyme and Reason

From: Theo Devlin, The Woodland Winds

November 25, 1944

Dear Poppy,
If there's one thing I know about grief, it's that people like to give you advice on how to feel about it. I don't have much to say, except that you won't forget Al. You couldn't forget Al. He's your brother, and as long as you and your family and your shop live, a part of him lives too.

You reminded me once to look deeper for the good. Don't forget your own advice. For example, I've noticed recently that poppies are this amazing red, and the bookshop smells like pine trees when it's having a good day, and my mother laughs at my jokes, even when she doesn't think they're funny.

It may not feel like it now, but things still shine, Poppy. Don't be afraid to see it.

Yours,
Theo

Chapter Thirty-Six

❦

April 9, 1945
Sutton, New York

I stand on tiptoe and lean over the ladder, searching through the books shoved in the top corner of the classics section.

"What did you say it was called again?" I ask as I push aside a particularly thick wisteria vine.

"*The Emerald Kingdom*," the customer says. Her name is June, like the month. She has red curly hair and bright eyes and is visiting from 1995. "I hate for you to go to so much trouble, but my sister used to read it to me when I was little. I've been thinking about it a lot lately."

"Don't worry, it's my job to look for things." I shift a multivolume copy of The Boxcar Children out of the way.

"We used to sneak it under the covers at our foster home in the middle of the night." She laughs and then she's crying. "I'm sorry. My sister is getting married, and she and her husband are moving overseas. I thought if I could give this to her as a gift, it might connect us even after she's gone."

I look down at her sympathetically, and then back at the shelf, which I have now scoured top to bottom. I climb down the ladder. "I can write another bookshop to see if they have a copy."

"Oh, no. I was hoping to give it to her as a wedding gift tomorrow. Thanks anyway."

I frown. June has been nothing but kind ever since she walked in. I want to help her.

I start to follow her to the front of the shop when I hear a dull thump behind me. I turn to find a book lying faceup on the rug. I peer at the title, *The Giver*. I straighten and glance around suspiciously.

Another dull thump startles me, this book just ahead of the other one.

"What are you playing at, Rhyme?" I stoop to pick it up when a third falls on top of it. *The Emerald Kingdom*.

"June! I found it!" I pick up the book and she rushes at me.

"It's exactly as I remember. It's perfect!" She clutches it to her chest.

I smile and wipe a hand over my sweaty brow. I'm not sure how I missed it. "Let's head to the front and I'll ring you up."

She follows me to the counter, telling me all about

the plot of *The Emerald Kingdom*. Papa is behind it, and he shifts to the left so I can get to the register.

I show June how to use the currency exchanger, and once she's paid, I hold the basket of pins out to her.

"Take one of these, and please come again."

She fishes one of them out, pockets it, and leaves the shop with a spring in her step. I let out a breath.

"Difficult customer?" Papa sets a copy of today's newspaper down, and I catch a glimpse of the headline: WAR IN LAST WEEKS—GERMAN RESISTANCE COLLAPSES. Memories rise to the surface unbidden, the smell of smoke, the sound of gunfire.

"No, she was nice." I sit on the stool behind the counter and try to push the thoughts away. Papa sorts a stack of inventory, setting one book aside. "What is that?"

"A book about the *Titanic*," Papa says.

We stare at it solemnly. Al had been collecting and reading books about the *Titanic* since he was twelve. The pain on Papa's face cuts me in two. We both miss him, but Papa lives with the guilt every day.

"I still keep them out for him." Papa rests his hand over the cover.

It has been five months since we lost Al. Somehow, it still doesn't feel real.

Papa clears his throat and pushes back from the

counter. "Cyrus is coming in later. I need to get some things in order for him."

The Council has Rhyme and Reason on probation. Cyrus comes once a week to inspect the shop, and Papa has to keep a daily log that is looked over thoroughly. It will last another few months, and then the visits will be less frequent. But I suspect they will watch Rhyme and Reason warily from now on.

"Can you take over for me? I need to grab something from the apartment." Papa glances down at his watch. "What time does your club start?"

I raise my eyebrows. "It's not a club," I say teasingly. "It's a society."

"Ah, yes, your society. My apologies." He gives me a smile, which is rare for him these days. "I'm so proud of you, Poppy."

I tilt my face up. That surprises me after all our conversations about me finding life outside of Rhyme and Reason. "Really?"

He puts a hand on my shoulder. "All I've ever wanted was for you to have a chance to find your own voice separate from Rhyme and Reason's. To be your own person, and you're doing it. You're really doing it."

"Thanks, Papa." My eyes blur with tears, and I swipe at them with my sleeve. "I can take over for a minute. But hurry, I don't want to be late."

He walks down the aisle between the fiction shelves, and I marvel that months ago he was on his deathbed. He has come so far. We all have. Just not without a cost.

I get to my feet. There's been so much to do to get ready this morning I haven't had a moment to sit down. I just need one more thing to make our setup behind the lilac hedge complete. The old ivory clock in the back corner of the shop is going to be the perfect final touch.

As I move through Rhyme and Reason, the fireflies appear in the air around me, their soft glow filling me with affection. I pass through the fiction stacks and see Kosma and Prosper and James in one of the aisles. They've built a massive fort out of pillows and blankets.

Prosper reads from a stack of comic books they've commandeered. "'Once again assuming his identity as Superman, Clark Kent launches himself up into space at breathtaking—'"

"What do you think it's like to be able to fly?" Kosma interrupts him.

"I don't know, who cares! You interrupted the story," Prosper scolds her.

"I think it would feel like floating in water." James answers her question, and Kosma beams up at him.

I move on to the reading area, where Katherine and Whitney sit side by side.

"That's the thing about the suffragist movement. We want to show the world that we have our own thoughts and opinions, that we're capable of so much," Katherine tells him, and Whitney nods, taking notes on a pad as he interviews her for his newspaper.

In the back corner, I reach the round table with the antique clock, and stop. Our framed family photographs are positively stuffed on every square inch of the surface. A thin layer of dust coats each one. I look at them, a timeline of our lives. There's Al, and me, and James. Then Al and me. Then just Al. Mama and Papa's wedding photo. Papa in the Great War.

Papa looks young, standing tall and proud with his fellow soldiers. I didn't understand what it was like before, but now I see what war can do to a person and how that led Papa to the choices he made. I wish he had told us sooner about the hard times in his life, before things unfolded the way they did. Maybe it all could have turned out differently.

I grab the ivory clock and turn to leave when I notice a crop of blue wildflowers have grown around Al's picture. And I remember that day with Prosper behind the lilac hedge when he was missing his mother.

Do you know that love is really just a type of magic? I asked him. *Whisper whatever it is you want your mother to know, and this flower will deliver it to her.*

I lean into the wildflower and shut my eyes. "Al." His name is like a long-lost friend on my lips. "When I look around the shop, I see you everywhere. In the quotes on the chalkboard, and the birds-of-paradise that have suddenly bloomed along the stairs because they were your favorite. I miss you." I pause to push down the emotion that floods through me. "I'll see you on the other side."

The bell above the door rings.

I kiss the flower, just the way Prosper did, in goodbye.

"Hello?" someone calls out. "Anybody home?"

I rush to the front of the shop to meet the customer.

"Hi, welcome to Rhyme and—" I stop, the breath knocked from my lungs.

"Hey, Sunflower. What's buzzin'?"

Carl stands in military uniform, a grin on his face. He swipes off his hat.

"Carl?" I rub my eyes, not sure if I'm dreaming or not. "How are you here? I don't understand."

"That day in October with you and Al . . . I was wounded. The doctors said it was a concussion." He brushes his bangs aside, revealing a large scar on his forehead. "I spent months in a field hospital, barely able to open my eyes. They had some trouble identifying me until a few weeks ago . . ." He trails off.

Wounded. He was wounded at the Siegfried Line. I feel woozy, and he reaches out a hand to steady me. When he's sure I'm all right, he pulls a folded newspaper clipping from his coat pocket and sets it on the counter.

The date is from the first week of November. It talks about a town in Germany on the Siegfried Line and how the Allies lost a lot of soldiers trying to conquer it. The reporter describes a strange storm that scared the Germans so much they surrendered. A massive victory that led the Allies farther into Germany.

I look up at Carl. "Did you—did you see Al? Did you see what he . . ."

Carl blinks back tears. "I saw. The grenade hit that cloud, and it was like an accelerant. Took out everything in its path. That's when I got hit too. I'm so sorry about Al. Sorry that it ended the way—" He stops, unable to finish as emotion grabs hold of him. "I keep replaying it in my head. I should have come back with him when he asked. I—"

"No." I cut him off. "No more should-haves. Al did what he did to save all of us."

Carl looks down at his hands, then back up at the store. "I miss him."

"Me too," I whisper. "But don't let his death destroy you, Carl. Don't make the same mistake he did. You have to let him go."

"Is that what you're doing?" Carl asks.

The question is heavy on my shoulders; I wish I could say yes but it wouldn't be true. "I'm trying."

"Then I'll try too." He looks around. "Are your folks here?"

"Papa is upstairs. He'll be shocked to see you. Be careful with him?"

Carl swallows and then nods.

"You remember the way?"

"Of course." He steadies himself, then gives me a sad smile. "See you later, Lily."

"See you, Carl."

After he's gone, I sink down on the stool behind the counter, feeling shaken. Carl is here, alive and breathing. It means Al's sacrifice set things back to the way they should have been. Maybe we can find peace in that.

I look around the shop, my heart in my throat. I used to think it could protect me from all of the bad. I needed the magic to be my strength, to keep me from feeling pain or embarrassment or sadness. But Rhyme and Reason can't do that for me, because all of those difficulties are just a part of living. Now I know that I am strong enough to face things on my own and that together, Rhyme and I can be unstoppable.

The *scritch-scratch* of the chalkboard grabs my attention and I look back at it.

"She, In the dark, Found light, Brighter than many ever see." —*"Helen Keller,"* Langston Hughes.

The lilac hedge morphs, a doorway opening as Ollie emerges.

"You coming?" she calls. "It's almost time."

I pick up the ivory clock and start toward her. "I thought this would look nice with the centerpiece. What do you think?"

I hold it up and notice something I've never seen before. Engraved on the wooden back are the words *For Ada Elaine Fulbright.*

"It's beautiful," she says.

"I think so too," I say, running my finger over my great-aunt's name.

I follow Ollie into the children's section, where we have set up our meeting space. We've moved the long ebony table from the reading area and borrowed eight of the mismatched chairs. Mama's gold candlesticks sit in the center, and the surface is positively drowning in flowers. Shimmering yellow marigolds, glittering dahlias, bursting peonies in peach and magenta and lavender. Lush green vines snake between plates and teacups and cutlery. A copy of *Estefan Gonzalez and the Elixir of Life* sits at every place setting.

I place the ivory clock next to the books and candles I've stacked for the centerpiece.

"What do you think?" I ask Ollie, nerves dancing in my stomach.

Ollie looks up from a piece of paper in her hands. "Great. Hey, I was thinking, what if we do poetry for our next meeting? I've got some great recommendations."

"Poetry." I nod. "You make a list, and I'll help you get copies of whatever you want."

Ollie beams and takes a seat at one end of the table, scribbling away with a pencil.

I pull nervously at the bottom of my cream-colored sweater. I'm worried no one is going to come. Rhyme and Reason has never done anything quite like this before. I first had the idea for a book club a few weeks ago. I mentioned it to Ollie, and together we made it bloom into something so much bigger.

The enchanted forest mural on the wall behind the table is glimmering today. The fairy hollows showcase brightly colored roofs and windows, and the branches of the trees glow. Above it, on the wall, we've placed a banner with the name Ollie came up with for our group:

The Society for Bookish and Adventuresome Young Readers.

"Are we early?" Two new regulars move toward me and Ollie. They're sisters, Peach and Pearl Cook, who have been visiting Rhyme and Reason for the last few weeks. At fifteen and twelve, they come from 1922. Their parents are archaeologists off working in King Tut's tomb while they stay with their aunt for a few months. They stumbled into the shop and have hardly seemed to leave since.

"Right on time." I glance at my wristwatch.

"Where should we sit?" Pearl, the younger and shyer of the two, looks up at me, a blush in her cheeks.

"Anywhere you like." I motion for them to choose a space. "Make yourselves comfortable! We'll get started as soon as the others arrive."

I head toward the opening in the lilac hedge and wait, hands clasped in anxious excitement. I greet them as they show up. Liliana Martinez, fourteen, from 1895; Nevaeh Johnson, twelve, from 1987; Mona Nakamura, thirteen, from 1973. I hung posters around the shop, inviting anyone around our age to join us. Today there will be eight in all, but I hope to add more soon.

As I wait for our last society member to arrive, I look at the shop. The lemon tree stands lush and full, the voices of the regulars fill the air, and the chalkboard writes a new quote. I wish Al were here to see me. I wonder what he'd think of my being brave, trying to make friends, and starting on this new adventure.

As long as you and your family and your shop live, a part of him lives too, Theo wrote, and I see that reflected here.

Rhyme and Reason ensures that a part of all of us will go on forever through the stories and moments we share.

Somewhere there's a past where Al and I sit behind the front counter, trying to read the same book, bickering over pace and page turning. Somewhere there is a past where we are drifting between stardust and daydreams. The memories we made cannot be erased or forgotten. They will always be the light that guides me through the dark.

"Sorry I'm late!" Alexander Erickson, twelve, from 2005, slides into view. "I'm always running behind."

He pulls my attention away from Rhyme and Reason and memories of Al. I smile at him. "You're just in time."

Alexander leads the way, and I follow him to the table. The group has all chosen their seats, and a spark fills the air as they chat excitedly. Alexander takes the empty place on Ollie's left. I watch them all for a moment, my heart full of hope.

Five months ago, I never would've put this together. I would've been too frightened of rejection. But I'm starting to see someone different inside of me. Someone who stands on her own two feet and uses her voice instead of running from it. I'm excited to get to know her more, to find out how far she can go.

I move to the head of the table and clear my throat.

The group settles down, and the fireflies float in the air around us, their glow soft and friendly and warm.

"Welcome," I say, "to the Society for Bookish and Adventuresome Young Readers. Shall we begin?"

Acknowledgments

Just like Poppy needed Rhyme and Reason's regulars to make it all the way to the end of her story, I could never have made this book happen alone. So many people have waved stardust over these pages. I would truly be nothing without them.

First, to my parents. Dad, thank you for your love and support. Through singing, you tell stories in a different way than I do, but it was from you I first learned how. Mom, thank you for teaching me to love books, for the endless Scholastic orders and trips to Barnes & Noble. Thank you for reading so many of my manuscripts and drafts. And thank you both for believing.

To my brother Ryan and my sister-in-law Amber. Thank you for giving me the gift of time. Without you, I'm not sure this book would've ever come to fruition. Your constant love and support have meant the world to me.

To Kim, my sister, my roommate, my best friend. I don't have words. Thank you for frantic late-night plotting sessions, for long car rides, for your unwavering faith in me, and for reading and rereading my drafts.

Thank you for giving *Bookshop* its title and celebrating every step of this journey. I may not have a significant other to thank, but you're a close second.

To my brother Josh and sister-in-law Maddy. Thank you for your excitement and support, and for always showing up on my doorstep with cookies exactly when I need them.

To my sister Ashley. Thank you for loving my characters and my books, for showing me the edge of the cliff and how far I was away from it. For conversations over Marco Polo and all of your encouragement. I have learned so much from you.

And lastly, to Russell, my nephew. For the adventures and the magic. We have walked on the moon, explored the Arctic, and traveled to the Emerald Kingdom, traversing pretend worlds from our imaginations. You inspired me to believe in myself again, and my life is forever changed because of you. Dream big, Russell. You are full of so much light.

To my agent, Sarah Landis. I am forever grateful to you for your guidance and wisdom. Thank you for seeing so much potential in *Bookshop* and in me. From our first emails, I knew you were special, and I feel so lucky to have you as my agent.

To my editor, Maggie Rosenthal. Thank you for loving *Bookshop*. Thank you for your enthusiasm and encouragement. The first time we spoke, I knew you really saw this story, and I feel like fate brought us together. I'm so grateful to have had the chance to learn and grow from you. Your notes and your wisdom helped *Bookshop* bloom so bright.

To the rest of the team at Viking Children's Books and Penguin Random House, thank you for all of your hard work in championing *Bookshop*. Special thanks to Maddy Newquist and Krista Ahlberg. Thank you to Jessica Jenkins for the cover design. And a massive thank-you to Quang & Lien for your stunning cover art. You truly brought the magic of Rhyme and Reason to life.

To Kathy Dawson. Thank you for working on early drafts of *Bookshop*. Your notes and suggestions helped me and *Bookshop* grow. Thank you for the stardust you sprinkled over us, and thank you for believing in me.

Thank you to my 2018 Pitch Wars mentors, Gabrielle Byrne and Julia Nobel. You made my wildest dreams come true when you picked me as your mentee. You saw the potential this book had to become a middle grade, and you had faith I could get it there. I cannot thank you both enough for your mentorship. *Bookshop* wouldn't be what it is today without you.

Thank you to Brenda Drake, for creating Pitch Wars, and to all of those who work so hard behind the scenes. My experience as a mentee has forever shaped me.

Thank you to the Pitch Wars class of 2018. So many of you have encouraged me and lifted me up. Special thanks to Lorelei Savaryn, Summer Rachel Short, Jessica S. Olson, Rochelle Hassan, and Erin Bledsoe for letting me take up space in your DMs.

I had so many amazing teachers who inspired and encouraged me along the way, I wish I had space to thank them all. To Debbie Bennion, your eighth-grade class allowed me to stretch my writing wings. To Sharon Hanson, my high school creative writing teacher, who let us dream and create and explore our own imaginations. And last, to Alan Heathcock (no relation to Allan Fulbright), you let me take your class three times and tirelessly cheered me on over and over again. It was in your class I started to believe in myself. Al, you taught me everything. I wouldn't be half the writer I am today without you.

To Kendra Kellis. Thank you for counseling me through one of the toughest times of my life. Not only did you help me find a missing piece of this story, but you also helped me find the missing pieces of myself.

Thank you to my lifelong friend Brenna Wasser, who started a fan club for one of the first books I ever wrote and has been a fierce believer ever since.

And to the staff of Ada Community Library from 2007 to 2014: so many of you encouraged and built me up. I couldn't have done it without you.

Thank you to all of the friends and extended family who have supported me along the way. So many of you believed that I would get here someday.

And lastly, to my grandparents, Verla and Bob Allen, and Sam and Ann Thompson. Thank you for your love, your legacy, and your light. I hope I made you proud.